FORTUNATE SUM

FORTUNATE SUM

by

M. Ullrich

2016

FORTUNATE SUM

ISBN 13: 978-1-62639-530-5

This Trade Paperback Original Is Published By
Bold Strokes Books, Inc.
P.O. Box 249
Valley Falls, NY 12185

First Edition: March 2016

Credits
Editor: Jerry L. Wheeler
Production Design: Stacia Seaman
Cover Design by Jeanine Henning

Acknowledgments

I have this black binder—it's old, beat up, and bursting with the most random bits of dialogue and scenes. I've had this binder for over ten years now; it even came to Philadelphia with me when I went to see my first Madonna concert. Since then I've expanded into several spiral notebooks of outlines and character summaries, but that first binder was special because it represented my daydreams of maybe writing a book one day. I wrote that book, finally, and not one bit from that binder made it into *Fortunate Sum*. I think that's for the best, really.

First and foremost, I'd like to thank the wonderful team at Bold Strokes Books. I was welcomed warmly, and everyone has been nothing less than fantastic to this rookie. Radclyffe has built such a great company with a solid foundation of incredible people. I was an avid reader before, and now I'm honored to be part of this team.

My editor is really something special. Jerry Wheeler, your patience and willingness to share your knowledge made this green writer feel more comfortable and confident throughout the process. Your suggestions were invaluable, and this finished product is so much better because of you. Thank you, sir.

When I finally revealed my secret life as a writer to my friends and family, I've felt nothing but support from them. Thank you all for that. Sharing my excitement with everyone has been one of the best experiences thus far.

Heather, I'm incapable of putting together the right words to acknowledge what you mean to me and your role in making this happen. Simply put—it wouldn't have happened if it weren't for you. You've supported me since day one and you've been by my side every step along the way (and enjoying it). You're my lovely wife, my partner, and my PRIT. Thank you for your love, encouragement, and for believing in me. You're not just arm candy, that's for sure.

Finally, and far from least, if you are holding this book in your hands right now—thank you. From the bottom of this very nervous debut author's heart, thank YOU.

To Heather,
For believing when I was skeptical.

CHAPTER ONE

I'm not quite sure you understand the position this is putting me in. What you're asking me to do is something my family's company has never done since the day our doors opened in 1952." *What I'm telling you to do*, Catherine Carter thought as the deep voice continued to grouse into her ear.

She sat at her large desk, phone cradled against her ear as she typed information into her latest spreadsheet. Her back was to the floor-to-ceiling windows taking up two walls of her executive corner office. She was unaware of the world outside, all her concentration on the figures before her. Glancing quickly at the small screen on her office phone, she realized the conversation had been dragging on for almost fifteen minutes and she had yet to say a word beyond a monosyllabic greeting.

"Mr. Santiago?" Catherine tried to speak up, but the older man on the other end of the phone barely paused to acknowledge her firm voice.

"I read over the paperwork you sent to the office, and I have to admit, Ms. Carter, I don't really understand what it is you are expecting of my company." Mr. Santiago's slight accent added melody to his words.

"Mr. Santiago, if you just give me—"

"You expect me to put a stop to bonuses and cut back on management's vacation time. How am I supposed to explain this to my employees?" His small pause gave Catherine the opening she needed.

"Tell them they either take these cuts, make these small sacrifices, or they won't have a job by this time next year." She sighed as her patience waned. "Mr. Santiago, I don't think I can stress the importance of openness and honesty with your workers enough. Your business is in big trouble, and if you don't make these cutbacks, you'll lose everything you've worked so hard for. I know things were different in 1952, but my focus is on getting your family's company to see 2052." Catherine paused and wondered why some businessmen had such a hard time understanding the sink-or-swim world of business management. She pulled at the collar of her black turtleneck sweater, a wise wardrobe decision that frigid morning, but the stress of the afternoon caused her to regret it. As her blood pressure rose, so did her temperature.

"Is there any other way?" the older gentleman asked. He'd been reluctant to work with Catherine initially, so she wasn't surprised he was fighting the idea of listening to her now.

"No," Catherine answered quickly, trying to think of a way to end the conversation. As if on cue, her assistant entered the office with a steaming cup of coffee in one hand and a green folder in the other. Catherine watched with wide, relief-filled eyes as Vivian Rinaldi approached quietly.

"I'll see you at our meeting on Friday morning. Any further questions and concerns will be addressed then. Good-bye, Mr. Santiago." She placed the handset on its cradle and rolled the tension from her shoulders. Her head fell forward, and she closed her eyes before she spoke quietly. "Vivian, I am so happy to see you."

Most people at Marcati and Stevens saw Catherine Carter as the firm's driving force, even Anthony Marcati and Phillip Stevens themselves. But it was Walter Adamson whose opinion mattered most. He sat at the helm of the ship and he was more than happy with the direction his company was heading. The firm had become a household name in the world of finance since they had taken Catherine under their wing seven years prior. They may not have been located on Wall Street, but the sprawling office building they occupied deep within the business district made up for that. Catherine was a first for them. She was brilliant, determined, dedicated, and the first woman to make it onto the team. Their youngest financial advisor approached each client with a unique combination of care, dedication, and brutality. That technique spelled success.

"A few of us will be going to the new Cuban place down the street for lunch if you'd like to join us. I've heard they have deliciously strong margaritas." A sly smile tugged at Vivian's ruby red lips. Catherine looked up at her assistant and grinned.

"I'd love to, but I'm swamped." She waved at the stack of files with her left hand as she smoothed the lapel of her charcoal pinstripe suit. Catherine had purposely kept her distance from her coworkers over the past three years. She always made sure to adhere to her number one rule: Keep her business life and personal life separate.

"I guess I'll just have to drink your share, then?" Vivian placed the green file on Catherine's minimally decorated desk. It matched the rest of her large office—very few personal effects lined the walls and large bookcases. One family photo stood proudly amongst several diplomas and awards for Catherine's greatest professional accomplishments to date.

"As long as you don't slur your words later, have a few in my name." Catherine chuckled and turned in her chair, looking out at the view for the first time since she had arrived that morning.

"Very well, dear. Would you like for me to bring you back something for lunch?"

"No, thank you. I'm sure I have something to eat around here. If not, I'll get delivery from the deli on the corner. Go enjoy our drinks." Catherine turned to spare a small smile for her assistant and immediately returned her contemplative stare to the window, watching the large snowflakes that had begun to fall across the city.

The rest of the workday passed too quickly for Catherine to keep track. She didn't realize it was past eight o'clock until the sky had gone from gray to black. She finished up the report she had been working on for well over an hour and turned off her computer. She left the files where they were and cleaned up the remnants of the small salad she had eaten for lunch earlier that afternoon. With a briefcase full of work to do at home, and her thick, black wool coat secured around her lean frame, Catherine made her way from the empty office building to the local PATH station to wait for the next train home. Catherine rarely drove into the city during the winter. She didn't trust the rear-wheel drive of her Mercedes-Benz to keep her safe on slushy nights, nor did she trust aggressive taxi drivers to think twice about the accumulation of snow and ice around them.

The trip back to her top-floor luxury condominium took less than forty minutes. She stepped across the threshold and was greeted by complete silence. The open space matched her office in its lack of decorations and its large size. Oversized windows let in the moonlight and the sun, whenever it decided to grace the people of Hoboken, New Jersey, with its presence. For now, the beams of silvery light guided Catherine on a well-worn path toward a light switch and a phone with a flashing red number signaling a new message. She flipped the lights on, taking in the muted grays, blacks, and whites of the large living room with expensive leather furniture and a large-screen plasma TV. Connected to the living space was an up-to-date kitchen accented with granite and stainless steel. It was all safe and neutral, sleek and professional, just like its owner's wardrobe. After hanging her keys on their designated hook, Catherine pressed the play button on the phone and listened intently as she hung her jacket in the small coat closet by the front door.

"Hey, Cat. I don't know why I expected you to be home.

You'd think I'd know better and try your cell or the office first. Anyway, I just wanted to remind you about my party this Saturday. You better be there!" A warm chuckle filled an otherwise chilly condo. "It's not every day that your best friend turns thirty! Dennis and the kids send their love. Call me back!"

Catherine couldn't help the smile her best friend always seemed to put on her face. Alice Garner had been Catherine's rock since their freshman year at Rutgers University, although Alice was a Montgomery at that time. Graduations, a wedding, and two kids later, Alice and Catherine's friendship was as strong as ever, a great blessing in a monotonous life. Now Catherine felt as though she had a family all her own. When Alice had married her soul mate, Dennis, Catherine was afraid she'd be lonelier than ever, but the complete opposite had happened. She was welcomed into the fold and even became godmother to both the couple's children.

After microwaving dinner and consuming it without a breath between bites, Catherine shuffled her way to the large master suite. She secured her long, deep brown curls atop her head with a large clip and started the water for her bath. When her claw-footed tub was about half-full and steaming, she added a handful of expensive lavender-scented bath salts. Catherine wouldn't admit it, but she loved the sexy, feminine air that surrounded her when she used them. She may have been alone and lonely in her empty home, but she made sure to enjoy all the small luxuries she allowed herself. After taking a deep breath of the relaxing aroma, Catherine undressed and put her clothing away before she allowed herself to sink into the bath that awaited her. The stresses of her day slowly washed away, replaced by the personal stresses she tried so desperately to drown in a sea of numbers.

Her best friend was turning thirty, a milestone Catherine herself would be achieving in just four months. Once the streets of Hoboken started to thaw and flowers bloomed triumphantly, she'd be facing a deadline that had been in place for the better part of a decade. At the naïve age of twenty-one, Catherine had believed she could achieve anything, and she had accomplished most everything she'd planned. *Most.* Once the water had turned cold, along with Catherine's mood, she rose from the tub and dried off before putting on her black silk robe. Thoughts continued to swirl around in her mind as she washed what little makeup she wore from her youthful face. Staring back into the large, curious brown eyes in the mirror, she wondered what was stopping her from making that final check on her list.

As she got ready for bed, slipping nude between expensive sheets, she looked to the picture on her nightstand and smiled. A tanned, pink-cheeked version of herself smiled back, one arm around Alice with two goofy children seated on their laps. It was a wonderful, albeit short, vacation in the Hamptons that past summer. The Garner family and their plus-one had enjoyed long days on the beach with the kids and evenings in front of a campfire with fine wine for the adults. She had never been so relaxed, so happy since graduating from college.

Every night Catherine would stare at that picture and wonder exactly what she could add to her life to get that feeling back into her every day. She knew the answer. The cold, empty space next to her practically screamed it at her. She had everything else: the job, the apartment, the car, and the cushioned bank account. The echo of her furnace kicking on only served to highlight the void left empty by a missing puzzle piece. Her eyes grew heavy as she calculated the population and the statistical variables that could point her in the direction where a suitable man could be hiding.

CHAPTER TWO

Death was inevitable, but it was still hard to deal with. No matter how old the deceased, their death would hit their loved ones with a force no one would be prepared for. Tears would be shed during the preparations, sobs would accompany the eulogy, and every day that passed after the burial would be under a dark cloud for a long time before it finally dissipated to a dull ache. Some unlucky people suffered more than their fair share of losses, but their frequency didn't make them hurt any less. Imogene Harris sat paralyzed on her best friend's couch, tears slowly falling down her cheeks in a well-traveled path. She had buried her grandfather less than six hours earlier, and the disbelief still shook her to the bone.

"Sweetie, are you sure you don't want to be with your mother?" Sophia sat down beside Imogene's slumped form and thrust a steaming cup of tea into her shaking hands.

"I can't." She looked to her friend and continued, "It's like burying my dad all over again. I had to be strong for her then. I can't do it this time. I need to feel this. That doesn't make me a bad daughter." She hesitated before asking, "Does it, Sophia?" She didn't dare look in the other woman's eyes. She kept her gaze on her lap and counted each piece of fuzz that clung to her long black dress.

"Oh, honey." Sophia wrapped her strong arm around

Imogene, encouraging her to rest a tired head on her shoulder. "Of course it doesn't. You need to grieve. We're all entitled to that."

Sophia Glass had been at her side through the toughest times since grade school, so Imogene didn't have to specify what she meant when she said she needed to feel "this." Imogene's father had died over a decade ago, and she hadn't been the same since. A small part of her died along with Francis Harris when the second tower fell on that day in September. No matter how many flags were flown in his memory or how many other firefighters had sent their support her family's way, Imogene and Mary Harris had been left without the man who had loved the women in his life more than anything in the world. In the years that followed, Imogene had turned to her grandfather for the guidance her father used to provide, and now she had lost him as well. In a way, she was grieving the loss of both of them.

At thirty-three, Imogene knew she should have felt lucky to have such a wise man in her life for so long, but the selfish side of her expected Winston Harris to live forever, to guide her until *her* dying day. She remembered the day after her nineteenth birthday when she shared her deepest secret with him. She stared down into the cup of tea Sophia had brought her. The steam rising from the surface of the deep amber liquid hypnotized Imogene, and she heard her grandfather's voice as if he were standing beside her.

"Grandpa?" Imogene stood at the white kitchen counter, cutting an apple into slices.

"Yes, Immy?" He worked a small ball of dough with a rolling pin. Seconds of silence passed, the dough becoming thinner and thinner, the young woman becoming more and more nervous.

"I think I'm gay." The knife in her hand stilled as the words left her mouth, and when a response didn't come, she risked a glance. Winston was still working the dough, lifting it carefully onto a pie dish and making sure he hadn't missed a tear or space.

He wiped his hands on his apron, smiled triumphantly at the perfect crust and then at his granddaughter.

"Do you think or do you know?"

"I know." Imogene stood tall, but her heart hammered violently as she waited for his response. He caught her off guard by pulling her into a tight embrace. When he finally released her, tears shimmered in both their eyes, and they wore equally large smiles.

"There's one thing you need to realize." Winston turned his attention to making the perfect scalloped edges on his crust.

"What's that?" She didn't bother to hide her grin as she went back to the task at hand.

"Whether it's a boyfriend or a girlfriend, your father and I will still kill them if they break your heart." He punctuated his words by picking up the rolling pin and tapping it against his broad palm several times before going to work on the top crust. They both laughed and continued their work. Later that night, they ate the best apple pie they'd ever had while feeling closer than before.

"I heard your mom talking about your inheritance," Sophia said, bringing Imogene back to the present. "Seems..." Imogene watched as Sophia tucked a strand of her sandy blond hair behind her ear and searched for the right word. "Hefty." The change of subject was obvious.

"Yeah." Imogene wasn't one to speak of money. She hadn't uttered a word about the settlement she received after her father's death, and she was just as tight-lipped now.

"Any plans for it? Travel, cars, a small hut in Belize?" Sophia encouraged.

"I'm just putting it into the shop." Imogene had opened Cowboy Fran's a month after the settlement money was in the bank. She wanted to do something in her father's memory, but she also knew it'd put her associate's degree in business to good use, a degree she only got to make her mother happy. After stepping foot into the vacant storefront on Washington Street, she had fallen in love and signed the lease papers immediately. Shortly after, the small boutique had become a staple on the busy Hoboken street, catering to women in the area by providing them with clothing, jewelry, and household items that stepped outside the business casual box most were forced to live within during weekday hours. Once the apartment upstairs had become available, Imogene jumped to move in. Now Cowboy Fran's wasn't just her job, it was her home as well. She loved it, but she would gladly give it all back if she could have her father and grandfather in her life for just one more day.

"You should look into some investments," Sophia said nonchalantly. "Chris's friend knows a great advisor if you'd like me to get the number."

"Listen, Sophia…" Imogene stopped her friend from going any further. She was too exhausted to think beyond her sadness. "I appreciate everything you and Chris have done for me, I really do, but I'm not worried about the money right now." A silence fell over the room, uncomfortable enough that Sophia's husband, Chris, stepped in the room, then spun on his heels and left again. Imogene got up to take her full cup of tea into the kitchen and deposit in the sink before returning to the living room in search of her coat.

"I should get home. You know how cranky Vixen gets when I'm away for too long." Imogene smiled every time she talked about her beloved orange tabby cat.

"There's a time she's not cranky?" Sophia flinched slightly as she spoke.

Imogene thought back to the last time one of Sophia's belly scratches had gone wrong and felt pity for her traumatized friend. "You just bring out the best in her." Imogene chuckled, even managing to make that sound sad. "I'll see you later." She slipped her long tweed jacket on and started for the door.

"Oh!" Sophia's deep blue eyes lit up. "I'm working a party this weekend for Chris's best friend's wife. You should come and be my assistant. It's been a while since we worked a room together."

With a hand on the doorknob, Imogene grinned at her friend. Sophia always knew exactly what she needed to get through a hard time. Free food and great entertainment always helped. "When and what time?"

"Saturday night, meet me here at seven."

"You got yourself a faithful assistant, Miss Glass." Imogene bowed slightly, her auburn hair tumbling over her shoulders.

"Thank you. No great psychic could perform without one." The two women shared a hug and a wicked smile before bidding each other a good night.

Chapter Three

Catherine took a moment before knocking on the door. She rolled the cool glass bottle of expensive wine between her palms and braced herself for an evening surrounded by complete strangers. It wasn't that she had never met these people, she just never got to know them. Never had the desire to, either. Catherine was there to wish her best friend a happy birthday and help out in any way she could, not to make friends. She made sure she arrived early enough to avoid walking into a crowd but late enough not to be mistaken for anyone of real interest—a strategy she'd perfected over the years. After a deep breath, she opened the door and was greeted immediately by a flustered Dennis.

"Cat!" He rushed over and took the bottle, putting it on the nearest table. "Thank God you're here. I'm trying to make sure that all the food is properly displayed and the drinks are easy access, but I'm not sure anything is up to Alice's standards." She felt his panic seeping from every pore.

"Where is the birthday girl?" Catherine scanned the open space.

"I told her to take her time getting ready."

"Good. I'll do a casual walk-through and fix whatever needs fixing. You just worry about what your wife needs." She smiled and patted his muscular shoulder. Relief immediately flooded his young, bearded face. Dennis was five years older than Alice but looked younger than Catherine's own twenty-nine. His boyish good looks and dark features had drawn Alice in immediately, but his charm and goofy humor were what sealed the deal. Catherine couldn't have picked someone more perfect for her dear friend.

"You're a lifesaver." He was gone before finishing his words.

"And you owe me," Catherine mumbled to herself as she removed her coat and hung it in a nearby closet, one she knew wouldn't be used for any strange coats. She hated leaving a party smelling like someone else's perfume or cologne. She smoothed out any wrinkle that could have formed on her perfectly tailored shirt and slacks during the short drive over. She spent many hours a week at the gym and, as a result, she was proud to properly display her tall, trim, athletic body. Catherine looked long, strong, and in charge dressed all in black. It gave her the necessary confidence to make it through tough meetings as well as small parties.

She walked through her friend's large, open home not too far from her own condominium. Instead of a busy city feel, it was tucked away into a neighborhood for growing families. Every time Catherine visited, she'd think of how it'd be the perfect place for her to settle down when the time came to start a family. She wandered about slowly, making sure all the preparations would please Alice, and they would.

More and more guests filled the living area and large kitchen within the next half hour. Catherine hadn't had the chance to manage even a small "happy birthday" to Alice before someone dragged her away to greet her guests. She hadn't even caught a glimpse of her. Catherine remained tucked away with a glass of the wine she brought and found herself somehow having a one-on-one debate about the Super Bowl with a man she believed was named Eric. Catherine hated sports. Thankfully, she was part of a family that enjoyed entertaining and worked in a field that required her to address large groups of people at a time. Catherine managed to handle herself just fine. She only caught herself wishing the kids were there to take her away from the stifling adult once. Finally she couldn't take it anymore.

"I'm sorry, Eric," she held up her glass, "too much wine on an empty stomach."

"It's Jeff. My name is Jeff." She flinched at her mistake.

"Excuse me, Jeff." She slithered away, feeling guilty, bored, and tired. Deciding she was ready to leave, Catherine scanned the large crowd in hopes of finding Alice. No such luck. Instead of weaving in and out of bodies to find her, she decided to fill a plate at the impressive buffet. She had a lot of work waiting for her at home, but at least this way she'd get to it with a full stomach while avoiding another sodium-packed prepared meal.

As Catherine grabbed a plate, a redheaded woman who seemed more eager to get to the shrimp cocktail than any other partygoer bumped her. Catherine stumbled back a step and almost dropped the dish. Just as Catherine was about to bite off a remark, the redhead turned around to offer an apology.

"I am so sorry! I probably look like some sort of fool, stumbling over myself just to get to some food!" A megawatt smile spread across her beautiful face, rendering Catherine speechless. "I didn't get a chance to eat all day, and I have been waiting patiently for an opening to get at least a little something to nibble on." Catherine tried to follow what she was saying, but the other woman gripped Catherine's shoulder to steady herself as she slipped back into her runway heel. "When my opportunity came, so did you. That's when I forgot how to put one foot in front of the other without losing a shoe and, well, crash." Giggles fell from her full pink lips.

Catherine couldn't stop staring at her, even though she hadn't heard a word the woman had said. Her thick, long, auburn hair framed her face well. She looked so young and yet so mature. She possessed a timeless, old-Hollywood beauty Catherine thought magnificent. The sprinkle of freckles across her pink cheeks added to the charm she saw in the woman's large, crystal blue eyes. She took her hand off her shoulder, and Catherine realized she should say something.

"Me either." The woman looked confused, and Catherine thought to elaborate. "I haven't eaten much either." When the redhead smiled brightly, Catherine's stomach did a little, unfamiliar flip. She swallowed hard as the other woman looked her up and down. The movement was subtle, but she felt as though it was a physical caress. Catherine reached over and grabbed a large platter overflowing with peeled shrimp. "It'd be a shame if we both starved. Shall we?" Together they walked toward the empty couch.

The two women sat, laughing and joking as they ate. Catherine learned quite a bit about the bubbly redhead beside her. She knew she liked shrimp immensely and could spot a finely tailored shirt a mile away. Though her red hair fell in waves, she was jealous of naturally curly hair, she had a love for heels but couldn't quite master anything higher than two inches, and she absolutely adored parties and white wine, but not as much as her Aunt Rita. She was everything Catherine wasn't and enjoyed all the things Catherine shied away from. Thankfully, she was so talkative, Catherine didn't have to share anything too personal.

Without prompting, the crowd shifted to the perimeter of the room, clearing space in the center for a woman with blond, chin-length hair. She was slim and tall, authoritative in posture and air. She waited patiently for the quiet murmurs around the room to die down.

"What's this all about?" Catherine whispered, leaning in closely. She wouldn't let herself acknowledge the dizzying feeling that accompanied the scent of the other woman's perfume. It was a delicate, addicting scent.

"That's Sophia Glass. She's a psychic," the other woman offered. She never took her eyes off the blonde as she started speaking, opening up to the crowd.

"Hello, everybody. My name is Sophia, and I'll be your

entertainment for this evening." A few men hooted at the idea and Sophia laughed. "Not that kind of entertainment, although it would probably increase my pay rate." The rest of the room joined in on the laughter. "I'm a psychic, and I'm here to talk to the believers and possibly even intrigue the skeptics."

"A psychic? Are you kidding me?" Catherine could barely contain her disbelief and giggles. *What was Alice thinking?*

"Sophia has a large following and a very well-respected practice in town."

"A practice? She's not a doctor," Catherine said. "She may be a quack, though."

"She's not a quack."

"You believe in this stuff?" Catherine pointed toward Sophia. "That woman is here to make money. She'll tell these people anything they want to hear." She shook her head and laughed again as she looked around at the interest on everyone's faces.

"You should be more open-minded," the redhead whispered.

"I am open-minded, but I'm not stupid." Catherine looked into the blue eyes suddenly boring into her. Gone was the laughter, gone was the light, gone was the magic and the connection that had no name. Before she could ask why, the psychic started talking again.

"I'd like to call up my dearest friend to assist me. Imogene, come up here."

Catherine realized she had put her foot in her mouth, and she didn't like the taste of it when the woman next to her rose and joined in the spotlight at the center of the room. She sank into the plush sofa and waited patiently for an opportunity to escape with her tail between her legs.

❖

It was almost an hour before Catherine managed to catch a glimpse of Alice and feel any hope of getting out of there before she had any further uncomfortable interaction with Imogene. On her way over to say good-bye, Sophia stopped her. *Great,* Catherine thought, *now I have to deal with this?*

"Hello." Sophia extended her thin hand toward Catherine, who hesitated before taking it. "I'm Sophia—"

"I know."

"You seemed to have made quite the impression on my assistant." A playful smile appeared on Sophia's face. Catherine took in her sharp features and midnight blue eyes. White teeth peeked from between her thin red lips. They weren't perfectly straight, but Catherine thought the imperfection added a pleasant character to an attractive face. The woman was beautiful, but she wasn't nearly as captivating as Imogene. Where one was warm and inviting, this one was fierce.

"I guess you could call it that." Catherine wasn't looking to make conversation. She wanted to get out of there as quickly as possible.

Sophia crossed her arms over her chest. "I do enjoy the challenge of a good old-fashioned skeptic."

"I'm not looking to challenge you."

"Oh, I know."

Catherine thought the statement was delivered the same way as any of her other party tricks. After her failed attempt at socializing earlier, the last thing she wanted was the runaround from this woman. "Listen, Sophia, I'm sure your assistant gave me rave reviews and my sitting alone with my head in my hands just reinforced them, but—"

"You're much too proud to believe in this whole shtick, aren't you? Much too successful in a real business to be bothered with something so abstract. I don't fit into your black-and-white world, do I?" Catherine just stared as Sophia continued. "Maybe it wasn't your skepticism that drew me to you. Maybe it was the sadness that surrounds you." She brought the words to life by tracing a circular shape in the air. Catherine didn't have the chance to argue before she was accepting a business card from the psychic. "I can tell you if you'll have it all by May," Sophia whispered to her. And with that, she was gone.

"Hey, Cat. I'm sorry I haven't had a chance to talk to you all night. Dennis really outdid himself this time, didn't he?" Alice looked at her friend. "Are you all right? You look pale." She held Catherine's shoulders and looked into her eyes. "Cat?"

"Yeah. Yes. I'm fine. Sorry, I'm just heading out." She looked everywhere in an attempt to find the woman who had just shaken her to her core. When she noticed that Alice wasn't letting go, she settled her gaze on her friend. "Your hair!"

Alice ran her left hand through her freshly cut black locks, but the other remained on Catherine's sturdy shoulder. "I needed a change." Her normally long, straight hair was now cut pixie short and styled off her face haphazardly with a funk unique to Catherine's eccentric friend.

"It looks fabulous. *You* look fabulous." Catherine wrapped her arms around Alice and held her tightly, whispering a birthday wish into her ear before reluctantly letting go. "I'll talk to you tomorrow. Give the kids a kiss for me." With a gentle parting smile, Catherine headed for the door.

Sophia's voice followed her home and into bed, where choppy dreams invaded her subconscious. Catherine awoke in a cold sweat several times that night, thinking of past failures, mocking laughter, and faces hidden by a dense fog. It wasn't until the early morning sun wrapped itself around Catherine's curled form that she found some form of peace. Sophia's voice repeated ten very specific numbers in sequence until Catherine was lulled into a light sleep.

CHAPTER FOUR

Almost a week had passed since the disaster that was Alice's birthday party, a week full of snow, sleet, and gloomy days that forced Catherine to work from home. Unlike the rest of the advisors at her firm, Catherine didn't have a hard time focusing on work while she was surrounded by home comfort. She actually thrived in it. It allowed her to start earlier, work through with any necessary meals, and continue until she fell asleep atop her sheets with her laptop and files scattered across her king-size bed. Truth be told, Catherine's clients benefited from Mother Nature's latest temper tantrum.

Catherine didn't look beyond her front door for more than a takeout meal and the newspaper until the Friday afternoon that followed the party. Alice begged her to come for a cup of coffee at the little café down the street from Catherine's apartment, saying she needed to escape two kids who had been snowed in for far too long. Catherine sat and stirred her espresso, waiting patiently for her friend to arrive. Usually punctual, Alice arrived a few minutes late due to the closed lanes and icy back roads.

"I cannot get over this weather." She shrugged off her green coat and hung it on the back of the chair across from Catherine at the small round table. Catherine looked up from the swirling bronze and mahogany colors on the surface of her drink and greeted Alice with a welcoming smile.

"It is winter in the northeast," Catherine said as Alice settled in and looked over the small menu.

"It's droll, and it's making me bitter." Alice's frown perked up as she made a quick decision. "I'd kill for a vanilla cappuccino and one of their almond biscotti."

"Let me." Catherine rose from her chair and started to make her way to the counter to order before stopping to add, "It's the least I can do since I barely saw you for your birthday."

"Oh, we'll talk about that when you get back."

"Great." Sarcasm dripped from the single word as Catherine gritted her teeth and repeated Alice's small order over and over in her head.

Five minutes in line—two waiting patiently for the right portion of foam to be added and another minute to make it back to the table without spilling a drop—wasn't nearly enough time for Catherine to put together enough of the right details of her story to satisfy her friend and keep out what she was reluctant to share.

"Here you go." She set the drink down along with the biscotti before settling back into her seat. "I really do love your hair like that." Today, Alice's new short do was left flat, but its natural body allowed it to fall into its own style, highlighting her deep green eyes.

"It saves me twenty minutes in the morning. Dennis and the kids are wonderful, but," she looked around before whispering as if sharing a great conspiracy, "I'm beginning to think this was the best decision I've ever made." Alice pointed to her hair and laughed out loud, a hearty, deep rumble that Catherine joined.

"It suits you. It goes perfectly with your style," Catherine said, gesturing toward the magenta cardigan over a vintage Aerosmith T-shirt. "I'm jealous."

"There is a world beyond suits, you know. Remember those days?"

"This isn't a suit," Catherine challenged. She raised her arms to allow an appraisal of her current, slightly relaxed outfit of jeans and a sweater. Alice stared blankly, clearly unimpressed. "Fine. You win. We can't all be as fashionable as you."

"Flattery will get you everywhere *except* out of telling me what happened Friday night." Alice dipped her upper lip into the foam on her cappuccino.

"Damn." Catherine chuckled. "I don't know where to start—with insulting the assistant or the fortune teller?" She ticked off the two options on her fingertips.

"Psychic," Alice corrected.

"There's a difference?" Catherine noted Alice's glare. "Fine. *Psychic.*" She took a deep breath and relayed the evening step by step, every minute she hadn't been able to forget since that night. She ended the tale with the words Sophia had spoken so clearly, so confidently, that they still sent a shiver down her spine.

"Wow." Alice looked away. Catherine could tell she was processing the new information, looking back at her when she asked, "So, are you going to meet with Sophia?"

"I don't know. I don't believe in what she's trying to sell, but there's a small part of me that's curious about what she'd say."

"She's not technically trying to sell anything if the card says that the first appointment is free," Alice pointed out.

"True." Catherine looked down into her now empty cup, the fine grounds outlining the bottom in a shape that resembled a heart. "What if she has nothing good to tell me?" Her voice was small, ashamed of the fear it held.

"Such as?"

"I won't achieve the goals I have set for myself."

Alice rolled her eyes. "Why is that so important to you? You've been obsessed with this idea of having a perfect life by the time you're thirty for so long I'm pretty sure you've missed out on living most of it."

"You know my family. By the time my brothers were thirty, they had the career and the family. I already have a career that my father doesn't approve of…" She let her voice trail off as the painful memories all came rushing back.

"Just because you're not a lawyer like daddy, Patrick, and Russ doesn't make you any less successful."

"And I go home to an empty house every night. I figured that by now I'd have a guy to bring home that my dad could be proud of, you know? Someone who'd play golf at the club and chat about cars or whatever. My brothers have wives who spend time in the kitchen with my mom. Well, they make believe they do."

"Do they even know what a kitchen is?" Alice quirked an eyebrow.

"Being with someone my dad actually likes would be the one thing I could have over them." Catherine chose to ignore Alice's accurate quip.

"You're talking a lot about what *they* would like for you, not what *you* would like."

Catherine spotted the challenge in her best friend's eyes. "Alice…"

"Fine." Alice raised her palms in surrender. "I think the only solution is to just go see Sophia," she said with a dismissive shrug.

"How's that the *only* solution?"

"Well," Alice took a sip of her beverage, "if Sophia says something you're not satisfied with, your skepticism can easily discredit her words and you'll continue on as if nothing happened." She took a bite of her cookie and chewed slowly, leaving Catherine in suspense.

"And?"

"And if she says something positive, the hopeless romantic that I know is buried under those business suits will have a glimmer of hope to cling to." One more bite and the biscotti was all gone, save a few crumbs scattered across the tabletop. "Maybe you'll actually come home after a date and call me to say something positive for once."

Catherine pulled back, offended. "What's that supposed to mean?"

"You usually just complain about the guy chewing with his mouth open or not holding the door for you." Alice brought her mug up to her lips, but paused long enough to add, "Or dirty fingernails."

"No one wants to date someone with dirty—okay, you know what? I'm not arguing about this with you. I just have standards and whether you view that as romantic or not doesn't matter." But she knew Alice was right. She had nothing to lose by going to see Sophia, nor did she have anything to really gain.

"Speaking of your romantic side, remember the paper you wrote for the creative writing final sophomore year?" Alice asked.

"That was a terrible segue."

"I'm proud of it." Alice smiled.

"The story about the businessman and the artist?" Catherine laughed at herself and cringed slightly. "I still can't believe you made me take that class. I was happy with my roster full of math courses."

"Ms. Nguyen really liked it, as did I. You're not all about numbers, you know?"

They had been at this crossroads many times before. Neither would add more. Catherine knew Alice had her suspicions, but she could never bring herself to confirm them. Linda Nguyen. That was a name Catherine hadn't thought of much in recent years. Hearing it brought about a whole new set of memories and a pain that still resonated until this day.

After they had taken that class, both passing with flying colors, Catherine knew she had changed. A new lightness accompanied her footsteps, balanced out by the kind of heaviness that accompanied a dangerous secret. No matter how many times Alice tried to bring up Ms. Nguyen, Catherine would change the subject. And that was how it went for two years until the end of junior year when Catherine wouldn't eat or leave their apartment for two weeks.

"Both of you were delusional. It was an old story of forbidden love retold from the mind of someone who lacked imagination." Catherine tried to keep her tone light, tried to keep the conversation from going any deeper into dangerous territory. With as much time as had gone by, Catherine should've been able to talk about it, to confide in her best friend about that time of her life, but the secret had become such a part of who she was, Catherine was unable to form the words.

"Ms. Nguyen saw your potential. I wish you would."

You have no idea what she saw in me. Neither do I, Catherine thought to herself. A flash of beautiful, sharp almond eyes invaded her mind.

"I can't do this anymore." Catherine had been practicing that one sentence in the mirror for over a week.

"Can't do what, exactly?" Linda wiped at the corner of her mouth with her cloth napkin and pushed aside her empty dinner plate.

"The hiding and the sneaking. I'm tired of it, Linda."

"We've talked about this many times, and you said you understand. I could lose my job, you could get expelled—any scholarship you worked for could be revoked." Linda spoke evenly. "We both knew this going in."

"I know, but I didn't expect it to be so hard. I've been lying to my family and my friends—"

"Alice is the last person who could ever know!"

"I know." Catherine shrank back into the dining chair. "I don't see the harm in my family, though." This had been a conversation they needed to have for a while now, and she wasn't about to let her girlfriend intimidate her. "My mother keeps asking if I've met anyone…"

"And you keep telling her no. It's really quite simple." Linda stood and grabbed their plates before heading to the kitchen. Catherine was on her heels.

"But that's just the thing! I have met someone, I am with someone, and I want to share that with them." When Catherine didn't receive a response except the sound of running water, she

continued. "I am so in love with an amazing, brilliant, beautiful woman, and I want them to see how happy she makes me." Linda's rigid shoulders fell, and she turned to look a hopeful Catherine in the eye.

"And when your mother asks how we met, when we met, what will you tell her? Will you tell her how you'd linger after class and ask for special attention on your writing assignments?" At Catherine's soundless, dry stutter, Linda asked, "You didn't think of that, did you?"

"No, but—"

"There's not one parent who'd want to hear about their child getting involved with a teacher." Linda shut the water off, leaving a deafening silence. "Things will change once you graduate."

Catherine watched as Linda threw the damp dish towel down and walked away. She was both angry and sad, not just at the situation she had willingly gotten herself into, but at how easily Linda seemed to accept their hidden romance. As a woman, why should she be content with being someone's secret?

"That won't work for me." She said the words quietly at first, but as they tumbled from her lips, she found a bravery she had lacked over the past year and a half. That newfound courage carried her to the living room where Linda was sitting on the edge of the sofa with papers sprawled out on the coffee table before her. "That won't work for me. This isn't working for me."

Linda sighed and sat back, her movements clearly indicating her growing frustration. "What's the solution, then?" Linda stared with hard eyes as Catherine stood in front of her.

"Quit."

Linda frowned.

"I'm serious."

"Quit?" Linda said.

Catherine nodded.

"My job?" Catherine nodded again. "Are you giving me an ultimatum?" Linda asked.

"No, I'm giving you the solution you asked for. You've told me about an opening at Stockton, you constantly complain about the faculty at Rutgers, your relationship with the dean is less than ideal, and we won't have to keep us a secret anymore." Catherine saw nothing but skepticism looking up at her. "We do want the same thing, right?"

"Yeah, of course." Linda looked away a second after she spoke, and Catherine knew what was coming next. "But I can't just quit my job. I'm sorry, Cat."

"I am, too." Catherine wiped away the tear from her left cheek with the back of her hand. She gathered her bag and jacket from where she'd dropped them only hours earlier and rushed for the back door. She didn't want Linda to know how much hope she had had for the two of them. Catherine didn't want to accept the reality of that misplaced hope either.

"Wait!"

Catherine paused in the open doorway. Linda gripped her wrist, pulled her back into the entryway, and closed the door. "Give me until the end of the semester." They were standing so close that Catherine could feel Linda's breath against her lips. It weakened her knees as well as her resolve.

"You'll quit?"

"Yes,"

"Promise?" Catherine was earnest.

"I promise. But," Linda raised her index finger in the air, "I need to get everything in order first. I can't quit without another job lined up." Linda released Catherine's wrist and settled her hand on her hip. "I have bills that need to be paid and a girlfriend who really enjoys shrimp." Her eyes softened when Catherine smiled.

"I can wait until then." Catherine kissed Linda softly, then asked, "Do those papers need to be graded tonight?"

"Yes." Linda leaned forward and captured Catherine's mouth with a much deeper, exploratory kiss. When they separated, *she started working the button of Catherine's jeans and added, "But who cares? I'm quitting soon anyway."*

Catherine shook off the memory. "Numbers and I were meant to be, that's all there is to it," she said with finality. She pushed her empty cup away and stared blankly at the tabletop linen.

"Dennis has a potential client for you. Apparently it's a pretty desperate case."

"A business?" Catherine relaxed at the subject change and perked up at shop talk.

"I think it may be more of a private situation, I'm not sure. I didn't get many details other than a hefty inheritance that needed to be put someplace safe."

"You know I prefer to work with a company's money, not individual bank accounts." Catherine hated clients who rarely worked for the money they had and acted stupid when it came to handling it beyond spending.

"Consider this a favor for a friend of a friend." Alice paused, looking thoughtful. "A friend of a friend of a friend would be more accurate, I guess. Whatever. Anyway, if you're interested, I can arrange for them to come over for dinner one night, and you can do the initial evaluation then. Think about it." Alice rose and slid into her jacket, and Catherine mirrored the action with her own black leather bomber.

"You know I'll do it."

"Great. Will you call Sophia?" They were buttoned and bundled and walking out the door.

"I think I will." Catherine pulled the business card from her pocket and turned it over in her hand a couple times. Standing beneath the café awning, hiding behind thick white puffs as they breathed in and out, the women smiled at each other and hugged good-bye.

"I knew you would," Alice whispered into her frigid ear.

❖

Just two blocks down the street, Cowboy Fran's was a bustle of activity as Imogene weaved in and out of several racks of the latest arrivals, deciding whether anything else needed to be added to the display she had just finished in her front window.

Imogene prided herself on running a shop that not only carried the highest quality clothing and accessories but also had antiques and handmade furniture for sale. Just about everything in the shop was available for purchase, which made Imogene's place stand out from the competing businesses on her street. One day, a customer could leave with a hand-woven scarf from Morocco, and the next a van could pull up outside to cart away a chair Imogene herself had fought to acquire at an antique auction earlier in the month. The variety of her goods drew in a diverse crowd of people that made her proud to own the place.

She stood outside in the cold winter afternoon, rubbing her arms frantically to keep the blood flowing, and appraised her handiwork. With a big smile, she bounced back inside in search of her coat and scarf.

"Amanda?" Imogene called out to her only employee. The young woman, somewhere in her early twenties, perked up at the mention of her name and pushed a magenta tendril of hair behind her over-pierced ear. "I'm running to pick up lunch, so I need you to watch the floor. I'm taking my car, so I shouldn't be long."

"You got it, boss," Amanda said as she went back to assisting her customer.

After securing each button and wrapping a blue scarf tightly around her exposed neck, Imogene walked out onto the busy streets of Hoboken, weaving between pedestrians and patches of ice. Although it normally bothered her that she owned a business and lived on the street but was never able to find a parking spot on the same block, today she welcomed the short walk. The cold air lifted some of the sadness that still lingered, invigorating her for another busy workday.

❖

Catherine walked along with her phone against her ear and her eyes on the sidewalk.

"Sophia Glass's office. This is Gladys, how may I help you?" Catherine fought an odd combination of relief and disappointment that Imogene didn't answer.

"I'd like to make an appointment?" The words came out as a question, Catherine not knowing how anything worked in the psychic world.

"For when?"

"As soon as possible." She surprised herself with her own eagerness.

"We have a one thirty available today."

Checking her Stuhrling watch, Catherine noted it was just after one o'clock. "I'll take it." Catherine relayed her information to the receptionist and checked her watch one last time to calculate how much time she had before her appointment, almost dropping her phone as she collided with another pedestrian.

"Get off the phone and enjoy your life!" A gentle voice called out without an ounce of aggression as Catherine tried to regain her balance. She turned to tell the other person just what she thought, but all she saw was a retreating form bundled in a black coat and sky blue scarf. Catherine grumbled to herself and continued in the direction of the address Gladys had provided over the phone.

Swinging open the large glass door of the storefront, Catherine was surprised by the office space she walked into. She wasn't sure what she expected; maybe bright colors and decorations that would make her feel as if she was transported to the days the gypsies ran the fortune-telling racket, but not this.

The space was large, with an open waiting area and a saltwater tank full of colorful fish tucked away in the corner. Several chairs looked comfortable enough to curl up in with your favorite book if not for the small reception desk occupied by an older woman.

"You can go right back, Sophia is waiting for you." The older woman, who Catherine felt confident to assume was Gladys, spoke up and pointed toward an office door in the back of the room.

"How did you know who I was?" Catherine asked with narrowed eyes, wondering if the receptionist was psychic as well.

"Not many people brave the ice to come here, and you're right on time."

"Right." The large wooden door was slightly ajar, so Catherine poked her head inside. Sophia was seated behind her desk, resting the back of her head against her large chair. She knocked gently to avoid startling her.

"Come in," she said, not opening her eyes right away. "You must be my one—" When she saw Catherine, she paused. "Hello again. I wasn't expecting to see you this soon, if at all," she teased.

"I thought for sure *you* would have been able to see this coming," Catherine teased back as she stepped further into the office. She immediately relaxed in her surroundings. The office smelled of lavender and was decorated in a modern style. Light neutral colors covered the walls and thriving plants sat on the long windowsills.

"I can't see everything," Sophia said. She reached out her right hand and waited for Catherine to take it, looking surprised when she actually did.

"Catherine Carter."

"Please have a seat, Catherine. There's no need to be nervous."

"I'm a little out of my element. I can't help but be a bit jumpy."

"I'm not talking about that, although that's pretty obvious as well. I'm talking about life in general." Sophia sat back and steepled her fingers together. "You're fighting the clock, and it makes you nervous."

Everyone hears their clock ticking, especially women. Catherine tried to school her features, wanting to keep from silently telling her whether she was right or wrong. *Next she'll say something just as generic in an attempt to get me to hand over my checkbook.*

"You will find happiness in time." Sophia closed her eyes when Catherine laughed at her words. "But the sadness you carry now? It's bleeding into everything, everyone around you. They see it and feel it along with you, ever since it started." Catherine started to fidget in her seat. She picked at a loose string on the arm of the upholstered chair. Sophia inhaled sharply. "You've been deeply hurt by someone you put on a very high pedestal."

Catherine watched as Sophia's eyes moved rapidly beneath the thin skin of her eyelids. When they opened once more, Catherine tried to discern the look directed at her. Sophia looked confused, bewildered, and maybe even a bit ill.

"What's your favorite color?" Sophia asked, the question catching Catherine off guard.

"I don't know. Blue, I guess. Why?" The way Sophia smiled led Catherine to believe she'd answered the question correctly.

"It's going to have a great impact on your life."

Catherine sat in silence for a moment and thought of everything she could take from this ten-minute meeting. Sophia had focused more on pain from the past as opposed to the happiness she was so desperate to find in the future. *Why should I waste another twenty?*

"Thanks for everything, Ms. Glass." Catherine stood up and extended her hand. Just because she felt a fool didn't mean she should be rude. Sophia's hand was warm and soft, but her eyes were still closed.

"You will be happy, in time," Sophia said. Catherine felt

Sophia's reluctance to let go of her hand, but she tugged it free and made her way to the door quickly.

❖

Catherine hurried back in the direction of the café in order to retrieve her car. She kicked herself for thinking Sophia would be able to help. Sure, the psychic said she'd be happy, but wouldn't she say the same to any other person who sat across from her with money in their pocket? Catherine fisted her hands at her sides, regretting the choice she made to waste an afternoon on a silly whim.

"Son of a bitch!" She didn't care who was around or who heard her. The seven-year-old on the corner who gave her a shameful look probably heard worse at home, so she wasn't about to feel guilty now. Stepping back to take a look, Catherine cursed again as she saw a long scratch along the driver's side of her silver Mercedes. "Dammit." She kicked at a nearby pile of snow. After she glanced again at the vehicle, she noticed a note on the windshield. She unfolded the small piece of paper and read the unruly handwriting: *I'm so sorry!*

The simple apology was followed by a phone number and a scribbled name. It could have ended with an *E*, but Catherine wouldn't be willing to bet money on it. She looked at the damage one last time and started to calculate how much it might cost her to get rid of the electric blue blemish.

CHAPTER FIVE

Catherine kept herself buried deep with proposals, numbers, and reports for days on end, only leaving her office for sleep and bathing. Thankfully, the weather had been cooperative, and the several meetings postponed from the previous week were finally had. She was all caught up by Friday. With a sigh of relief, she leaned back and checked the time. If she left the office then, she'd be able to stop by the store and grab a couple presents for the kids and a nice bottle of wine for the parents. As much as she loved her work she wasn't looking forward to a dinner filled with financial talk, and a potential client that would most likely have many inane questions. She was, however, looking forward to some quality time with her favorite family. Surely Alice wouldn't mind if Catherine paid her children in toys to keep distracting her from the business at hand. She leaned forward and hit the intercom button on her phone.

"Vivian?" She waited a beat.

"Yes, Ms. Carter?" The receptionist's rich voice crackled through the small speaker.

"Am I free to go?" She was already pulling on her long wool pea coat.

"I won't tell if you don't." Vivian's slightly mischievous tone matched that of her boss's.

"Good." Vivian jumped when the voice came from beside

her desk instead of the phone. "Go home, Vivian. Enjoy your weekend."

"You, too, Ms. Carter."

Just a little over an hour later, Catherine stood outside Alice's door for the second time in two weeks with a bottle of wine in one hand, but the smile on her face was due to the bag of goodies she held in the other. Tonight was casual, with no party and no guest list. It was quality time with the four people who were more family to her than any of her blood kin were. Catherine didn't bother to knock. She walked into the house and announced her arrival, happy to be pummeled by an energetic child.

"Aunt Cat!" A little girl with a head full of dirty-blond knots shrieked as she threw her body at the tall woman.

"Hey there, Mac!" Catherine refused to call the six-year-old by her full name, claiming Mackenzie had far too many letters for such a small person. She scooped the small pajama-clad bundle in her arms and swung her to and fro. "Did you miss me?"

"Not as much as you missed me!" Mac giggled as she was bounced around.

"You got that right!" Catherine covered her chubby cheeks with kiss after kiss.

"What are you two up to?" Alice said, coming out of the kitchen while she dried her hands on a dish towel.

"No good." Catherine placed the child on her feet and walked over to hug her friend. "You look nice." Even in a simple, purple sleeveless dress, Alice managed to look stunning.

"You don't look so bad yourself, boss."

Catherine grinned at the nickname. Alice only used it when Catherine showed up wearing a suit. "Thanks." She blushed slightly. "Where's Dennis?"

"Giving Daniel his bedtime bath."

"Oh man, I was hoping to give him this before bed." She raised the small bag in her hand, but the nosy Mac snatched it away.

"For me?" Her little face was already buried in the gift bag.

"For you *and* your brother," Catherine clarified.

"If it's a noisemaker, I will kill you. And I'll make it painful." Alice crossed her arms.

"Two plush teddy bears and one *very* educational video game. I promise." Catherine crossed her heart with her long index finger.

"Fine. Let me check on Dennis and Daniel." She bent at her knees to get eye level with her daughter. "And then it's bedtime for you, missy." Alice stood and walked out of the room.

"One Cat ride before bed?" Catherine looked down at her short accomplice, getting an enthusiastic nod.

Catherine heard Alice laughing when she reentered the room to find her on her hands and knees, the expensive suit jacket thrown across a nearby chair and a giggling Mac on her back. Mac's laughter echoed through the room as Catherine crawled back and forth and bounced her body all around. Both their faces were red with exertion, making Catherine look years younger.

"Hey, Cat?" Alice said, still grinning.

"Yeah?" Catherine answered from the floor but never stopped moving.

"There's something you need to know about this little meeting tonight."

"What's that?"

"Our guest, and your potential client is, well..." Alice hesitated a moment too long, and the doorbell rang.

"Here! The guest is here!" Catherine finished. She rolled the child gently to the floor before flipping onto her back and lifting Mac into the air, letting the little girl feel as though she were flying.

Catherine could hear the small exchange as Alice greeted her guests, but she couldn't see the new arrivals from behind the couch. The voices came closer, and then suddenly seemed to be standing over her. Catherine pushed up on her elbows and rose to steady herself on her knees. She looked up just as Alice entered the room with two women. Catherine froze.

"Cat, you remember Sophia and Imogene, don't you?"

"They're here!" Mac screamed, and she tackled the flustered Catherine to the floor before she had a chance to speak. The last thing Catherine saw before closing her eyes against an unidentifiable emotion was two sets of black shoes and a pair of blue heels. Catherine was a professional, and she would handle this situation like one. Despite having her face in the carpet and her shirt untucked, baring an inch or two of her taut abdomen, Catherine was about to rise to the occasion. Literally and figuratively.

"Did you know about this?" Imogene whispered from the corner of her mouth to Sophia. Instead of answering, Sophia changed the subject.

"Alice! So good to see you again. I'm sorry Dennis couldn't make it, he's feeling a bit under the weather." She embraced Alice loosely and pointed to the two-body pileup in front of her. "Is she yours?"

"No, she's not mine, but the child is." A short burst of laughter cut through some of the tension that filled the room. "That little spitfire is Mackenzie, and she is how old?"

"Six years old," the little girl answered immediately while continuing to climb Catherine like Everest.

"That's right! And my son, Daniel, is four. He's getting his bedtime bath, so he won't be joining us this evening."

"Good thing, too," Catherine said. "I'm not sure these joints would be able to take it." She collected herself, shaking off the surprise that temporarily paralyzed her. She stood and made her way over to her fellow adults, giving Sophia a narrow-eyed look that let her know not to speak of their meeting.

"This is my friend and experienced financial advisor, Catherine Carter. I'm not sure if either of you remember her from the party—"

"Oh, I remember her," Imogene said, locking eyes with her.

"Catherine." Sophia extended a hand. "So nice to formally meet you."

"You, too." Catherine shook Sophia's hand and turned to Imogene after. "Imogene, right?"

Imogene took Catherine's offered hand in a warm, tight grip. "Right."

Before Catherine could say anything more, possibly even apologize for her harsh words during their last conversation, Imogene had turned away and followed Alice toward the dining room. Catherine watched her voluptuous hips sashaying beneath a simple black dress and released a heavy breath.

Great. This should be fun, Catherine thought as she followed the small group, tucking in her shirt and straightening her trousers along the way.

Dinner went by smoothly, conversation flowing between everyone. Catherine made sure not to engage Imogene directly, and she kept her eyes away from Sophia's knowing gaze. Thankfully, Alice and Dennis were wonderful hosts and never had a lack of subject matter. Whether it was the kids or Dennis's job as a high school English teacher, they made sure an awkward silence never fell.

"So!" Alice's warm voice got everyone's attention as she turned to address a silent Catherine. "What's going on with you lately, how's your car?"

"It's still gouged." Catherine sat back into the cushioned dining room chair and sighed in contentment at her full stomach. She felt relaxed for the first time that evening.

"You haven't called the number that was left? Cat, it's been a week! The person that hit you probably thinks they're going to get off scot-free. It's so unlike you to let something like this slide."

"Don't let it go too long," Dennis added quietly. Imogene and Sophia just watched the exchange as they sipped at their coffee.

"I won't. At first I was waiting because I was pissed and

didn't want to overreact. I knew if I called that day, I'd be awful to whoever scribbled that note with their second grade handwriting. I can't even read the name on it!" She chuckled as she swept her thick curls off her shoulder with her left hand. "I don't know what to say. 'Hi, is this the person who hit my car and left a giant blue scratch down the entire side and then fled the scene? I got your note.' I think I can do better than that, Alice."

"What are you going to do, then?" Alice continued, "Just let it go and pay to fix it yourself? A Mercedes can't be that cheap when it comes to bodywork."

"Oh shit," Imogene said. Her head was down, and Sophia fought to hide a smirk. After a moment, Imogene looked up and stared at Catherine before saying, "I'm sorry."

Each person at the table looked from one to the other, realization dawning on each face at separate times. Catherine kept her eyes on Imogene, watching as shame and embarrassment crawled across her freckled face. Her cheeks were rosy, and her eyes sparkled slightly with what looked like latent tears. For the first time that evening, Catherine allowed herself to look at and admire Imogene. She remembered just how beautiful Imogene was. A familiar warmth spread through her at the opportunity for a fresh start with her.

"Well, it seems as if we were destined to meet again," Catherine said. She looked at Sophia, who was chuckling softly. *Psychic humor.* Catherine shifted and leaned forward with her forearms on the table. "I suppose we should pour ourselves another cup of coffee, exchange information, and get down to business." Catherine smiled as she delivered her words in a calm, gentle tone. Her anxious feeling melted away the instant Imogene smiled at her.

Sophia wore a knowing look while Alice looked both confused and relieved.

Catherine and Imogene talked at the table while Sophia

and Alice went into the living room. Dennis checked on their sleeping children.

"Catherine is quite a puzzle." Sophia didn't soften the statement.

"Excuse me?" Alice said, sitting back on the couch.

"She seems so tense, almost cold most of the time." Sophia looked over her shoulder to make sure no one else could hear her. She wasn't normally one for gossip or talking behind anyone's back, but the way Catherine's moods and emotions shifted behind her dark eyes genuinely intrigued her. "But at other times, she seems like the most warm, friendly person you could ever want in your life. She has me curious, I'll tell you that much."

"She's been through a lot." Alice looked at her hands and remained silent after offering what little information she had.

"We all have," Sophia argued gently.

"It's her job. The warm Cat is the Cat I've always been friends with. She's just become a lot more business oriented over the years. That's all."

Sophia wondered if Alice truly believed that or if she had noticed a hint of worry in her words. Judging by what she had seen when she had the chance to read Catherine, Alice was giving her a basic reason for her friend's behavior. Maybe Alice didn't know the real reason after all. Whatever the truth was, Sophia believed she knew who could bring back the Cat everyone knew and loved.

"I was driving along at a painfully slow pace, and all it took was a small patch of ice to send me right into the side of your car. It happened in slow motion. Literally! I could have gotten out of my car, taken a picture of the impending doom, and gotten back in before impact. But I couldn't stop it."

Catherine realized she truly enjoyed listening to this woman talk, but she enjoyed watching her even more. She felt hypnotized by her face, her smile, the expressions she made with each word and the little things she did with her hands and fingers in order to express herself fully.

"So I waited around for a little bit, but you never showed up. I figured a note was a fool-proof plan. I guess I never took my terrible handwriting into consideration, though." Imogene's small smirk was playful, but Catherine still received the message.

"I suppose it's my turn to apologize?" Catherine shifted uncomfortably. "I'm sorry for that comment, and I'm very sorry for my behavior at the party. I had no idea you were close with Sophia, but that doesn't make what I said okay. I can be very opinionated sometimes, especially when I'm outside of my comfort zone."

"Something tells me it's not very difficult to find yourself outside your comfort zone." Imogene swallowed the last little bit of cold coffee at the bottom of her mug.

"I concede." Catherine tipped her head.

"Listen, Cat, I—"

"Catherine. It's Catherine." She saw Imogene's chagrined expression and felt the need to add, "Only Alice and Dennis get away with that nickname." Her explanation didn't prevent some awkwardness. *How did we get so personal so quickly?* she wondered.

"I get it," Imogene said. "Only my grandfather was allowed to call me Immy."

Catherine smiled warmly at the thought of a boisterous, young Imogene running amok with a head full of fiery red waves, being scolded by an older man for doing something she had been told not to so many times.

"Catherine, I think we should put everything behind us and move forward. I do believe we are here for a consultation."

"I was here for the pot roast, but I suppose you're right." Happy to see Imogene smile, Catherine broached the subject she knew she'd be much more comfortable with. "Tell me about your financial situation."

"I'm not really sure where to start."

"I usually recommend the beginning," Catherine said with a lopsided smile.

Imogene shook her head and took a deep breath. "I own a boutique on Washington Street."

"Name?"

"Cowboy Fran's."

"What do you sell?" Catherine questioned quickly.

"Would you like for me to tell you about my situation, or would you prefer to interview me?"

"I'm sorry." Catherine sat back and crossed her arms over her chest. "Please, continue." She encouraged Imogene with a slight flourish of her hand before covering her troublesome mouth with three fingers.

"My boutique is my greatest investment and my life. That's where my money went before, and that's exactly where I plan on putting it now." The certainty with which Imogene delivered her words clued Catherine in to just how much of this meeting was actually Imogene's idea. "I have been successful thus far, so I'm really not looking to fix something that isn't broken." *She doesn't need me.*

"If you don't mind me asking, this meeting wasn't your idea, was it?"

"No, it wasn't." Imogene smiled abashedly.

"Whose was it?"

"Sophia's," Imogene admitted.

"I should've known," Catherine replied quietly. After listening to Imogene reason away the need for help and considering her already packed client list, Catherine was ready to dismiss the whole case and wish Imogene the best of luck. Just as she started to push her chair from the table, Imogene came to her friend's defense.

"She's my best friend, and she just wanted to make sure I handled my inheritance cautiously."

"That's right," Catherine said. "When Alice told me about a potential client, she mentioned a hefty inheritance."

"I'm sure it's not hefty compared to what you deal with daily. Do you even speak to clients with under a million? A little over eight hundred thousand dollars is probably chump change to you." Imogene laughed at her own joke, and Catherine froze. She looked to a smiling Imogene with narrowed dark eyes.

"A little over?"

"Well, most came from multiple accounts and his property, but there's more in a few stocks he'd invested in decades ago. I'm no stocks expert but, yeah, I think it all puts me somewhere between eight hundred and nine hundred thousand." A simple shrug punctuated Imogene's rapid and casual calculations.

"Wait here." Catherine rushed from the room, returning a moment later with her jacket and a business card in her hand. "Call my office Monday morning. It was nice seeing you again." With that, Catherine left.

Imogene remained seated, running her fingertips over the raised letters on the small card. *Catherine Carter*. Bold, black lettered, and in the palm of her hand. The quiet authority the other woman exuded had pushed Imogene from knowing she didn't need financial help to feeling she couldn't go on another day without it. *How did she do that?* Imogene thought as she sat stunned. She ignored the little voice in the back of her mind that wondered if she wanted Catherine's help or Catherine herself.

Chapter Six

Imogene spent her weekend struggling with what to do next. It wasn't until her weekly phone call with her mother Sunday evening that Imogene made her final decision.

"How's my daughter?" Dorothy Harris asked in a tone that held genuine concern.

"I'm fine, Mom, just very busy with the shop lately. The spring collections come in earlier and earlier every year. I feel silly unpacking short-sleeved blouses when it's below freezing outside." She looked out her small bedroom window to check on the snow that had yet to stop falling.

"Have you managed a date anytime recently?" Straight to the point, as usual.

"No, Mom, I haven't." Imogene barely held in her exasperated sigh. Every week, every conversation was the same.

"Are you at least trying?"

"Of course I'm trying!" This time, she let her annoyance show. "I just haven't met anyone worth my time since Aria and I split." She removed her heavy sweater and threw on a thin sleep shirt.

"That was over a year ago, sweetheart. You're so kind and beautiful, I find it hard to believe that it's so difficult for you to find someone."

"And we were together for four. It takes time to heal, I

haven't been ready." Her jeans were next, quickly replaced by soft cotton shorts. It may have been the arctic tundra outside, but her apartment got a little too warm in the peak hours of the night.

"Believe me, I know that." Dorothy didn't have to speak specifically of the loss she and her daughter shared. "I just want to see you happy."

Imogene listened carefully and heard the sadness, the slight pity each of her mother's words held. She was alone, not lonely, but the difference didn't mean a thing to Mrs. Harris.

"If I told you that there may be someone, but it's too early to tell, would that satisfy you for now?" Imogene asked playfully. Nevertheless, she winced at the mere mention of her possible future advisor. *You'll say anything to get your mother off your back, won't you?*

"For now." Dorothy's response was flat. "I'd feel better if you'd tell me a bit about her."

"It's too soon, but you'll be the first to know if something develops."

"Why do you insist on lying to me? We both know Sophia will hear everything first. Your poor mother will always be in second place." She spoke in defeat, an overexaggerated melancholy echoing with each word she spoke.

"Your guilt won't work this time." Imogene smiled at the playful sigh she received in response.

"Fine. I'll try harder next time."

"Good night, Mom."

"I love you, Imogene."

"Love you, too."

Imogene sat on the edge of her bed and wondered if what she had told her mother was true. Was something there? A hidden potential between her and Catherine Carter? Despite their rocky start, could it be more than a mild flirtation? *There's only one way to find out*, Imogene thought as she threw herself back into a pile of pillows.

When Monday morning rolled around, Imogene sat at the

front counter of Cowboy Fran's and held the phone in her hand. It took a few pep talks, but she finally dialed Catherine's number.

"Catherine Carter's office, this is Vivian speaking. How may I help you?" Imogene shouldn't have been surprised when the phone was answered on the first ring, but she still was.

"I was actually looking to speak with Catherine."

"May I ask who is calling?"

"Imogene Harris." For the tenth time that morning, she had started to doubt her decision.

"Ms. Harris, I was told you may be calling this morning. Ms. Carter is in a meeting, let me see if I can interrupt." Imogene was put on hold before she had the chance to insist Vivian do no such thing. Monotonous instrumental music filled her ear. She must have been on hold for close to five minutes, apologizing to each customer who needed help and only received half of Imogene's attention, before the line came to life once again.

"I wasn't sure you were going to call." Catherine's smooth voice replaced the music with a melody all its own.

"I wasn't either. I hope I made the right decision." Imogene grimaced when she heard just how low she let her voice drop. *Not even a minute in, and I'm already flirting with this woman!* The effect that Catherine had on her was immediate and unsettling, but Imogene felt possessed. She listened as a quiet rustling sound filled her ear.

"Would I sound narcissistic if I told you it's the best decision you'll make all day?" Catherine's tone conveyed a smile.

"Only a little." Imogene giggled.

"Good. I don't want my true colors to be showing just yet. Dammit."

"Are you okay?" Although they were speaking over the phone, Imogene shifted uncomfortably after Catherine's odd, gentle outburst.

"Yeah." Catherine's warm laughter traveled through the phone and straight into Imogene's chest, where her heart picked up its pace. "I wore wool pants today."

This small, intimate detail caused Imogene's smile to grow wider. She twirled a thick lock of her hair around her fingertip several times before speaking. "Itchy?"

"Unbelievably so. I knew I pushed them to the back of my closet for a reason."

"I bet they look fantastic, though." A beat of silence passed before Imogene realized what she had said and not just thought. Imogene held her breath. When a response didn't come, she added, "Because wool always looks classy." She slapped her forehead and hoped the sound of skin on skin wasn't audible to Catherine.

"Classy, yes. Comfortable? No. They're slim fitting, too." Catherine's tone had changed slightly and if she didn't know any better, she would have sworn Catherine was egging her on, but before Imogene could match flirtation for flirtation, Catherine continued. "Do you think you can come by my office today? I'd like to go over a few ideas with you and get a feel for your business." Her tone was neutral, and her professionalism was back in place.

"Where is it?" As many times as Imogene had looked over the business card over the weekend, she'd never noticed anything beyond the name and phone number embossed on it.

"Lower Manhattan, not too far from Wall Street."

An icy chill ran down Imogene's spine at the mention of such an address. She wasn't sure why she was surprised by the office's location, but it caught her unaware. "I can't," she quickly choked out. "I have to be at the shop all day."

"Okay." Catherine paused as if she were expecting more of an explanation. When Imogene didn't offer one, she asked, "What time are you there until?"

"We close at nine." She answered automatically, still fighting against the nausea and anxiety gripping her gut tightly.

"Do you mind if I come to you, then? I'd like to get started as soon as possible. I can be there by six."

"That's fine."

"All right, then." The silence stretched on and became awkward. "I have to get back to my meeting."

"Right!" Imogene snapped out of her painful reverie. "I'm sorry to take up your time."

"It was a welcome interruption, I assure you." Catherine laughed lightly before saying good-bye and hanging up the phone.

Imogene sat and stared at the phone, wondering what she had just agreed to. When she looked around her store she didn't want to think of the way a straight-laced, professional Catherine would judge it, just like she had her best friend. She wasn't at all sure if someone who wore a suit every day and was so business oriented could see the heartbeat that was within the small boutique.

"Oh well. We'll just have to wait and see." Imogene whispered to herself as she went to take inventory of some newly arrived jewelry.

Chapter Seven

As Catherine went from the railway station to her home, she tried to ignore the way she felt. She was dreading this private work, but had been urged into it by her best friend and charmed into caring by the charismatic Imogene. It was a deadly combination she didn't even bother to try to fight. Her watch read five forty-five by the time she stepped into the garage of her condo. As much as she would have liked to run upstairs to change into a comfortable pair of jeans and a sweater, she didn't have time for it. She said a small, thankful prayer for the comfortable penny loafers she had chosen that morning. Sliding behind the wheel of her Mercedes, she pulled out onto an empty road, making her way to Washington Street.

It wasn't hard to spot Cowboy Fran's amongst the other storefronts. Catherine wondered how she hadn't noticed it until now. It was bright, inviting, and charming with its colorful exterior and carefully decorated front window. This place was clearly well cared for, and that made all the difference in the success of a small business. The bell above the door that signaled Catherine's arrival went unnoticed by Imogene. She was so engrossed in helping an elderly woman that she didn't tear her eyes away to greet her latest customer, but that didn't stop her from speaking up the best she could.

"Hello!" She was so cheerful and bubbly that Catherine couldn't help but smile. "I'll be right with you."

"Take your time." Catherine stepped a little closer and stood with her hip against the counter.

Catherine could tell Imogene recognized her voice by the way her body stiffened slightly before she relaxed and turned to her. Catherine's breath caught as their eyes met and Imogene graced her with a warm smile. Her heart pounded, and all Catherine could think of was how that mouth had to be made of sugar and spice. When Imogene returned her attention to her customer, Catherine shook off her slight stupor.

Catherine took the opportunity to observe Imogene in her element as well as drink in the sight before her. Imogene wore her long red hair pulled back and bundled into some sort of bun at the top of her head. A few small tendrils escaped and danced along a creamy white nape exposed by a flowing green blouse. Catherine had knowledge, albeit minimal, of materials and she felt it was safe to guess that this one was a silk blend. It looked soft enough to beckon to her fingertips, but not as soft as the skin that was exposed by the low V-neck collar. Her tight blue jeans hugged her shapely thighs and calves that tapered down to black ballet flats.

Shaking her head, Catherine turned her attention to the store, taking in the wide array of goods and the charming decorations. Cowboy Fran's was indeed warm and inviting, but it also had the same feel that most high-end boutiques had. Catherine was genuinely impressed. In less than ten minutes, Imogene had rung up her customer and was at Catherine's side.

"Well, don't you stick out like a sore thumb?" Imogene pointed at her black and gray ensemble. That prompted Catherine to take another look at her very colorful surroundings. "So? What do you think?"

"It's lovely." At Imogene's eye-roll, she continued. "I mean it! It's lovely and quite unique. Very eclectic. It seems like the type of establishment that draws in the general public as well as regular clients."

"As a matter of fact, the woman who just left is Ruth Ann. She comes in at least once a week for a new pair of earrings. I often wonder what her jewelry box looks like since she's been a customer of mine from the moment the doors opened in 2003." After they shared a short laugh, Imogene motioned toward the back of the store. "Let me show you to the office."

"But what if a customer comes in?"

"Cameras in every corner, and the bell is anything but quiet. Come on."

Catherine followed her through the store, pausing to check out various items of interest. A colorful, watercolor style floral print silk robe caught Catherine's eye. *Alice would love that.* She made a note to check the price on the way out. They made it to the office moments later, and Catherine removed her jacket and took a seat across from Imogene, behind a small desk overrun with piles of papers, order forms, and empty paper coffee cups. Catherine watched as Imogene looked her over.

"Does the wool look as classy as you suspected?" she asked.

"Are you a swimmer?"

"Excuse me?" The question caught Catherine off guard.

"You're built like a swimmer."

"I run." Catherine was bewildered. She thought she'd seen an attraction in Imogene's eyes as they swept her body, not just innocent curiosity. Sure, she had been out of the dating game for a while, but was she really that out of touch with reading people?

"I hate running." Imogene sat back with a look of concentration on her face. "The last time I ran was over the summer when it started to rain on my way back from the deli three blocks away after picking up lunch. It was the *worst.*" An adorable cringe overtook her features. She looked again at Catherine and smiled.

Not really knowing where to take the conversation and not daring to acknowledge just how charming Imogene was,

Catherine returned their attention to the business at hand. "I have to ask, why the name Cowboy Fran's?"

"I named it in memory of my dad. He was born and raised in Texas, overflowing with Houston pride. He was all about the Cowboys, the Longhorns, and the Alamo. He'd bring home a bouquet of bluebonnets for my mom every holiday, even after we moved."

"Bluebonnets?" Catherine asked. She wondered how she had never noticed Imogene's slight Southern accent before.

"The Texas state flower. Anyway, I wanted to name it after him, but I knew very few women would shop at a clothing boutique called Frank's, so I took his birth name, Francis, cut it down and added a nickname some knew him by. Cowboy Fran's was born on the spot."

"It definitely adds intrigue." Catherine smiled at her, happy to receive one back, the dimple in Imogene's right cheek fascinating her.

"So where do we start?" Imogene seemed eager, and Catherine appreciated that.

"Where do you keep your records?" Imogene pointed to an old, rickety file cabinet against the wall. The forest green metal monstrosity stood about four feet tall and housed four separate drawers all labeled "paperwork."

"Payroll and employee information is in the top drawer, invoices are in the second, and the third and fourth are dedicated to miscellaneous papers I didn't really know what to do with but seemed important." Catherine sat stunned. "Listen, I may have opened this place with money I didn't earn, but I kept the doors open for ten years. Ten *years*. That was all me." Her tone was growing more defensive and louder with every word. It occurred to Catherine that Imogene mistook her silence for an insult. "So don't look at me like I don't know what I'm doing."

"Actually," Catherine looked to Imogene to make sure the tirade was over, "I wasn't doubting your ability to run this place. Like you said, you've kept it open this long. I'm not here to fix what's not broken." Catherine was sure Imogene recognized her own words the moment she said them. "I'm here to help what you already have grown and hopefully ensure a comfortable future for you and your family." This wasn't the first time Catherine had to calm a balking client, but it was the first time she cared about whether the client believed her.

"I'm sorry."

"Don't be. I know what it's like to be underestimated, I get it. It's just a lot to go through. Receipts?" It was a quick topic change, one that Imogene seemed grateful for as well.

"On top of the filing cabinet." When she looked again, Catherine notice three shoeboxes stacked there. She looked at her curiously. "It's my system," Imogene said.

"Your system needs help," Catherine said with a tilt of her head.

"Isn't that why we're together?"

The question played over and over in Catherine's mind. Why else would two very different women be together? She hadn't even realized how nice the thought of Imogene being interested in her was until it was no longer there. The reality sobered her immediately.

"Right." Catherine rose and walked over to the files. "I guess we'll start with taxes. Where's last year's paperwork?"

"Top drawer. My mother does all my filing for me, and I also took a night course in tax preparation. We try to keep everything in house, it's another way I try to limit output."

"*Great.*" She couldn't hide the sarcasm in her voice, which immediately caused Imogene to stiffen. "I'm sorry." She followed her grimace with a sympathetic smile before getting back to work.

Catherine admired the way Imogene kept an eye on her expenses, but she was frightened by the potential mess self-filing could cause. With a deep breath, she opened each drawer in turn and removed all the necessary files. Catherine then did the same with the boxes of receipts and payroll information.

They spoke casually, but very little. Catherine was reluctant to share anything more than business knowledge, and Imogene seemed content with just observing. It took over an hour for the two women to collect everything needed, but once Catherine was satisfied, she stepped back and took a breath.

"Here's the plan." She looked up to make sure Imogene was listening and noticed that she looked tired. "I'm going to take this back to my office and look everything over. I'd like to get an idea of what last year looked like for Cowboy Fran's so I can make sure everything will be in good shape for this year. If it's all right with you and your mother," Catherine added with a wink, "I'd like to take over your taxes for last year. I'm assuming that you haven't filed yet?" Imogene nodded. "Good. Then after I get all of this sorted, we can talk about your inheritance. Would you like to hear the idea I'm working with now?" Again, Imogene nodded. Catherine frowned at Imogene's silence. She was normally so talkative and inquisitive. "I'd like a fair amount of that money to sit right where it is in order to support this business. Whatever is in stocks will remain there, and the rest I'd like for you to invest further in any way you feel most comfortable. My main goal, however, is to make sure Cowboy Fran's and your father's memory are around for as long as possible."

Imogene looked up at Catherine with shining eyes. "Thank you." Her normally strong voice crackled.

When the urge to wrap the emotional woman in a warm embrace became too strong, Catherine cleared her throat and shrugged off the thanks. She was here because Alice asked her to help out a friend of a friend. Her desire to do her job the best she could had nothing to do with the glimmering blue eyes looking up at her at that moment.

"I'll be in touch soon." Catherine put on her jacket and collected the many boxes she had put together. After a few trips out to the car, she finally had everything she needed as she closed her trunk, or at least she thought she did.

"Last one." Imogene ran outside and handed over a blue file before they said their final good-byes on the sidewalk. She watched as Catherine climbed into her car and drove off, her red taillights disappearing before Imogene made her way back inside.

Once she locked up for the night, Imogene sat behind her desk once more. She stared into space as she wondered about her behavior throughout the night. She'd unabashedly checked Catherine out several times, but when Catherine tried to call her out on it, she feigned nonchalance and brushed it off. Every time Catherine put another tempting body part on display—whether she was reaching deep within the filing cabinet for a particularly stubborn folder or bending to fill an empty box—Imogene averted her gaze for fear of being caught staring again. She was never one to hide her intentions or attractions, so what was it about Catherine Carter that startled her?

Imogene stood and started to make her way out. She picked up her cell phone and dialed Sophia. Maybe she had some sort of advice to clear her frazzled mind.

"Hello?"

"Hey, Sophia, it's not too late to talk, is it? Did I wake you or Chris up?" She suddenly felt silly for calling her friend so spontaneously.

"Sweetie, it's barely nine o'clock. I'm not that old yet." A comforting chuckle traveled through the phone. "What's up?"

"Catherine Carter just left."

"Oh?"

"She came by to talk about the business."

"How did it go?"

"I'm not sure. I mean, it went good, I guess."

"You guess?"

"She had some good ideas. She seems like she has good intentions, but I get such an odd vibe from her." Imogene fought to make sense of her own scattered thoughts.

"What do you mean?"

"We were together for over two hours, and she still feels like a complete stranger to me." She paused long enough to unlock the door to her apartment.

"So she's not much of a conversationalist?"

"She's great at conversation, but it was all incredibly superficial or about the store. After a while, I just stopped talking because I felt like I was assaulting her."

"And…" Sophia encouraged.

"And nothing." Imogene kept the details to herself. She wasn't ready to tell Sophia about the easy conversation or flirtation she resisted, and she definitely wasn't ready to tell Sophia she was undeniably attracted to Catherine. "I'm just hesitant to trust a complete stranger with something that means so much to me." She shucked off her shoes and gave Vixen a scratch from head to tail, smiling fondly at the purr she received.

"I think you should give her a chance. Catherine could be good for you."

"Good for me?" Imogene guffawed. "Not only are we complete opposites in every way, but she's so black-and-white, judgmental, and incredibly square! Sure she's attractive, but that will only take a relationship so far before—"

"I was talking about your business, Imogene. Catherine could be good for your business." Imogene was glad Sophia wasn't there to witness the many shades of red she was turning. "It sounds to me like you're being a bit judgmental as well."

"Are you meddling?"

"Excuse me?" Sophia said, obviously offended.

"Did you read something? Did you see something?"

"I promised you years ago that I'd never read you without your permission, and I intend on keeping that promise until I die."

Imogene couldn't believe she'd accused her. "I'm sorry."

"It's okay. She's really got you out of sorts, doesn't she?"

"I hate not knowing someone I'm working with! It drives me crazy! Does Chris know anything about her?"

"Not really. All he knows is that she and Alice have been friends since college or earlier. Unfortunately, I don't know Alice well enough to ask personal details about her best friend. I could try to take a peek next time I'm around, you know."

"No thank you, but I appreciate the offer. I'm just usually so good at getting people to open up and feel comfortable around me, but she's all business most of the time. I offered little random tidbits about myself, and she'd respond with a question about the store. It's so frustrating!"

"I'm sure she has her reasons."

"I can't even tell if she's a lesbian."

"And that matters because...?"

"It doesn't," Imogene barely whispered. She sighed as she slumped into her worn sofa and brought her feet up to rest on the coffee table.

"I do know she's single."

Imogene sat silently on the other end of the phone, fighting a smile. "She's calling me soon so we can meet up and talk business. I guess we'll see what happens. If I can't trust her, if she doesn't open up a little to me, I can't work with her."

"That's understandable."

"I should let you go. I don't want to keep you from Chris." Her eyes were growing heavy and Imogene stifled a yawn. Talking about money for hours was exhausting.

"He's a big boy. He'll understand my best friend needs me."

"You truly are the best, Sophia."

"I know. Have a good night, Imogene."

"Good night."

"Oh, and Imogene?"

"Yeah?"

"That new cashmere sweater you got in the boutique would look fantastic on you. Especially in blue. It'd be perfect for a business meeting." Sophia hung up before Imogene could question her suggestion.

Chapter Eight

S unday lunch seemed like the perfect place for Catherine to discuss business. She'd be able to eat and keep a time limit on her interaction with her client. She sat quietly in one of three chairs at the round table and stirred the carefully measured dash of sweetener into her unsweetened iced tea. A large box of files was on the chair across from her, leaving the spot beside her open for Imogene. When she breezed through the front door, Catherine stared for a moment before waving her over.

Imogene approached slowly and removed her brown leather jacket along the way. Catherine appraised her cobalt blue sweater, woven of what looked to be the softest yarn, with a scoop neck low enough to hint at the perfect amount of cleavage. The top hugged her slim abdomen tightly, cut high enough to accentuate the swell of her beautifully rounded hips, hips that held Catherine's attention for longer than appropriate.

But Catherine wasn't thinking about Imogene's hips. Nor was she thinking about how they'd feel under her palms or just how decadent it would be to sink her short nails into them. Those thoughts were off-limits, as were the thoughts of counting each perfect freckle on her pale chest with her lips. Catherine shook her head and buried those feelings. *This is business*, she reminded herself.

"Hi."

"Hey. Please, sit." Catherine rose and indicated the spot next to her.

"I was so happy when you mentioned this place, it's one of my favorites." Imogene placed her jacket on the back of her cushioned chair and relaxed into it.

"Mine as well. If I'm not getting takeout for dinner on my way home, I'm usually sitting here for lunch on the weekends. Alone." *Why did I feel the need to specify alone? Now she probably thinks I'm pathetic.* Imogene looked at her with sad eyes. *Yup. She thinks I'm pathetic.*

"I usually get takeout and bring it back to the store." Imogene opened her menu and started to read, a relief to Catherine, who was ready to drown in her sympathetic gaze. Something about it was so soft, emotional and yet feral.

"Can I get you something to drink?" Their waiter approached quietly, startling both women.

"Thai iced tea, please," Imogene said. "I'm ready to order if you are." Catherine nodded. "I'll have the Pad Kee Mao, please."

"And for you?" The waiter smiled at Catherine.

"I'll have the coconut rice salad with shrimp. Thank you." Catherine handed her menu over and turned her attention back to Imogene. "How was the rest of your week?"

"Busy. I was actually quite shocked to hear from you so soon. I thought for sure that this," she pointed her thumb in the direction of the overflowing box, "would have taken you a lot longer."

"I pride myself on being quick, efficient, and thorough." Catherine sat back with a cocky grin on her face, one Imogene didn't look away from. "I was recommended for a reason."

"I never doubted that. Speaking of all the work you're doing for me, we never discussed your rates." Catherine raised an eyebrow. "I'm not sure how this goes. I've never worked with a consultant of any kind. Do you get paid hourly, per meeting, or at the completion of the job?"

Catherine took a long sip of her iced tea, chewing on her straw for a moment while she collected her thoughts and formulated an answer. Imogene looked back at her with innocent curiosity and lightness. "I'm not taking your money."

"What?"

"I'm not taking your money," Catherine repeated. She sat back and folded her arms across her chest, shoulders squared. "I'm doing this as a favor. Alice asked me to help out, and I want to do just that. This isn't about money for me, it's about doing what I'm good at and helping a friend in the process." Catherine watched as Imogene looked from her face down to her toned arms. Subconsciously, she flexed.

"I can't let you do that."

"Sure you can. I'll tell you what, buy me a cup of coffee sometime, and we'll call it even."

"I'll do you one better. Lunch is on me." Before the innocent argument could go any farther, the waiter brought their food, providing the perfect distraction.

"Enjoy." Catherine fluffed her rice in order to make sure the dressing as well as the ingredients were evenly distributed throughout the whole bowl. Before she had the chance to indulge in her first bite, Catherine saw a look of pain and mild disgust on Imogene's face.

"Are you all right?" She placed a gentle hand on Imogene's shoulder. That sweater was just as soft as she thought it would be.

"Yeah." Imogene coughed. "I just hate spicy food."

"Did the menu not specify it was spicy?" Catherine looked around for their waiter, but Imogene stopped her with a gentle hand. Catherine immediately dismissed the slight jolt she felt.

"Yes, it did. I just really want to like spicy food. I keep ordering it in hopes of changing my mind. No such luck." Catherine eased back into her chair at Imogene's crooked smile.

Just when I thought she couldn't be any more charming!
"Well, I know you like shrimp, so why don't you have some

of mine." It wasn't a question or suggestion. Catherine dished some of her rice salad onto a small plate and pushed it in front of Imogene.

"I can't take your lunch from you!"

"You're not, I'm sharing. Besides, I never finish the whole thing anyway."

"Thank you," she said, taking a bite. "Oh my God. This is divine." She nearly grunted.

"I know, that's why I order it at least two times a week." An odd sense of pride wedged its way into Catherine's chest at knowing Imogene enjoyed one of her favorite things.

"How is it possible that I've never ordered this? How do you not eat it all? Are you on a diet or something?"

"No, nothing like that. I'm not dieting, but I do believe in portion control and plenty of exercise to stay healthy."

"It shows." When Catherine blushed, Imogene added, "I don't believe in either, obviously."

Catherine's eyes grew wide, and she spoke without thinking. "You have a perfect body." Silence fell over the table as they both reddened and stared at one another. Catherine was sure she could hear herself blink.

"Thank you," Imogene replied breathily.

Catherine changed the subject quickly. "Let's talk numbers, shall we?" Nearly an hour had passed, and they had yet to discuss business.

They got right to it as they finished their lunch and indulged in desserts and blended coffee beverages. Catherine went over the numbers she had worked on and proposed ways Imogene could invest and make her money grow. She had a wide array of options to choose from, several foolproof plans, and many more suggestions to make along the way. Catherine was satisfied with her work and the attention Imogene gave her every idea. She sat quietly and took in the information as she sipped her drink or twirled a lock of hair around her slender fingertip, an action that caused Catherine to stutter more than once. She wondered just how silky each glittery strand really was.

"I honestly think your best options are stocks and real estate. There's several more products out there, but after looking over your records and getting to know you, I'd say those suit your situation."

"I'm against the stocks idea," Imogene decided matter-of-factly. "Whatever my grandfather invested in years ago is enough for me."

"What about real estate? Do you own a home now?"

"No. I live above the store in a small apartment."

"You could buy a house with a nice piece of property. It'll be a smart investment and one you can enjoy for years to come," Catherine pointed out.

"I love where I live. I couldn't imagine living anywhere else or having a whole house just for myself." Imogene's tone was soft, but almost sad.

"I'll see if I can come up with other options." Catherine turned slightly in her chair to face Imogene more fully. "Keep an open mind about looking at some houses. The money you have now can promise you a comfortable future, but I'm also looking to make sure you'll have that for your future family." Imogene's bark of laughter caught Catherine off guard.

"I don't even have a partner yet. It's a little too early to be thinking about a family."

Catherine thought she was genuinely amused by such an idea. But her use of the term "partner" was a pleasant surprise. She felt the need for clarification. "Partner?"

"Well, ideally we'd be married, but I guess I'd buy a house with a girlfriend if I knew marriage was in the near future." When Catherine shifted slightly, Imogene asked, "Did I make you uncomfortable? I just assumed—"

"Assumed what?"

"I know that Dennis and Alice are huge LGBT supporters

since his sister is part of the community. That's how they met Chris and Sophia, actually. At a benefit." Imogene visibly swallowed. "I figured you'd be as supportive since you're so close to the family."

"You're right, I am." Catherine took a deep breath and relaxed. "You just surprised me, that's all." Catherine was surprised, but not at Imogene's assumption. She was surprised by the possibilities this new information presented. Thoughts she was ready to so quickly discard in the name of an overactive imagination were now real possibilities. That petrified her.

"What about you?" Imogene asked. "Investing in a house for a future family?"

"Condominium and no kids in the near future. I, too, am partner-less." She scrambled quickly to add, "But of the male variety. Men are easier, they fit my lifestyle better," Catherine explained lamely. *My heart breaks too easily when women are involved*, she thought. *This is for the best.* For a moment she was sure she noticed a flash of disappointment in Imogene's blue eyes. Catherine wanted to take the words back, but it was too late. They finished their drinks in silence.

Their lunch came to a close when the waiter brought the check, and Imogene immediately snatched it, making good on her earlier promise. After she paid the bill and left a substantial tip, both women bundled up and walked out to the parking lot. Catherine carried the box of files to Imogene's Mazda and packed it into her trunk. They stood on the sidewalk for a few minutes just looking at one another. The sun was shining on that brisk afternoon, making Imogene's hair sparkle with highlights of gold and copper. Her blue eyes seemed a shade lighter and held the kind of smile only people who appreciated life could wear. Catherine's puffy down jacket kept her warm, but she still shivered when she looked deep into Imogene's gaze. Catherine was powerless once they pinned her. Dark brown curls covered her stoic face as the wind whipped up the busy street. They wished each other simple good-byes before parting. Imogene went to her driver's side and Catherine jogged across the street to her silver luxury car.

Once her car door was shut, Imogene let out a heavy breath. *What* was *that?* She picked up her phone and typed out a quick message and sent it to Sophia before turning the key in the ignition.

She's straight.

Chapter Nine

Catherine was completely distracted on Monday morning, a rare occurrence for her. She stared out her large windows with a blank expression as thoughts of Imogene and Cowboy Fran's swirled through her mind, thoughts that had kept her mind scattered since she awoke at sunrise. It took two extra minutes on the treadmill to complete a mile, six attempts to button her shirt correctly, and two cups of coffee because she lost count of how many spoonfuls of sugar she had put in the first cup. For the first time in Catherine's adult life, she felt disordered, and she blamed it on her surprise at how well Imogene ran her business, not Imogene herself. Catherine was ashamed to admit she had assumed the eccentric redhead knew very little about business management, but after reviewing the store's file, Catherine was not only impressed but intrigued. She'd been intrigued by Imogene's brains as well as her spirit, and if Catherine had allowed herself to delve a little deeper into her feelings, she would have admitted that Imogene's beauty was on the list of things she liked about her also.

"Ms. Carter?"

Catherine started at the sound of Vivian's voice. "Yes, Vivian?" she answered after catching her breath.

"There's an Imogene Harris on line two for you. Would you like to take it or should I take a message?"

"I'll take it." A slight panic washed over her before it was tamped down by embarrassment. Imogene was her client and surely she had no idea she occupied a few too many of Catherine's uncharacteristic daydreams lately. She picked up her phone before the wait became prolonged.

"Hello, Imogene."

"Catherine!" The volume and excitement of the voice was unexpected. "I hope I'm not interrupting."

"No, of course not. What can I do for you?" Catherine relaxed into her chair and tried to imagine what Imogene was wearing and if she was smiling as broadly as her voice conveyed.

"Nothing. I have something to tell you, and it can't wait."

Catherine's mouth was doing its best impression of the Sahara. Anxiety always had that effect on her.

"Nothing bad, I hope."

"Nothing bad unless you're a mouse, then maybe."

"I'm not following."

"I was going through the boxes of receipts you returned. I thought maybe it was time to invest in a big-girl organization technique."

"Boot boxes instead of shoe?"

"Ha-ha. Very funny. I got another filing cabinet. Anyway, I found another box of miscellaneous papers and dumped them out on the floor. Everything was dated 2005 and earlier, and my guess is that the rodent corpse I found in there was just as old."

"No way!"

"Way. So I was just calling to let you know that you chose the wrong boxes and were not an instant winner this time, but please try again." Imogene's deep chuckle vibrated through the phone and made its way deep into Catherine's chest.

"I'll definitely choose more wisely next time."

"Well, I guess I should let you get back to work. I know I'd be upset if I were to find out that my financial advisor was taking personal calls during work hours. Oh wait…"

"Good-bye, Imogene."

"Buh-bye." The singsong tone Imogene used for her parting words played on repeat in Catherine's mind after she hung up.

The phone call did very little to calm the storm that had started to build that morning. Catherine's mind weaved between numbers and Imogene's bright smile, her curvy hips, or the way her bright blue eyes sparkled when she laughed and her freckled nose scrunched up when she wasn't pleased with something. Imogene Harris was much more captivating than Catherine had expected, and even more interesting than the pile of work that lay neglected on her desk. Vivian startled her for the second time that morning. "Catherine, dear, don't forget about the eleven o'clock interview." Catherine looked at her standing in the doorway, smiling gently. *How long has she been there and how long have I been sitting like this?* She looked down and noticed she still had her hand on the receiver.

"Thank you, Vivian. Could you bring me a coffee? Mine was dreadful this morning." Catherine checked the clock and noted she had ten minutes before she was expected in the main conference room down the hall. She wasn't a partner in the firm, but Marcati and Stevens valued her opinion when it came to new hires and let her have a say in decisions about the staff. She slipped her feet into the worn loafers beneath her desk. It was still icy outside so Catherine's shoe choice was more practical, not wanting to risk a broken neck or a ruined pair of Guccis.

Nine minutes later, Catherine sat beside the head of a long conference table with a steaming mug of perfectly sweetened coffee in front of her. An elderly yet spry man sat beside her. Walter Adamson was the head of the entire firm, but his name wasn't on the building because he preferred to remain behind the scenes as much as possible. Catherine admired the man, not only for what he had accomplished in the world of business finance, but also for his life and legacy. His employees looked up to him, many liked him on a much more personal level, his family adored him, and Catherine did as well.

He had taken her under his wing during her senior year internship and taught her everything he knew, impeccably grooming her to be the company's leader once his own time was up. That had earned Catherine her fair share of dirty looks in the office, but she hadn't given a shit what they thought. His support meant the world to Catherine after the way her father had turned his back on her for her career choice. Even now that she'd won her father's recognition after years of fighting for it, Walter Adamson was more of a father figure to Catherine than he was.

They spoke briefly about Catherine's client list, and she found herself wanting to discuss Imogene with Walter. His dark eyes willed her to open up in a way she never experienced, but she kept the focus on the matter at hand instead.

"Are you ready? These things are dreadfully boring," he whispered in a gravelly, aged voice.

"If you'd like to take a nap, I'll take notes for both of us." They shared a laugh and Catherine smiled warmly. He wore the same black pinstripe suit and red tie combo every day he was at the office, which became fewer and fewer at his old age. Catherine always found comfort in the scent of his Old Spice and how he usually missed a small patch of gray hairs on his chin.

She waited patiently for the rest of the team and the potential hire to arrive, scribbling notes on possible alternatives and Realtors for Imogene. A minute later the door swung open and Anthony Marcati and Phillip Stevens entered. They always arrived together to meetings and interviews, both impeccably dressed in three-piece suits. Mr. Marcati was often drawn to the darker suits, with colorful ties that had a tendency to be obnoxiously bright. Mr. Stevens, on the other hand, enjoyed his browns and earth tones. Summer found him in khaki suits with oddly matched mint green shirts and darker ties. Whenever she saw him, Catherine often found herself thinking all his money couldn't purchase good fashion sense. She smoothed down her blouse and the front of her pressed black trousers at the thought.

"Good morning," both men said in unison.

"Do they have to do everything together?" Walter whispered into Catherine's ear and she barely suppressed her laughter.

"Good morning, Phillip, Anthony." With a nod of her head, all morning pleasantries were completed.

"We have one interview this morning for the entry-level position that just opened. Let's get it over with as quickly as possible, I'm starving," Anthony said, his rounded belly shifting beneath his large suit jacket as he laughed at his own words. He had a kind face, aged and tanned from many family vacations to his home in Florida.

"Anything we should know about before we get started?" Walter said.

"Yale business graduate, just moved here from Chicago and we were his first choice in the city," Phillip answered and then added, "Good to know we still have an impressive reputation."

"Bring him in," Walter said. Phillip left the conference room and returned a moment later with a younger man by his side.

"Everyone, this is Richard Thorton. Have a seat, Richard."

Richard had a matured yet youthful look and was thirty-six, according to his résumé. His jaw was strong and chiseled, his black hair brushed back from his forehead and sculpted into a classic style. His olive complexion highlighted his long eyelashes and dark eyes. Richard's good looks didn't capture Catherine's attention at first, but the way he dressed certainly did. He wore a tailored black suit with a starched white shirt that accentuated his tall, muscular frame. What caught Catherine's eye was the horrifically mismatched navy blue tie Richard paired with such a classic wardrobe combination. The navy and the black looked as if they wanted to match, which left Catherine wondering whether this man had dressed in the dark that morning. Suddenly, a thought hit her. All of her attention was drawn to his navy blue tie. *"Blue will have a great impact on you."* Sophia's words echoed in her mind. *Could this be him?* The lack of a ring on his left hand gave her hope.

The interview went quickly and well. Richard Thorton got rave reviews from everyone around the table, including Catherine. He had the kind of experience and knowledge Marcati and Stevens valued. On a more personal front, they learned the Chicago native was used to brutal winters, and the worst New York had seen was like a walk in the park for him. The meeting finished with Walter giving his secretary the go-ahead to contact Richard Thorton later that afternoon with the good news that he'd be the latest addition to their already stellar team.

❖

After a brutal morning spent dealing with plans for a private bridal shower reading, Sophia Glass sat in her office and traced circles on her throbbing temples. A light knock on the door drew her from her slight meditation. "Come in."

"I know you had a rough morning," Gladys started timidly, "but are you willing to take a walk-in?"

Sophia rolled her dark blue eyes and released a sigh. "How does the rest of my afternoon look?"

"Wide open."

"Fine. Send them back." Gladys retreated quickly, and Sophia scolded herself for not being kinder to her receptionist. Gladys was kind and dedicated, and she made a note to tell her as much by the end of the day.

"Hello again," Catherine said in a shaky voice from the threshold, and Sophia jumped at its familiarity.

"Catherine!" Sophia's mouth fell open in surprise. "Please have a seat." This was the last person she expected to see in her office again. She remembered how much time Catherine and Imogene had been spending together and wondered if that had something to do with her spontaneous visit.

"I need to know more," Catherine said, sitting down across from Sophia. "You said something about the color blue. Is it directly connected to me finding happiness by my thirtieth birthday? Will he be wearing blue? Is it an article of clothing? I need to know."

"Catherine, it's hard for me to answer specific questions like that. Any psychic who says they can is most likely a fraud who is after your money. I can tell you a hundred small things like stay away from making any major decision in August and your lucky number is eleven—"

"Will eleven o'clock be significant?" Catherine interrupted.

"*But*," Sophia emphasized, "I can't see what's not there. It's impossible." Sophia smiled softly as she tossed Catherine's own words back at her. "All I can tell you is what I saw the last time we were together, and if there's anything more now."

Catherine let out a heavy breath of disappointment. "Just tell me what you saw," she said curtly.

"When I close my eyes, I see you surrounded by blue, everywhere." She purposely left out the mention of blue eyes she saw so clearly, feeling the need to protect her best friend. "All I know is that it will lead you on the path to happiness."

"Thanks." Catherine started to rise but fell back into the cushioned chair when Sophia continued.

"I also see how sad you are, how lonely you feel." Catherine nervously fiddled with her jacket's button. "I also see a time you were happy, genuinely happy, in the arms of a beautiful woman." Catherine's head snapped up so quickly that her curls fell across her face. "Tell me about the woman in room two-fourteen."

Catherine remained quiet. The silence filled with a thick tension as the two women sat and stared. Sophia wouldn't allow Catherine to fall back on avoidance. She'd have to be patient, but she would wait. She noticed Catherine swallow hard before clearing her throat.

"I don't want to talk about that."

"You'll feel better—"

"It's off-limits!" Catherine said decisively.

After a moment of discomfort, Sophia took a risk and spoke again. "I can't control what I see."

"But you can control what you talk about." This time Catherine stood and remained standing while she shrugged on her coat. "And don't mention that to anyone else."

"Anything we speak of here is private." Sophia looked offended. Whoever Sophia saw in Catherine's past, it was someone who was and always would be a vital piece of who Catherine Carter was and why she walked cautiously through life beneath a cloud of mournfulness.

"Good." With that final curt word, Catherine spun and made her way from the building, leaving Sophia in a stupor.

Chapter Ten

Imogene was surprised when her phone rang early on Friday morning. The boutique was a couple hours from opening, and Sophia rarely called during the morning hours. Friends and family never made it a habit to call at all. Imogene preferred quiet mornings where she could lie around and catch up on the latest book she'd purchased or browse the many catalogs she received in the mail. It was eight o'clock and a groggy, sleepy Imogene grumbled as she looked at the bright display of her phone. Her heavy eyes shot open wide when she saw Catherine's name in bold lettering.

"Hello?" Imogene cringed at how deep her morning voice sounded.

"Good morning, it's Catherine. I hope I'm not calling too early."

"No!" Imogene cleared her throat, "No. Not at all. I've been up for a while." *Twenty-five minutes is a while, right?* She tugged awkwardly at the tie on her terry-cloth robe.

"Okay, good. Listen, Imogene, I was wondering if you'd like to come by the office today. I have another list. This one has a few products as well as Realtors. I'd like to go over it with you as soon as possible. Are you available to meet me at my office this afternoon?"

"This afternoon?"

"Yes."

"At your office?"

"My office."

"In the city?" Imogene's grip on the thick sash increased.

"That's the one. I can give you directions if you need." Catherine offered so easily it reminded Imogene of just how oblivious the caller was to her distress.

"No, that won't be necessary. I'm very familiar with the city." She thought about all her time spent there and how her father and brothers on duty chased her around the large firehouse when she was growing up.

"Hey, Cowboy! You better watch out. Your little one is going to be trouble when she gets older." A rotund man spoke from behind a large, red fire truck. When he stepped out from behind it, the rest of the company started to hoot with laughter at the sight of a six-year-old Imogene hanging from his broad shoulders.

"My Imogene? Never!" Frank Harris ran up and snatched his small daughter up into his arms, causing her to squeal with delight. When her giggles subsided, they looked at one another, eyes locking and faces set in similar expressions. He continued to speak softly. "She's my little angel."

"Imogene?" Catherine's voice brought her back to reality. Imogene was embarrassed to feel tears on her cheeks.

"Yeah." Her response was soft. She didn't trust her voice to keep from cracking.

"So I'll see you around two." It wasn't a question; it was set. Imogene could picture her name spelled out in Catherine's calendar, and her chest felt inflamed.

Imogene fought to calm her racing heart and the familiar feeling of panic and take a full breath. She wasn't ready. The city was no place for her. It was a collection of intersecting streets that all told the story of a life, many lives taken too soon, and she wasn't ready to forgive it. Before she knew what she was saying, Imogene blurted out the first thing she could think of to get herself out of her current position.

"I'd much rather cook for you." *I'd much rather* what?

"You'd much rather *what*?" It was the second time Imogene put off meeting at her office for someplace more intimate instead. It was only a matter of time before she would question Imogene. "I have meetings with sales representatives all afternoon." *Lie.* "But I'm free this evening and was planning on cooking up something delicious." *Another lie.* Imogene covered her face with her free hand. "Why don't you change into something comfortable and come over around seven?" Imogene started to make a mental list of all the things she would need to do before then, like food shop. "I'd feel more comfortable talking about my finances at home anyway. It makes this feel more like my idea." She laughed in an effort to calm herself and sound natural. She failed.

"Okay. It's been a while since I've had a good, home-cooked meal. I'd be a fool to decline."

"Great! I'll see you at seven."

"See you at seven." The phone went dead.

Imogene released a breath and plopped her body down on her bed with force, earning an evil glare from her furry bedmate. "Don't you dare look at me like that, Vixen." A small meow came from the grumpy tabby's mouth. "Your mother is an idiot." She reached over and scratched between the feline's ears. "And now I have to figure out what I'm going to cook." She sat up suddenly. "I have to clean!"

She spent the two hours before the boutique opened dusting, vacuuming, searching the Internet for recipes, and, finally, showering. She barely opened Cowboy Fran's doors on time. Once she made it through the busy afternoon, she ran to the store and bought all the necessary ingredients for the simple pasta dish she planned on preparing that evening. She hoped Catherine enjoyed pasta, but she wasn't riddled with panic and insecurities over the menu alone.

She was afraid Catherine wouldn't feel comfortable in her simple world. She was obviously used to the finer things in life, from custom-tailored suits made from the finest materials to the sizable diamond studs that sparkled on her ears. Beyond that, Catherine seemed to construct her world within a monochromatic spectrum that left little room for the wondrous prism of color Imogene lived on a daily basis. Being such complete opposites was a recipe for disaster, or at least an evening full of discomfort and awkward moments. Imogene wondered if she had made a terrible mistake, but before she could dwell on it, the bell above the shop door chimed.

"We're closing in five minutes, but I could help you find anything you may need." Imogene spoke before looking up from the register she had been trying to balance.

"I'm just looking for a good meal," Catherine said with a smirk when Imogene snapped to attention. "Hi."

"Hi," Imogene replied. She looked at the small clock on the wall. "Are you always early?" She laughed despite the pounding of her heart. *Calm down!* she told herself.

"Yes, but I think fifteen minutes is hardly that early."

"It is for an unprepared hostess."

"Then I guess the imposing party will just have to help out in any way she can." Imogene took a step closer to Catherine, lost in her clean scent. Somehow, just a slight inhalation had cleared Imogene's mind of not only her work, but all the reasons she had decided to write off her attraction to Catherine.

"Help me close up?" Imogene quietly requested, trying to shake the inappropriate shift in her own thoughts and mood.

"It's not too early?" Catherine pointed to the small sign that noted the store hours.

"This weather has been killing business lately, so I've been closing early."

"Makes sense." Catherine shrugged and turned back to Imogene. "What would you like me to do?"

Imogene and Catherine closed up Cowboy Fran's in record time. Imogene turned the heavy lock into place and directed Catherine to a small alcove to the left, illuminated by a small, warm amber porch light. Switching to another key on her overstuffed ring, Imogene unlocked her apartment door and stepped inside.

"This is me." They ascended a narrow staircase that delivered them to the landing of Imogene's small loft apartment. "It's not much, but it's home." Between bouts of self-conscious worry, she wondered why the other woman's opinion mattered to her at all.

Imogene watched Catherine as she scanned the open space, but she couldn't read much on Catherine's face until she looked at the large bookcase that separated the living space from the bedroom. Catherine stepped closer to read a few titles.

"I needed some kind of privacy for the bedroom, and I had so many books that the solution seemed obvious," Imogene said as she stepped up bedside Catherine and placed her hand on one of the shelves. A smile of pure pleasure spread across her lips.

"I can't remember the last time I read a book for pleasure." Catherine's confession tugged at something deep inside Imogene. *What does she do besides work?*

"I'm an addict. All the dignified, classic titles are on this side and the racier ones are in my bedroom," she said with a wink when Catherine's mouth fell open. "Can I take your coat?"

"Th-thank you," Catherine stuttered out. She took off her heavy, black coat and handed it to a waiting Imogene.

"I thought I told you to change into something comfortable," Imogene gently scolded as she took in Catherine's formal attire. "My apartment isn't exactly a black-tie establishment." She wasn't sure why she was so pleased to see Catherine blush at her words, but she reveled in the pleasure.

"I, uh…" Catherine looked down at her suit. "I didn't have time. I didn't want to be late."

"God forbid," Imogene teased as she walked toward the kitchen. "I hope you like pasta."

"I do. A little extra time at the gym can erase anything."

"Any allergies?"

"Nope."

"Good. Have a seat and make yourself comfortable. I'll be quick." Imogene started to make her way around the kitchen, setting out ingredients and utensils on the counter.

Most of her attention was dedicated to the task at hand, but Imogene couldn't keep her eyes off Catherine on her sofa. She was struck by the vision of such a dark woman engulfed by multicolored throw pillows. Catherine contrasted with her surroundings, but Imogene was surprised by just how welcome the sight was. Suddenly, Vixen meowed, and Catherine jumped in alarm.

"That's Vixen. Do you like cats?" Before Catherine could answer, Vixen jumped up in her lap and kneaded her expensive slacks. Catherine's eyes were wide with fear. "My guess would be no. She tends to be drawn to people who prefer to be left alone." Imogene went back to inexpertly slicing the red bell pepper.

"Can I touch her?"

"I wouldn't recommend it."

As Imogene continued to make dinner, she didn't hear many sounds from the connected room. Catherine never moved and neither did Vixen. Imogene only heard one hiss over the sizzle of vegetables in olive oil and the boiling water. Imogene considered that to be progress on her feline companion's behalf. If Sophia were to occupy the spot where Catherine was now, she'd have a few teeth marks on her hands as souvenirs.

"Dinner's ready!" she announced from the kitchen as she dished several scoops of the fragrant meal into bowls. Imogene giggled as Catherine nearly jumped from the couch and approached. The excitement that lit up Catherine's eyes added to the prideful thump of Imogene's heartbeat. "I knew you'd prefer something on the healthy side, but I still wanted some flavor." Imogene chuckled awkwardly. "Whole wheat pasta, every vegetable I could get my hands on, and a light sauce made from chicken stock, spices, and a small amount of butter. I don't care what anyone says, I'll never give up my butter or olive oil."

"Thank you." Catherine's face fell into a sullen, unreadable expression. Her brown eyes softened in a way that was all new to Imogene. She didn't know how to respond. Instead of focusing on the delicacy of the moment or the way it warmed her stuttering heart, Imogene picked up the bowls and walked to the small kitchen table.

"Let's eat."

Catherine poured two glasses of wine before digging into her dinner with an unrestrained enthusiasm that kept Imogene smiling throughout the silent meal. They didn't talk because they were busy eating. Finally, when there was nothing more than the sound of silverware hitting empty dishes, Catherine spoke.

"That was incredible." She sat back in her seat and unbuttoned her suit jacket.

"I'm pretty proud of myself." Imogene smiled as she stood up. "Top off our glasses and bring them over to the couch. I just want to clean up real quick."

"No." Catherine stood immediately and took the dishes from Imogene. She jumped at the slight brush of Catherine's fingers against hers. "You cooked, I clean up. It's only fair," Catherine continued. She was already at the sink before Imogene could attempt to protest.

Five minutes later, Catherine sat beside Imogene and took a sip from her freshly poured glass of wine. As if on cue, Vixen plopped herself atop Catherine's thighs. Imogene giggled at Catherine's thinly veiled look of annoyance.

"You're really not an animal person, are you?"

"No. I'm not." Catherine cringed. "Sorry…"

Imogene dismissed it with a wave of her hand. "No need to be sorry." She wiped her palms along the front of her skirt. "Did you have any pets growing up?" Imogene tried to hide her earnest curiosity by focusing her attention on her own hands.

"We weren't allowed pets, and when I got older I just didn't feel the need to get one."

"I'd be so lonely without Vixen." Imogene picked up her adored tabby from Catherine's lap. "She's always here for me when I get home, makes me laugh when I'm down, and she's a great listener." They both laughed. "When the silence gets to be a little too much for me to handle, I can count on her to knock something over and cause a much-needed ruckus." She scratched below a pointed ear and smiled sadly. When she looked over at Catherine, she saw the same indescribable softness she'd seen before, shimmering in her deep mahogany eyes. "So," Imogene said roughly through the overwhelming emotion she felt at the way Catherine was looking at her. Something about the look shook her very foundation. "Let's talk business." She released Vixen and folded her hands on her lap.

Catherine launched into a thirty-minute-long proposal, listing several buildings and storefronts available to rent if the business owner was looking to expand, as well as a few other fitting opportunities. Imogene listened with rapt attention, and when the words became too technical for her to really understand, she just stared at the lips they fell from so poetically. She found herself wondering where such a passion came from.

"Did you always want to do this?" This was her chance to learn more about the woman behind the suits. Imogene rested her head in her hand and burrowed her elbow into the pillowed back of the couch. She turned her whole body in order to face Catherine more fully. She tucked her legs beneath her and let the wine relax her further. She waited for what she hoped would be a detailed, lengthy reply.

"Yes. Well…" Catherine took a deep breath. "I come from a family of lawyers. My grandfather, my father, my brothers."

"How many brothers?"

"Two older that both followed in my father's footsteps. The old man expected me to as well, but I didn't." Catherine's face set into a hard façade.

"A house with no pets and full of lawyers, sounds exciting." Imogene's light tone got Catherine to smile, a sight that caused a torrent of feelings to course through her and settle low in her belly.

"Yeah, well, I broke that tradition," she said curtly with a resigned finality. "What about you? Did anyone influence Imogene Harris's path in life?" Catherine mirrored the smaller woman's position.

"I had planned on going into design—fashion or interior, I wasn't sure—but I was interested in it all," Imogene stated wistfully.

"What happened?"

"I had just started my junior year when my dad died, and I decided to come home to be with my mom. Thankfully I had enough credits to get my associate's. I took a couple business courses, and those certainly helped me when it came time to open Cowboy Fran's."

"Do you ever think about going back to school?"

"Every once in a while, but the shop has been so busy that I don't want to risk splitting my attention and letting something slip between the cracks. Ultimately, I'm very happy with my decision. I have no regrets."

"You're a very wise businesswoman, much wiser than most of the clients I meet with on a daily basis. Multimillion-dollar corporations included."

"From Catherine Carter, that has to be quite the compliment." Imogene blushed as she tried to deflect the effect Catherine's words had on her with humor.

"Do you mind me asking about your dad?" Catherine tried.

"I don't mind, but I'd much rather talk about happier topics."

"That seems fair." Catherine reached into the inside pocket of her jacket and retrieved a small elastic ring. She captured her abundant curls in both hands and secured them atop her head in a haphazard bun. Imogene's eyes were drawn once again to a long throat sculpted of fine muscle that dipped down into a defined clavicle. The half-moon of flesh that peeked out of the collar of her black shirt caused Imogene to lick her pink lips. "But for once, I'm tired of talking about numbers."

Catherine poured the last few drops of wine into their glasses, and they continued to talk about the unusually long winter. Imogene talked about how she lost three deliveries already due to the snow, and Catherine countered with how many nights she spent on the leather couch in her office. They laughed and they drank, each passing moment bringing them closer together on the sofa. Imogene indulged in the feel of Catherine's muscular thigh where it met her knee more times than she could count. Soon enough, the topic of conversation turned to their disastrous first meeting.

"I'm sure I sound like a broken record at this point, but I am really sorry for how rude I was."

"It's long forgotten." Imogene waved her hand about. "I'm used to skeptics saying things like that. I was just so angry because I was really starting to like you." Imogene's heart started to race. Her words were so innocent, but the implications were anything but.

"Really?" Catherine's eyes dropped, and she started to fidget.

"Really. My grandfather had just died, and I was in a really bad place. Sophia asked me to assist in an attempt to take my mind off things, and before I almost tackled you, I was bored out of my mind." They shared a small smile at the memory. "You were charming, a great listener, and willing to feed me as many shrimp as I wanted. It was exactly what I needed. You were my hero."

"Hardly! I went on to insult your best friend!"

"Minor hiccup along the way." A half smile pulled at the corner of Imogene's full mouth and then blossomed into something full, something sinful.

"Can I make a confession?" Catherine asked quietly.

"Please." Imogene sat up straight with intrigue.

"I've gone to see Sophia since then. Twice."

"You *what*?"

"She said a few things at the party that night that caught my attention. Alice convinced me I had nothing to lose, so I went."

"And? Tell me everything." Imogene drained her wineglass and listened carefully as Catherine recounted the tale from the beginning.

Catherine shared all the details: the timeline of her life plan, how her deadline was less than four months away, and, lastly, how she was convinced Richard Thorton had to be the answer.

Imogene's jealousy simmered as she listened to Catherine go on about her handsome subordinate, but an odd sense of peace settled over her as Catherine described him as someone who "would do." Imogene listened intently, or rather she watched intently. She watched as Catherine's dark eyes lit up and her brows arched along with her tone. Imogene noted the small amount of makeup Catherine wore in order to soften her features, and she couldn't help but notice the way the small buttons barely hidden by her suit jacket strained against her small breasts. She listened to Catherine for fifteen uninterrupted minutes before finally asking a question.

"What makes you so sure Richard Thorton is your guy?"

"His tie, and his interview was at eleven," Catherine stated with certainty.

"I'm not following."

"Oh! I forgot that part. Sophia told me that my lucky number is eleven, and the color blue was going to have 'a big impact' on my life." Catherine hooked her fingers into air quotes as she spoke. "He was wearing a blue tie the first time we met at eleven o'clock." Imogene felt herself blanch. Catherine continued with the story and finished with her and Sophia's last, less comfortable meeting, telling Imogene she was interested in hearing about her future, not the past. Imogene sat speechless.

"It's late, I should get going." Catherine stood and made her way to the door.

"You don't have to go." Imogene jumped up to meet Catherine, already buttoning her coat.

"I'm pretty tired, and I'm sure you had a long day as well." When Catherine turned to look at her, Imogene noticed their position. Imogene was leaning with her back against the door, her left hand gripping the doorknob. Catherine was close, too close for comfort. But no matter how loud the voice in her head shouted for her to move, Imogene felt pinned by Catherine's dark eyes.

"I had a wonderful time with you, Catherine." Imogene spoke just above a whisper and worried her bottom lip between her teeth.

"Me, too." Catherine was quick to respond. "Thank you for dinner."

They were both smiling, and Imogene wondered if she was the only one having trouble breathing beyond a shallow gasp.

The spark was there, the invisible pull to be closer, the want, the need to feel Catherine's lithe body pressed against hers simmered just beneath Imogene's skin. And she could swear she saw the same emotions in Catherine's face. Imogene looked from Catherine's chocolate eyes to her mouth, subconsciously moistening her own lips in response to the temptation she felt. The thin tethers holding Imogene's self-control in place started to fray as Catherine bit her bottom lip. As soon as Imogene shifted forward, Catherine moved away.

"I'll see you soon." Catherine reached past Imogene and opened the door, squeezing between her and the frame awkwardly and quickly descending the stairs.

Imogene closed the door and stood with her forehead resting against the cool wood. So many thoughts and feelings swam inside, all fighting for her immediate attention, but one in particular made its way to the forefront. "I'm going to kill Sophia for meddling," she said to Vixen.

CHAPTER ELEVEN

Sophia cursed the gray area she constantly lived in as a psychic. She'd be bombarded with the private pain strangers tried to hide as she stood in the bread aisle of the supermarket and tried to focus on her own mundane decisions. She'd hear small messages from loved ones who had passed on as she tried to decide which dressing she'd prefer on the house salad. Sometimes the idea of going to a concert or party exhausted Sophia because it took too much energy to shut out the voices and the visions. But she wouldn't trade her gift for peace even if she had the option.

She had helped so many people that a small difference in her genetic makeup felt more like a blessing than a curse no matter how she looked at it. The only major flaw she saw was her inability to help herself, and that was a predicament she was faced with Saturday morning. Chris said Imogene had called him and asked him to tell Sophia they'd be having lunch at one o'clock. No matter how great her gift, she had no idea what that warning sign was telling her.

In all of their years as friends, Imogene and Sophia spoke directly with one another. Imogene had never used Sophia's husband as a middleman before, and this new development alarmed her. She hadn't heard from her friend at all before lunch, no calls or texts, which was another red flag. The final warning, the one that sent chills down her spine was the look of anger on Imogene's face as she stood in her open doorway at one o'clock on the dot. All the clues pointed to one very obvious conclusion: Sophia Glass was in trouble.

"You said you wouldn't meddle!" Imogene didn't even bother to remove her tweed coat before sitting in the empty seat opposite Sophia. "You promised!"

"I didn't meddle." Sophia's attempt at defending herself was shot down.

"I should've known when you told me to wear that damn blue sweater to my meeting with Catherine. It was weird, but sometimes you're just weird so I overlooked it. I overlooked it because I didn't think my friend, my *best* friend, would try to play matchmaker and push me toward a confused straight woman!" Sophia sat quietly on the receiving end of Imogene's tantrum. "A woman who is hell-bent on finding happiness with a man she's not even interested in, by the way. You're going to tell me why, right now."

"Imogene, you know I can't tell you anything that took place between myself and Catherine."

"She already told me about your two meetings."

Sophia was surprised Catherine had shared that information with Imogene, but the shock wore off and was replaced with satisfaction at knowing Catherine was opening up to Imogene.

"Don't do that!"

"What?" Sophia jumped at the sudden volume of Imogene's voice.

"That look you get when you either see something, have a secret, or know you're right. It's infuriating!" Imogene stood and started to pace. "Just tell me what you can."

Sophia could tell how frustrated Imogene was by the way she was frantically batting at her thick hair covering her face. "You obviously know about the blue thing."

"And the number eleven. Really?"

"What are you talking about?"

"You gave her my apartment number as her lucky number. I'd expect something more creative from you."

"Holy shit." Sophia looked at her friend with wide eyes, a bright smile soon following. "I didn't even think of that."

"You are so full of—"

"And I saw you." Sophia stopped the accusation. "I think you're going to be the reason for Catherine's happiness."

"How?"

"I don't know, I didn't see that much." Sophia furrowed her brow, thinking another meeting with Catherine could be beneficial for all three of them.

"So for all you know, I could be the one to introduce her to Mr. Right," Imogene said sadly, leaving Sophia to wonder if there was more to her friend and Catherine's relationship than Imogene let on.

"It's possible."

Imogene ended the conversation abruptly and walked to the door. "You're buying me lunch."

"It's the least I can do," Sophia said as she got her coat.

"Damn straight." Imogene quirked an eyebrow. "Are you going to a funeral after work?"

"What?" Sophia looked down in confusion and remembered the all black ensemble she had put on that morning. "Oh. My twelve thirty believes our readings are more successful if we wear all black." She shrugged.

"Are they?"

"No." Sophia smiled.

"You sure are dedicated to your work." They left the office smiling, but the tension between them hadn't fully melted away.

❖

On the opposite side of the Hudson River, Catherine was lost in a sea of graphs and numbers. Her desk was uncharacteristically cluttered with files and papers that didn't have a home. Two of her largest corporate clients had figures to be worked out and delivered via email by the end of business on Monday, and she preferred to deliver results at least twelve hours prior to deadline. When Catherine closed her eyes, she saw large sums. When she reopened them, she saw paper evidence of those exact numbers. It was dizzying.

Not many people were in the building on a Saturday afternoon, and that made Catherine all the more grateful to have Vivian at her side during the weekdays. Whether it was delivering a fresh cup of coffee or reminding her that she needed food to continue at the pace she was going, Vivian always knew what was best. Catherine was hungry and grumpy without her. A headache had come to life behind her right eye. She made a mental note to make sure fresh flowers and a basket full of goodies would be waiting for Vivian early Monday morning.

When her cell phone rang, she swiped the screen to answer without even glancing at the ID. She needed to talk to someone, anyone other than herself. "Catherine Carter," she answered almost mechanically.

"Catherine, it's Sophia Glass."

"Sophia! This is unexpected." She stood up and started to pace her office. She wondered if Imogene had asked her to call because of the way she'd run out on her the night before.

"I know. I just wanted to call and apologize for the way our last meeting went. It's been weighing on me lately, and I wanted to clear the air between us."

"It's okay. It's my fault, really. I should be the one apologizing."

"No. You're my client, and I should do everything in my power to make you comfortable." Sophia soothed, her voice becoming undeniably soft.

"Apology accepted."

"I'd like to make it up to you with another meeting—"

"That's not necessary." Catherine wanted to avoid that at all costs.

"I'd like to try to answer your questions, at least some of them. I won't push you, but I want to help."

"I don't…" Catherine paused as a casually dressed Richard Thorton walked by her open office door. "I don't have any time right now, do you have anything available after four?"

"Of course. Come whenever you'd like. I'll be here until six."

Catherine hung up and returned to her work while thinking about what she had gotten herself into. She cast one last glance at her empty doorway.

❖

Sophia heard the arrival bell above the door chime a little after five o'clock, and she went to see if it was Catherine taking her up on her offer. She peeked into the waiting area and witnessed a short, eerily quiet exchange taking place between Gladys and a visibly uncomfortable Catherine. Gladys was a woman of very few words, one of the things Sophia loved most about her. With a dirty look and a flick of an extended thumb, Gladys signaled for Catherine to go straight to Sophia's office. Sophia smiled and opened her office door to usher Catherine inside.

"Is she that warm with all of your clients?" Catherine removed her jacket and hung it on the back of the chair opposite Sophia.

"Gladys?" When Catherine nodded, Sophia laughed. "You left in such a hurry last time you didn't stop to pay your bill." She leaned in to whisper the rest. "She thinks you're a thief." The expression on Catherine's face was priceless.

"Oh my God, I am so sorry! No wonder why she hates me! How much do I owe you?" She started to reach into her coat pocket for her wallet.

"Don't worry about it." Sophia put up her hand. "You're a friend of a friend, I can't charge you."

"This is your business."

"Are you charging Imogene?" The knowing smile Imogene

hated so much blossomed on Sophia's face. "I'll make sure to tell Gladys to tone it down."

"Please don't. She doesn't need any more reasons to hate me." Catherine rubbed nervously at her forehead.

"Okay." Sophia sat back and observed Catherine. The gut-twisting sadness that accompanied her everywhere she went was back, as was her determination to ignore it. But Sophia saw it all, felt it all along with her. This time though, something new weighed heavily on her shoulders, and Sophia couldn't help but hope Imogene had something to do with it.

"I want to try something new this time," Sophia said.

"Like?" Catherine asked wearily. "You're not talking tarot cards and crystal balls, are you?"

"I'd like for you to cooperate." Sophia tried not to smile. "I just want you to relax and open yourself up to me." She turned off the overhead light, leaving just her small desk lamp and the final traces of the winter sun to illuminate the small space. She took a seat next to Catherine in the partnering chair, hoping for a more personal connection this way. "Close your eyes."

Catherine took a deep breath, closed her brown eyes, and rolled her shoulders. She even managed to remain silent for close to three full minutes.

"Anything yet?"

"Shh…" Sophia had closed her eyes as well, was concentrating on everything that surrounded Catherine, but she just couldn't break through that outer wall. "I need you to really relax and let me in." She reached across the small gap that separated the chairs and took one of Catherine's hands in a firm grasp. Once the physical connection was established, an emotional one came to life. All the sadness and pain came flooding in, punching the air from Sophia's lungs. Before she could think her words through, she asked, "How long have you been carrying this pain with you?" She held on to Catherine's hand tightly, fearing she'd try to escape again. The last thing she expected was a timid response.

"Since college."

She sounded so small, so defeated, and so open. "I can't control what I see or feel," Sophia started to explain again, "and when I started to see clients, I made a vow to keep secrets buried and inner turmoil covered. Everything that goes on between us in this office is private. I'll never abuse my gift or tell another soul what we speak of, but I also won't tell you anything you don't want to hear."

"Richard Thorton."

"Excuse me?" Sophia was confused as to what the name had to do with everything she had just said.

"He's the new guy at the office. Just tell me if you see anything about him. Whatever else that pops up along the way I don't really care about."

Sophia felt Catherine relax and let her mind open wide, thoughts and memories coming to life like a wilted dandelion at spring's first rainfall. "I don't see a Richard or any man in particular, but I do see great happiness for a thirty-year-old Catherine."

"What can I do to make it happen?"

Catherine's query struck Sophia as odd. "You can't make the future happen, Catherine. You have to be patient and allow these things to come to you in time."

"I'm not very patient—"

"Quiet." Sophia tightened her grip.

Sophia got a sudden image of Catherine and Imogene seated beside each other. Imogene rested her hand lightly on Catherine's thigh, and they were both laughing loudly. Before she could analyze the image any more, it was replaced by another vision of a younger, worrisome Catherine. That beautiful Asian woman Sophia had seen before was also there. Everything appeared the same until something much more fiery came to life. Catherine was once a passionate woman, one who knew how to love easily and touch gently. Sophia felt as though she were blowing the dust off a long-lost treasure chest filled with adoration, glee, and ecstasy. She wanted to help Catherine discover it again for herself. Now that she knew the answer, Sophia dared to ask the question again.

"Will you tell me about Linda?"

A pained smile crossed Catherine's face at the name. "I'm not ready to talk about it." One lone tear made its way down her porcelain cheek. "I don't think I'll ever be ready." The tear let go of the hold it had on her squared chin, absorbed into black slacks.

"It'll be hard to move on if you don't let go."

Catherine pulled her hand out of Sophia's grasp. What was she so afraid of?

"Is there anything else?" Catherine said, wiping her tears with haste as she got out of the chair.

Obviously, the session's over, Sophia thought. "I'm seeing a lot of your past, but not much of your future. I'm sorry." Sophia sat back, exhausted from the roller coaster of emotions and disappointed in her inability to see more.

"I appreciate you trying." She pulled on her coat.

"Catherine?"

"Yeah?" She turned back on her way to the door.

"Stop looking so blue." Catherine dipped her head in a small nod and left the office. Sophia sat befuddled. She had never found herself in this position before. Catherine was the only client to ever deny her full assistance, and Imogene could get hurt because of it. *And people assume my gift is always glamorous.*

CHAPTER TWELVE

By midweek, Catherine was exhausted. She slumped in her office chair, staring at her computer screen as she tapped her ballpoint pen rhythmically to the tick of the clock on the wall. She was so tired of looking at pixilated numbers, she fought to keep her eyes open. Vivian had already told her to take a half day several times. She said she was worried, that she didn't look well. It wasn't a lie. She was dressed more casually and hadn't slept much since her last meeting with Sophia because memories of Linda Nguyen haunted her in the darkness. Each time she'd lain down to rest, everything flooded her mind with unwanted pleasure.

Catherine waited patiently as an eager student folded a piece of paper and tucked it into his back pocket before she tapped on the door frame to Ms. Nguyen's small faculty office. Catherine bit her lower lip when Linda looked up at the student with her gorgeous dark eyes. She dismissed him.

"I'll see you in class on Thursday, Peter. Don't worry about the mix-up with your schedule. We'll make it work." Linda stood from behind her desk and led the jittery young man from the tight space.

"Thanks." His deep voice filled the room before he hurried around Catherine into the hallway.

"Freshman?" Catherine asked with an amused smile. Being intimidated by the faculty and the older students seemed so far behind her now.

"How did you guess?" With a subtle tilt of her head, Linda invited Catherine into her office. She scanned the hallways, a practiced and perfected move, before closing the door.

"We should leave that open," Catherine said. She might not have been intimidated anymore, but now she was afraid of getting caught.

"Don't worry about it. As long as we don't make it a habit, no one will suspect a thing." Linda stepped closer slowly. Catherine felt like prey, and she tried to lean back against a barren desk with casualness she didn't have. "Do you not trust me?"

Professor Nguyen made people feel at ease even when she pushed them far outside their comfort zone. As a student, Catherine fell victim every time she'd read one of Catherine's stories aloud during class. As a lover, every ounce of Catherine's restraint and common sense would melt away at the feel of Linda's expert fingertips.

"I don't know if I trust myself," Catherine confessed just above a whisper. Her eyes dropped and she watched as Linda flexed her hands before gripping Catherine's waist.

"What are you afraid you'll do, Catherine?" Catherine felt the question hit her lips in small puffs of breath.

"I'm afraid I won't be able to stop…" The tip of Catherine's nose grazed Linda's. Her lips were burning with eagerness to taste her lover.

"My next class isn't for another hour." Linda kissed Catherine then, fully and deeply.

"I missed you," Catherine said in a whimper.

"Oh?" Catherine felt Linda's strong hands snake their way beneath her thin burgundy T-shirt. "Didn't have any fun back home for spring break?" Catherine's taut abdomen twitched as Linda fanned her fingers across the muscles.

Catherine supported her weight with her palms flat against the surface of the wooden desk. Her head fell back, her long curls tickling her bare forearms, exposing her neck for Linda's talented mouth. A year ago, Catherine would've been scared by this need, but now it had become a crucial part of her existence.

"I wanted you there with me, oh!" Catherine gasped at Linda's teeth scraping against her pulse point. "I can't wait to show you off this summer." Catherine raised her head and opened her eyes when Linda stopped what she was doing. Linda's sober expression morphed into something more lecherous. Catherine felt the button of her jeans pop open, Linda's fingertip skimming along the front of her damp panties.

"I missed you, too, love, especially your taste."

Catherine whimpered again and all apprehension died at the sudden pressure against her turgid clit. She looked on in awe as her girlfriend lowered her pants and underwear before settling on her knees before her exposed sex. Catherine was sure she saw love and adoration in her eyes.

"Dammit!" Catherine slammed her pen down. Even her pleasant memories were haunted with embarrassment at her own stupidity. How had she managed to judge a person, a situation, so poorly? She'd fallen quickly and powerfully for a woman she barely knew, and all she had in the end was her own tears for solace. Catherine wanted to chalk it up to young adult naïveté, but she had a nagging feeling the past was repeating itself with Imogene.

Imogene. Her name had been on Catherine's mind every day since they met, separated, and met again. Catherine could no longer deny Imogene had brought a piece of her back to life. All the spontaneity, humor, and liveliness in her life had been gone almost nine years, but Imogene made her feel all those things again. Every day seemed bearable, easy almost, around her. Catherine resigned herself to becoming addicted to that feeling, and she needed a dose of it if she wanted to feel better. She wondered how Cowboy Fran's had been faring during the most recent snow storm. Taking Vivian up on her brilliant idea, Catherine grabbed her coat and briefcase and powered down her computer on the way out of the office to find out for herself.

Catherine was more than surprised by the number of cars that lined Washington Street, but she was even more shocked by the number of people shopping in Cowboy Fran's late that afternoon. Apparently people got tired of fighting the weather and instead went on to live their lives normally. She spotted Imogene through the throngs of people. With moist palms and a beating heart, Catherine nervously made her way across the crowded space.

"Hey," Catherine said, flinching at how deep her voice sounded. Imogene spun around and a wide, brilliant smile spread across her freckled face.

"Hey!" Despite Imogene's cool exterior, Catherine could tell from her volume Imogene was excited to see her. "This is an unexpected visit."

"I hope you don't mind." Catherine stepped back for a moment to allow a middle-aged woman to pass between them. "I'm not usually one for dropping in unannounced, but I just had to get out of the office for the day."

"And here you are." Imogene crossed her arms over her chest and smirked.

"Here I am." Catherine swallowed hard. She could feel the warmth spread across her cheeks, surely leaving red in its wake.

The two women just stared at each other for a moment, Catherine looked over Imogene's flawless appearance. In something as simple as a sweater and jeans Imogene was stunning. Her wavy hair fell loosely around her shoulders in the slightly disheveled style Catherine found herself growing quite fond of. Her aquamarine eyes were lined with smoky colors that made them shine a shade brighter. Imogene shifted under Catherine's intense stare.

"No big meetings for The Suits today?" Imogene chuckled.

"No." Catherine smiled, shaking her head as she looked

down at the floor. *What am I doing here and why would Imogene want to spend time with me after the way I stumbled out of her apartment the last time we were together?*

"I was beginning to think I scared you away." She slid her hands into the back pockets of her jeans and kicked at an imaginary spot on her immaculate hardwood floors. "I ate the pasta, too, I didn't think it was *that* bad."

"You didn't scare me away," she said simply, with heartfelt seriousness. "I was actually wondering if you'd like to grab a late lunch."

"I can't," Imogene replied. "As much as I'd love escaping for an hour or two, we're so busy today that it'd be impossible for me to get away any time before dinner." Catherine thought she heard a slight inflection at the end of Imogene's sentence, as if she was timidly asking Catherine if that was an option as well.

"I can wait until then," Catherine said as more people swarmed around them. She weighed the option of going back to work, but she knew she'd never be able to concentrate. She didn't want to go home and sit in her empty, lifeless condo. Suddenly an idea hit her. "Need help in the meantime?"

"Excuse me? Seriously?"

Catherine enjoyed the shocked look on Imogene's face. "Yes, I'm serious. I have time to spare, and it looks like you could use another set of hands. I'm offering you free labor, Miss Harris. It'd be a wise business decision to take it. As your advisor, I'm insisting you do just that."

"Fine. I'd hate to upset my advisor," Imogene said with an infectious grin. She looked Catherine up and down quickly and fingered the cuff of her grey sweater. "If you're going to be a Cowboy Fran employee, this isn't going to work." To her right was a rack of silk blend button-up blouses ranging from a mossy green to a vibrant fuchsia. Imogene grabbed one the color of raspberry jam and thrust it toward Catherine's chest with a salacious smirk.

"I suppose you want me to wear this?"

"You look great in your usual black and white and gray. But if you're going to work for me, even for a day, you should wear my merchandise."

"Okay." Catherine wasn't about to argue something that made a lot of sense.

"You can use my office to change and hang up your coat."

Catherine nodded and made her way through patrons and racks of clothing to the office.

Imogene remained frozen in place, but she took time to watch Catherine walk away. She moved her slim hips ever so slightly, and her small, rounded backside left Imogene in a stupor until she heard the door to her office close.

"Do you have these in a size four?" asked a petite woman, startling Imogene. She looked at the print pants the customer held out.

"We do. They should be on the rack."

"They're not."

"I'm sure we didn't sell them all." Imogene smiled politely and walked her customer over to the display in question. She sifted through several hangers before finding the correct size. "Here we go." She handed the pants over and the woman stalked off without a thank you. Before Imogene could dwell on the display of rudeness, a middle-aged gentleman approached her with a frantic expression.

"My wife's birthday is today, and I've been in meetings all day so I haven't been able to get her a gift." His eyes were wide with worry. *You could've shopped a day earlier.* Imogene bit her tongue.

"Not to worry." Imogene pointed to a large table filled with various accessories. "Does she like jewelry?"

"Yeah, I-I think so." He looked to Imogene again. "Would you be happy if your husband came home with jewelry?"

"I don't have a husband, but I'd always be happy with jewelry."

Imogene jumped when Catherine chimed in from behind her. "Earrings are always a safe bet because you can match them to different outfits," she said. "I'd go with the amber studs by the register. They fit the season well."

"Thank you!" The customer rushed toward Catherine's suggestion. Imogene turned and regarded Catherine with a smirk.

"You know fashion?"

"I've picked up a thing or two over time." Imogene was charmed by Catherine's shy shrug.

"I would've never guessed."

"I'm offended," Catherine said.

"I'm so sorry!" Imogene gripped Catherine's forearm to stress her apology "I didn't—" She stopped talking as soon as Catherine's lips curled mischievously. "You're a bit of a jerk."

"That's what Alice always tells me." Catherine stepped back and smoothed a hand down the front of the borrowed blouse. "So?"

"Perfect fit." Imogene looked at Catherine's svelte torso, which was now encased in the silky garment. Her appraisal of Catherine's flat abdomen, perky breasts, and knowing mahogany eyes went beyond a professional assessment, but she wasn't about to apologize for it.

"And just as I suspected, you look wonderful in color." *Tread carefully, Imogene. The last time you let yourself flirt, she ran away! Back to work.* "Shall we?" Imogene cut her inner pep talk short and gestured to the sales floor with her right hand as Catherine stepped toward the crowd. Imogene followed behind her, struggling to keep her mind off her fresh scent. It was going to be a long afternoon.

Much to Imogene's surprise, the afternoon turned into early evening before she knew it. Working with Catherine not only proved to be easy, but she was quite helpful around the shop. They talked when they had some time to work on the stock between customers.

"You seem more than a little comfortable working around here." Imogene looked at Catherine across the table of cashmere sweaters they were folding. "I'm willing to bet you've done this before."

"Guilty." Catherine chuckled. "I worked at the Gap when I was a junior in high school, and then at various other stores in the mall once I was in college. It was a good way to help pay for school *and* be able to afford something other than ramen noodles for dinner."

"Then you hardly lived the average college experience," Imogene quipped. Catherine didn't respond, so she asked, "Will you tell me more about this hidden affinity you have for fashion?" She grinned when Catherine laughed and rolled her eyes.

"I wouldn't call it an *affinity* exactly, but I've always put care into how I look and paid close attention to what would look best when paired together. A lot can be said for someone who takes care of their appearance."

"Absolutely." Imogene knew she was staring at Catherine dreamily, but she couldn't censor herself. *Fashion talk is sexy.*

"What about you, Imogene? Any hidden passions or secret hobbies?"

As they started straightening another garment rack, Imogene's mind flooded with a hundred different trivial things she wanted to share with Catherine about herself. "I love to dance, anytime and anywhere. I'm pretty sure that's why my friends stopped inviting me out to bars." She laughed quietly.

"That bad?"

"I actually have a very good sense of rhythm, thank you very much." Imogene bumped her shoulder into Catherine's.

"Then what was their problem?" Catherine asked.

"I'm not exaggerating when I say anywhere. Even if we were at a bar with no dance space and a terrible selection of music, I couldn't stop myself."

"That's something I'd love to see," Catherine said with a gentle smile, and Imogene blushed.

"If you stick around long enough I'm sure you'll catch me."

"I hope so." Imogene didn't look away when Catherine spoke and their eyes locked. *I hope that means she doesn't plan on running away this time,* Imogene thought as a customer called Catherine away.

Several instances throughout the day, Imogene scolded herself for the territory her mind wandered into. From day one, all she wanted was to get to know Catherine better, and now that she was getting just that, she never wanted the wonder of the experience to stop. She was grateful for the blossoming friendship but alarmed by the desire she felt churning deep within. As Imogene watched Catherine Carter casually smiling and greeting people in her shop, she knew she needed more. She needed this Catherine around her as much as possible, and she wanted to be the reason for her smile.

"Thank God for pizza delivery. We would have never had dinner!" Catherine said in an exasperated tone as she locked the door behind the final customer. "Is it always like that?" She leaned with her back against the cold glass.

"Not really during the week. I would have asked Amanda to come in, but with the snow, I thought I'd be okay with just myself."

"You're lucky I came along when I did."

Imogene bit at the inside of her cheek as her heartbeat sped up. She had been mildly turned on for most of the evening as she worked closely with Catherine, but what had simmered beneath the surface moments before was now starting to boil low in her abdomen. *Alone at last!* she thought.

"I sure am." Imogene stood behind the counter as Catherine leaned in close on her elbows.

"You owe me now," Catherine said.

"Is that so?"

"Mmm-hmm."

The tiny hairs on the nape of Imogene's neck stood on end at Catherine's low hum. Catherine cocked her head slightly to the right before she leaned in a bit more. Imogene leaned in as well. *Anything you want.*

"Vivian, my receptionist, asked for next Thursday off. How would you like to come play secretary for a day?" Imogene's stomach sank. "You'll mostly be answering the phone and taking messages, but I'll also be expecting you to distract me as much as possible between meetings. What do you say?"

"Sounds fun, but I can't."

"Come on!" Catherine grabbed Imogene's hand. "Take one day off from the boutique to work with me. I'll take you out after. We'll go out to a show or just dinner. There's this amazing dim sum place that just opened not too far from the theater district." Catherine's enthusiasm was infectious, but Imogene still felt a churning in the pit of her stomach at the thought of being in the city again.

Imogene once held such love for it. The pace and attitude was infectious, and she felt as if she belonged. But then it betrayed her. Blaming the men responsible for the attacks wasn't enough—Imogene blamed the streets she once walked proudly, the buildings that provided her shade and refuge from the wind, and every nameless face that crowded each avenue. Each and every tall building would be steel and concrete reminders of September eleventh. She'd feel the pain again and feel the despair that came along with watching hours of news footage, waiting for days to just have her suspicions confirmed, days spent beside her sobbing mother when her father continued to not come home.

"I'm sorry, Catherine." Her breathing was heavy and labored.

"Okay. No show or dim sum. We could get a couple of dirty water dogs and hang out in the office. I have a pretty fantastic view."

"No!" Imogene said it so forcefully, she startled herself. She pulled back her clammy hand. "I can't. Now please, just drop it." She took a deep breath and excused herself to her office. Catherine hesitated before following silently.

"I'm going to go," Catherine spoke softly, cautiously. "I just have to change."

"Don't. Keep the shirt, it really does look amazing on you." Imogene's shame kept her from looking at Catherine.

"Thanks." Catherine collected her sweater and shrugged on her coat. She paused at the threshold of the office, tapping out a random rhythm with her index finger on the door frame. "Good night, Imogene."

CHAPTER THIRTEEN

It had been weeks since Alice had spent any time with Catherine. They'd had a few short phone conversations, but nothing beyond work and the weather. That wasn't normal. Catherine had tried to decline Alice's invitation to dinner Friday night, but Alice wouldn't allow it.

Catherine had sounded sad when she called early that morning, and Alice was desperate to find out what or who brought it on. Maybe she could help. As Alice feared, a shell of the Cat Carter she knew showed up Friday night. The difference was both astonishing and disconcerting. Alice made it through the main course and dessert without asking about it, but she was just waiting for the right moment to pounce.

"I'm going to put the kids to bed." Dennis collected the dessert plates.

"We'll do the dishes," Alice said, her eyes on Catherine. Her husband kissed the crown of her head, and she smiled at the way his beard tickled her scalp.

"I'll wash, you dry," Catherine said as she made her way to the kitchen sink. She turned on the water to its hottest setting and rolled up her sleeves before diving in. With a fresh dish towel in hand, Alice sidled up next to Catherine and watched her closely before speaking. She noted how tired Catherine looked. Something weighed heavily on her slumped shoulders, and Alice needed to know what.

"What's wrong?" she asked.

"What do you mean?"

"You've been unusually quiet all night, you're more doom and gloom than usual."

"Oh gee, thanks, Alice. You sure do know how to make me feel better." Catherine looked genuinely taken aback.

"Ha! I knew something was wrong!" Alice spoke triumphantly but sobered up the moment she noticed how deep the creases between Catherine's eyebrows ran. "Seriously. Talk to me."

Catherine took a deep breath and stared at the dish she held. She traced the design with her thumb until the suds had started to dry, but she remained silent.

"Are you going to wash that dish or just hold it for a while?" Alice's sarcasm seemed to jump-start Catherine back into action. "Now tell me what's got you so down."

"There's nothing to say." She washed the dish round and round. "It's just work stuff, I'm just under a lot of stress."

"I've seen you under stress at work, sweetie. This isn't that. Is it Imogene?" Catherine dropped the glass she'd been holding into the sudsy water with a splash. *Bingo*, Alice thought. *Now tread carefully.* "The job's a lot of trouble, isn't it?"

"It's…" Catherine looked around, and Alice wondered if she was hoping to find a response written on the cabinets. "It was very hard at first. A lot of disarray to sort through, but I think we're on the right track now." Alice thought she looked a little too satisfied with her answer as she went back to scrubbing the baked-on remnants of dinner.

"I knew it wasn't going to be easy," Alice said. "After dinner that night, I just got the impression that Imogene is a bit… flighty." Alice continued drying the glass in her hands. "That usually spells disaster."

"She's not flighty. Far from it, actually. She's quite brilliant. You know she's kept that business open for over ten years on her own? That's remarkable." Alice was surprised at how quickly

Catherine came to Imogene's defense. Judging by the blush that slowly crept up Catherine's cheeks, she wasn't the only one who felt the quick response was unexpected. "I thought the same thing you did, but it turns out Miss Harris really knows how to run a business."

"Oh." Alice eyed Catherine's downcast face suspiciously. "Well, that's good. I take it that you got your car fixed, then?" Catherine nodded. "So you've been spending a lot of time with Miss Harris?"

"I have to, I mean…" Catherine rinsed off, shut off the faucet, and leaned against the counter. She took the towel from Alice and dried her hands. "I had to evaluate the business and meet with her often to discuss her options."

Alice narrowed her eyes. She remembered Catherine doing the same thing years ago. She had a way of dancing around a topic by using the right words in the perfect combination to form a response you couldn't argue with because it was some form of the truth. But she was keeping details from Alice, and that hurt more than an outright lie.

"I saw you and Ms. Nguyen at the park today." Alice spoke the moment Catherine entered their small apartment off campus. She didn't even wait for Catherine to put her book bag down.

"You did?" Catherine's eyes were wide with fear.

"Yup." Alice crossed her arms and waited for the explanation she was sure would come. She was so confident that this was it, her best friend would finally tell her the truth and stop sneaking around. Alice was happy for Catherine. She had never seen her so content, and she knew that Linda Nguyen had everything to do with it.

"She wanted to use one of my papers from last semester as an example for her class. She asked me to meet with her to discuss it."

"That's it?" Alice ground her teeth together. She knew

Catherine was lying, she had been lying to her for quite some time.

"Yeah." Catherine reached into her bag to retrieve a thick book and a calculator.

"That's really great." Alice bit off her words as she went to her room and slammed the door behind her. She sat on her bed and wondered if Catherine knew how much it hurt her to be pushed to the outside.

That familiar pain filled Alice's chest as she watched Catherine close up again. Part of her was ecstatic since she knew it had been almost ten years since someone, anyone, had reached beyond Catherine's tough exterior. But she was still hurt that Catherine didn't trust her enough to share things like love and heartbreak with her.

"Sophia and Chris are really grateful that you took the job," Alice said as she went to the coat closet. She handed Catherine her jacket. "Don't forget about the St. Valentine's LGBT benefit next Friday. You bought two tickets back in October, remember?"

"I do *not* remember." Catherine laughed. "I'd lose my head if it weren't for you." She leaned in and wrapped Alice in a tight embrace.

When they let go, Alice smiled. "You'll need a date," she teased.

"There's someone at the office I have in mind."

"Oh really?" Alice was intrigued.

"You're leaving already?" Dennis reentered the room just in time to save Catherine from having to explain.

"Yeah, work's been kicking my ass."

"Well, I can't tell. You always look great. I love this shirt, by the way." He pointed to the raspberry blouse Catherine was wearing.

"Thanks, Imogene gave it to me." Alice perked up at this new information. "We'll talk soon." With a peck on two cheeks,

Catherine was out the door and on her way home, leaving a wide-eyed married couple in her wake.

"Thanks for bringing up the shirt." Alice wrapped her arms around her husband's waist.

"I knew you were dying to know about it but wouldn't ask yourself. Nobody ever suspects the husbands to be just as nosy as the wives."

❖

Imogene settled into her worn sofa with a full glass of wine in hand. It had been a long week, and after her less-than-warm good-bye with Catherine, she was in need of some liquid relaxation and good conversation to help clear her mind. That's why she called and invited Sophia over.

"You yelled at her?" Sophia pulled back in surprise.

"It wasn't so much of a yell as it was a stern, loud voice." Imogene scrunched her face as she described the scene. "I yelled at her." She slumped her shoulders in defeat.

"Did you apologize?"

"No."

"Imogene! That's so unlike you. I don't even know what to say!" Sophia frowned. "I almost forgot about my wine because of you!" She leaned forward and grabbed her glass with her long fingers. "Did you at least explain yourself?"

"No." Imogene took a large swig of her merlot before covering her face with her free hand.

"I knew something was wrong," Sophia whispered over the rim of her wineglass. "When you called me, I could tell by your tone. I didn't have to be a psychic to figure it out. Now are you going to tell me what's going on, or am I going to have to wait forever?"

"I don't know what to do." Imogene gulped the last of her wine and set her glass down. "I don't have anything to really apologize for. I didn't do anything wrong! And really, what are we? I can barely consider us friends, so what does that make us? Business associates? Acquaintances? She pushed a little too hard with trying to get me to go to the city, I had a sensitive moment, and it should just blow over, right?" She closed her eyes. "Then why do I feel so awful about it?"

Sophia gripped Imogene's knee. "Because you're a good person," she said. "And because you like her."

Imogene opened her mouth to deny it, but she sighed in defeat and hung her head.

"Oh well, there's nothing I can do about it now," Imogene said. "I've only ever called her office, and I can't show up on her doorstep to apologize for something I did two days ago. I'll wait for the next time she calls about the store, and I'll apologize then if she's upset." She sat back and took a deep, cleansing breath through her nose. "This is all your fault, you know?" she said to Sophia, who seemed more interested in her phone. "You just had to tell me that I'd be some significant person in Catherine's life, and now all I do is look for signs as to what I'm supposed to do or who I'm supposed to be! It's ridiculous!

"I haven't seen one damn thing to support this vision you insist you had, and what the hell is so important on that thing?" Imogene nearly snatched Sophia's phone away from her when her own phone signaled a new message.

"You may want to get that," Sophia said.

"Whose address is this?"

"It's Catherine Carter's address, in case you decide that you need it. Anyway, Imogene, I should get going. Chris is expecting me home early tonight." Sophia collected her jacket and purse before making her way to the door. "Apologize to her sooner rather than later. You'll both feel better that way."

Imogene didn't get up. She looked from the closed door to the clock and wondered if nine thirty was too late for a surprise visitor on a Friday night. After only a moment of debate,

Imogene decided if Catherine could surprise her, she could do some surprising of her own. She grabbed her coat and keys and left her apartment.

❖

Catherine jumped at the sound of her doorbell. She rarely got visitors, especially late Friday evenings. As she got up from the leather sofa and went to the door, she tightened the sash of her robe and ran her fingers through her damp head of curls. Her slippers echoed as she walked through her quiet condo. When she finally opened the door, Catherine was shocked to see Imogene.

Imogene was breathless, looking like she'd run there instead of taking her car. Her thick red hair was piled carelessly atop her head and her cheeks were pink. "I'm sorry to show up unannounced," Imogene said, "but I had to see you."

Catherine stared wordlessly.

"Should I leave or…?" She started to retreat, but Catherine didn't want to let her get away.

"No! I'm sorry, please come in." She stepped aside and ushered Imogene into her home. "I was just surprised. Stunned, actually." She laughed nervously. "Have a seat." She motioned toward the sofa. "Can I get you anything? Water, wine, beer, I think I may even have a leftover can of soda."

"Nothing, thank you. I hope I'm not intruding."

Catherine was standing a few feet away from where Imogene sat. She looked down at her attire and remembered where her evening was heading just before her doorbell rang. Her pajamas peeked out from her bathrobe and her hair was a mass of unruly, damp brunette curls.

"You're not. I had just finished up a shower and was about to settle in with a few procedural reports when you arrived. Truth be told, you saved me. Welcome to my home," she said as she sat beside Imogene.

"No wonder why you looked shell-shocked when you saw my place for the first time." Imogene laughed.

"Excuse me?"

"I look like a crazy hoarder compared to you. You have to have a cleaning lady. Tell me you have a cleaning lady, it'll make me feel better."

"A wonderful woman by the name of Rosemarie comes by every other Sunday to straighten up." Catherine smiled, feeling the familiar ease of being with Imogene. "I could give you her number, but I think your place is perfect the way it is. It feels like a real home." Catherine tucked one long leg beneath her and relaxed into the corner of the sofa, resting her elbow on the back.

"Oh please. I lose Vixen on a weekly basis, and my place is only a third of the size of this." Imogene leaned back into the sofa as well.

"If you'd like my theory, and stop me if you don't, I think Vixen gets lost on purpose. It has nothing to do with how cluttered or not cluttered your place is. It's that cat."

"Poor Vixen, she only has one real friend."

Catherine thought Imogene's fake pout turned her already plump lower lip into something positively luscious. "One real friend," Catherine repeated. "Isn't that all we really need to be happy?"

"Speaking of friendship," Imogene said, "I wanted to apologize for the other night."

"No need to. It's forgotten. It was a long day." Catherine waved off her apology.

"Catherine," Imogene said firmly. "I not only owe you an apology, but I also owe you an explanation for my outburst. I was incredibly rude to you, and it'll only make it worse if we act like it was okay." She shifted closer.

Catherine noted the seriousness in her tone and sat up straight. "I'm listening."

Imogene took a deep breath. "I hate telling this story." She shook out her hands. "Okay, like a Band-Aid. My father was a firefighter with the FDNY, and he died in 9/11. I haven't been back to the city since." Her words flew out in a rush, her voice wavering as she spoke. Catherine took Imogene's hands in hers, silently encouraging her to share as much or as little as she felt comfortable with.

Catherine listened intently as Imogene recounted it all, every detail from that day. She hung on every word, from what Imogene had for breakfast to the list of classes she had scheduled that day. Catherine held her breath when Imogene started to describe the way the horrible news had broken out across campus, slowly making its way to her. Catherine's chest tightened when Imogene started crying.

"I went straight home that night. My mom and I barely ate for weeks until his death was confirmed. The settlement money is what I used to open my store."

"I'm sure that didn't fill the void, though," Catherine offered sympathetically.

Imogene shook her head. "I know now that he was a hero and saved lives that day, but at the time I was so angry at him. He was off that day and didn't have to go, but because he did, I lost my father." Once she was finally out of words, full-body sobs overtook her. She slumped against Catherine, who held her tightly.

Catherine didn't realize what she was doing at the time, but she shifted to lie fully on the couch, holding Imogene. Nothing was in her mind except comforting her, letting Imogene know she was there and everything would be just fine. Catherine's robe soaked up Imogene's tears until she started to calm down.

Catherine then realized the position they were in. She noticed the way Imogene's stray hairs tickled her nose and that she'd been kissing the same spot of soft skin on Imogene's forehead without her permission. The ease Catherine felt comforting Imogene scared her, but no more than her need to do it. Catherine pulled herself away to retrieve a small box of tissues from the nearby bathroom, feeling cold air engulf her body. She fought against the urge to run back to the warmth of Imogene and resume her hold. Catherine avoided her reflection in the bathroom mirror as she grabbed the tissues and returned to Imogene's side.

"I'm so…" Catherine fought for the right words to say.

"You don't have to say anything." Imogene blew her nose and gave Catherine a pained smile. Catherine was stunned by how vulnerable she looked with her makeup running, and how her red-rimmed eyes were the clearest blue she had ever seen them. Imogene stood and put her jacket on quickly.

Catherine wanted to say so much, but she couldn't find her voice. She wanted to tell Imogene that she didn't deserve to suffer such pain. She was a beautiful, kind, lovely woman who deserved the good things life had to offer, including someone to shelter her from the bad. Catherine found herself speaking as she rushed to open the door for Imogene.

"I bought two plates for a fundraiser next Friday," she said to Imogene. "If you don't have any Valentine's plans, would you like to go with me?"

"The St. Valentine LGBT fundraiser, right? Sophia and Chris are going to that. I meant to buy a ticket months ago but kept forgetting."

"So, is that a yes?" Catherine asked, holding her breath.

"Yes. I'd love to." Imogene's smile stood out from the sadness that still stained her face.

"Great. Since we all know each other, we'll have a better time than if I brought a real date who sat like a bump on a log because he's a stranger. We'll figure out the details during the week."

"Sure." Imogene stepped into the hall and hardly turned back as she wished Catherine a good night.

"Imogene?" Catherine called out after her. "I'm really sorry about your loss."

Imogene's baby blue eyes sparkled as she nodded and left.

Chapter Fourteen

Catherine spent more time on personal calls that week than she ever had, making plans with Imogene and Alice for the Valentine's function. Everything was working out perfectly, until Catherine had an unexpected Thursday-evening date with Richard Thorton. At the end of a particularly long, drawn-out meeting, Catherine found herself in dire need of a drink. She surprised herself by asking Richard, but the fact that his excitement seemed genuine shocked her more.

That excitement didn't translate into reality. Once they got to a bar and ordered drinks, they stared at each other blankly across the small candlelit table. The uncomfortable silence stretched on and Catherine found herself wishing an empty glass would replace the full one that sat in front of her so she'd be able to excuse herself.

"So," Richard started, "that was some meeting." He straightened his burgundy tie.

"Sure was." Catherine ate the olive off the small martini pick. "One of the job hazards, I guess."

"I have a real love/hate relationship with this job," Richard confessed eagerly. "I enjoy what I do, but I hate having to explain it to other people, especially in a proposal that sounds a lot like 'please trust me with your millions.'" He took a healthy swig of his scotch.

"I know what you mean," Catherine agreed, relaxing as she treaded lightly on their singular common ground. "It's still better than what I originally thought I'd be doing with my life."

"And what was that?" Richard asked.

"Defense attorney," she said. "It's easier to convince people to trust you with their money than their lives sometimes." She laughed at her small joke.

"You made the right choice," he replied. "Most lawyers I know are terrible people."

Catherine stiffened defensively.

"You're incredibly talented in this field," Richard said. "You're brilliant with your numbers and very well accomplished amongst our most prestigious clients. Very impressive."

"Thank you." Catherine bowed her head modestly. Deep inside, she was uncomfortable with the way the conversation was going. She had asked him out in hopes of getting to know him personally, not to give him the green light to kiss her ass. "Tell me more about yourself, Richard."

"What would you like to know?" He looked at her over the rim of his glass.

"Family? Hobbies? Favorite sport?" *Anything?*

"Only child, parents are back in Chicago, and I'm not much of a sports guy." He kept looking at his drink after he spoke.

This is like pulling teeth, Catherine thought as she took another sip of her still-full martini. As the silence stretched on, her thoughts strayed, and she starting thinking about plans for the next evening. She knew what she was going to wear, but Imogene hadn't told her what she planned on wearing. No matter what Imogene chose, Catherine knew she'd look stunning. And she'd be better company than Richard. Hearing her name, Catherine felt Richard and the waiter staring at her.

"Would you like another drink?"

"No, thank you. One is enough for this lightweight."

He gave her a small smile before ordering a refill. Catherine silently calculated how much longer that additional drink would keep her there.

Richard was a kind enough man, but painfully dull. As much as Catherine tried not to compare Richard to Imogene, she just couldn't help herself. She hadn't really laughed with Richard, but Imogene left her breathless with laughter. And she wasn't attracted to Richard. She never even considered kissing him. Her belly didn't flop with giddiness when their hands accidentally touched. Catherine knew whatever part of her decided men were easier years ago was fueled by denial. They weren't easier. They just required less of her effort, time, and heart.

"Catherine? Are you okay?" he asked, furrowing his dark brow.

"Yeah, I'm fine." She looked at his fresh drink she didn't remember him getting, and she wondered how long she had been daydreaming.

"You seem distracted."

And you seem dreadfully boring was what she wanted to say in her defense, but she remembered her manners. "I have a few things on my mind." She finished her drink in one final swallow, wincing at the burn of the alcohol.

"Let's call it a night, then," he said, doing the same. "And maybe next time, if you're interested, we could do dinner instead."

Catherine wasn't sure she'd heard Richard correctly. It sounded as though he were asking her out on another date. Did she want to see him again in a more intimate setting? She found herself feeling flattered but unsure.

"I'll call you." Richard seemed satisfied with that.

Richard insisted on paying the bill for their drinks and walking Catherine to her car. They stood awkwardly in the frigid evening air. Catherine's cheeks stung from the bitterness but she didn't know how to end their date. Finally, for the first time that evening, Richard took the lead by extending his large, limp hand to Catherine.

On the way home, Catherine wondered if she could write it

off as an expense on her taxes before remembering Richard had picked up the bill.

She walked into her condo just as the phone in her pocket started to ring. Her mood quickly brightened when she saw Imogene's name light up the screen. "Hello?"

"Hey there."

The sound of Imogene's voice saved Catherine's night. "Hey, what's up?" she asked, holding her phone against her shoulder with her cheek as she unbuttoned her coat.

"I was just closing up for the evening and wanted to confirm everything for tomorrow one last time."

"Meet me here at six thirty. Everything else will fall into place." Catherine hung up her coat and unbuttoned her suit jacket. Her white blouse was next as she made her way to the bedroom.

"I feel stupid because I'm nervous, but it's been a while since I've been to any sort of formal get-together."

"Don't feel stupid and don't be nervous. You'll be hanging out with friends, just dressed to the nines instead of your usual eights." Catherine's voice was steady and comforting, but she felt wilted.

"Are you okay? You sound tired."

"Exhausted." Catherine plopped her tall frame down on the foot of her bed to unlace her wing-tip oxfords. "I had a long day at the office, and I'm just getting in from drinks with Richard."

"Blue tie guy?" Imogene asked.

Catherine smirked at the hint of surprise she caught in Imogene's tone. "One and the same." She rolled her tense shoulders and reminded herself to book a massage sometime in the near future.

"Like a date?"

"I guess? After an excruciatingly long and boring meeting, I needed a drink and I figured it was the perfect opportunity to get to know him." Catherine put Imogene on speaker as she entered the bathroom and set the phone on the dark marble vanity so she could pull her hair up.

"How'd it go?"

"About as well as the meeting," Catherine answered after a resigned sigh.

"Ouch."

Catherine could hear Imogene's smile in the single word she spoke. "Exactly. And he wants to see me again," she said as she removed what little eye makeup she'd put on.

"You're going to see him again?" The smile in Imogene's voice disappeared.

"I don't know," Catherine answered dimly. "Honestly?"

"Yeah."

"Going to this fundraiser with you tomorrow night feels more like a date than any moment I spent with Richard tonight, and it hasn't even happened yet." A beat of silence passed, and she wondered if she'd said too much. "I'm going to get going. I need to sleep if I plan on looking better than the walking dead tomorrow."

"Maybe I'm into that sort of thing," Imogene said playfully.

"If you're interested in arriving on the arm of a woman looking like a corpse, that is a request I can easily fulfill," Catherine countered with a laugh.

"I'm looking forward to it." Imogene's voice purred and echoed through the black-and-white bathroom.

"I'll see you tomorrow evening."

"Six thirty."

"Good night, Imogene."

"Catherine?"

"Yes?"

"I hope it's not a bad thing, tomorrow feeling like a date? I know I don't mind."

The words filled Catherine's heart warmly; excitement ignited every nerve ending.

"It's a good thing, Imogene, a very good thing."

"Good. Sweet dreams, Catherine."

Catherine put the phone down and walked slowly to her bed. *When was the last time anyone wished me a sweet anything?* She fell asleep easily that night, with a small smile on her face and dreams filled by someone whose name wasn't Richard Thorton.

Chapter Fifteen

Catherine checked the face of her oversized watch for the tenth time as she stood impatiently in the foyer of her building. It was nearing six forty, the limo was waiting, and Imogene had yet to appear. "Fashionably late" was a foreign concept to Catherine, who preferred to be "cautiously early." She was finding being late more unnerving than her anxiety at being a proper date for Imogene. She felt ill-prepared, seeing she and Linda had never been on a formal date. She couldn't think of any of her male suitors she wanted to emulate.

Closer to six fifty than she would have liked, Catherine heard a car door slam, and she stepped out of the foyer. She spotted Imogene rushing from her car.

"I'm so sorry I'm late! I was planning on being early because I know how important that is to you, but as I opened the front door Vixen escaped and I had to chase her around to get her back into the apartment." Catherine opened the limousine door for Imogene as she finished her rapid-fire apology. The annoyance Catherine felt earlier melted away as she smiled at a frazzled Imogene. She slid in next to her on the leather bench seat.

"Don't worry about it. You're here now, so just focus on having a good time." She fought against the surprising desire she felt to reach across the small space between them just to touch, to grab Imogene's fidgeting hand. Catherine wanted to avoid an awkward night, so she refrained from crossing any lines. Just because she said it *felt* like a date didn't mean it *was* a date. Catherine wished the limo had brighter lighting so she could see Imogene's face better. "Happy Valentine's Day, Imogene."

"Happy Valentine's Day to you."

Catherine smiled at how the moonlight illuminated Imogene's vibrant expression. They spent the short ride to their destination in a comfortable silence.

"Here we are," Catherine announced as the limo pulled up to the curb outside a large banquet hall a little after seven. "Ready?" The driver opened their door, and Catherine slid out with grace. A moment later, she extended her gloved hand into the limo for Imogene. While her exit of the vehicle wasn't as fluid as Catherine's, Imogene still smiled. Catherine took Imogene's hand and tucked it into the crook of her elbow as they walked through a large entryway. They went directly to the coat check and Catherine removed her long overcoat.

She wore a classic tuxedo with a tailored, slim, feminine cut. The flawless skin of her chest was on display thanks to the two pearl buttons she had left undone along her black silk button-up. The black-on-black color scheme combined with her height made her look stealthy and dangerous. Catherine felt sexy, and it showed in her confident gait. She watched as Imogene looked at her from her perfectly styled curls and darker-than-usual makeup to her black Louboutin heels. But she knew Imogene's attention would be drawn to one detail—a dizzying paisley print swirl of vibrant cobalt blue and muted navy she wore in the pocket of her tuxedo jacket.

"I figured that if I was going to be next to you all night, I needed to wear at least a little color." She grinned, but it faltered when Imogene didn't respond. "Does it look that bad? I can take it out." Catherine reached for the pocket square, but Imogene stopped her.

"No!" With visibly shaking hands, Imogene unbuttoned her long coat before letting it fall from her bare arms.

Imogene was wrapped tightly in a sinfully soft cobalt blue dress that matched Catherine's pocket square perfectly. The sleeveless design had thick straps that came down to a wrapped front cut in a low *V*, allowing a tasteful hint of cleavage. Her small waist was accented by the tight design and the tea-length flowing skirt, which danced in the slight breeze that accompanied the opening and closing of the door.

Catherine was torn between the awe she felt at her date's beauty and wondering whether their matching was a coincidence or not. With a small smile, Catherine extended her bent arm once again. "We may as well make it look like we did it on purpose."

"You look wonderful, Catherine. And you know, Sophia is going to have a field day with our matching colors."

"As do you, Miss. Harris, and not if Alice beats her to it." Catherine chuckled as she tried to imagine the look on Alice's face when she saw them. "If you're my date, and we're dressed to match, I'm going to have to insist you call me Cat." Catherine smiled nervously down at Imogene. "Unless you feel more comfortable with Catherine."

"I like Cat, a lot."

Catherine didn't think she was talking about the nickname alone, and her heart swelled with promising, budding affection. They entered the hall arm in arm, both looking pleased.

When they stepped into the throngs of people, Catherine thought the excitement of the evening was overwhelming in a pleasant way. The large ballroom was decorated tastefully but was muted enough to make the singles in the room feel comfortable as well. An open dance floor served as the room's centerpiece, surrounded by intimately placed circular tables for three couples.

"Shall we find our table or get a drink first?" Catherine asked Imogene.

"Let's find everyone else first." Imogene looked around and beyond Catherine.

They both looked from full table to full table. Straight ahead from where they were standing sat Sophia and Alice with their husbands. The two men were deep in conversation and the women were looking around the crowded room.

"There they are," Imogene said, pointing at them with her index finger. Catherine noticed her perfect French manicure, a detail so unlike Imogene and the colorful woman she was. The woman Catherine had grown so fond of.

"Let's not make them wait."

As they approached the table, Dennis and Chris offered quick hellos and continued their private conversation. When Catherine and Imogene settled into their seats, Sophia and Alice started to open up, talking freely about the week that had passed and how much they had been looking forward to the benefit. The conversation flowed easily as Alice shared stories of Mackenzie's latest adventures and of Catherine's college days. At one point, when Catherine was struggling for a breath between laughing fits, she looked over at Imogene beside her and felt a genuine contentment wash over her. She thanked her lucky stars for Imogene becoming part of her life.

"I'll get us the next round." Sophia stood and started to make her way to the open bar.

"I'll come along." Imogene stood, paused for a moment, and rested her hand on Catherine's shoulder. "Can I get you anything, Cat?"

"I'll have another dry, dirty martini. Thank you." Catherine nervously looked across the table to Alice as Imogene and Sophia left. "It's a great turnout tonight."

"I think we should dance," Alice said.

She's not fooling me, Catherine thought. She prepared herself for a thorough interrogation. She would tell the truth about the coincidental matching as well as the mutual decision to play it off as planned. She'd admit to a few innocent flirtations and tell Alice she was going with the flow. That's it. The plan was solid, and for the first time in years Catherine was okay with simply going with the flow. Tonight, she'd let Imogene take the lead.

Catherine stood in front of Alice and shifted her feet back

and forth to the beat. Alice had her own way of dancing. She was far from smooth, but she smiled happily with every move. Alice smiled sugary sweet, and Catherine knew the first question was about to drop at any moment…except it didn't. Alice continued to dance in silence with Catherine. From time to time, Alice would laugh and shake her head, but she didn't let Catherine in on the joke.

Catherine decided to finally break the wordless tension with a compliment. "You look stunning." She signaled to the strapless little black dress Alice wore.

"So do you. Very dapper," Alice said as she fingered the lapels of Catherine's tuxedo jacket. "I love when you break out the tux." She then changed the subject expectedly. "Imogene is absolutely breathtaking. Looks very good on your arm, too." She spoke loudly enough to be heard over the music. The two women stopped moving and stood awkwardly for a moment, staring each other down.

Catherine had to keep Linda a secret, but not Imogene. Not this time. She could scream her feelings from the rooftop, and she decided maybe it was time to talk to Alice. "Imogene is—"

"Mind if I cut in?" Imogene said loudly from behind Catherine, who jumped, her hand flying to her chest while Alice erupted with laughter.

"Of course not." Catherine was still breathing rapidly as she answered.

"You two have fun." Alice left the two alone with a wink.

They looked at one another for seconds before Imogene stepped closer and put her left hand on Catherine's shoulder, her right grasping Catherine's left hand. Catherine let out a shaky breath as her free hand settled on the swell of Imogene's hip. They moved together seamlessly, Catherine naturally taking the lead.

Catherine grew more comfortable in Imogene's arms, and the rest of the room seemed to fade away. Imogene released her grip on Catherine's hand and wrapped her arms around her neck.

Instinctively, Catherine wrapped her own arms around Imogene's waist and pulled her flush against her body.

Catherine's willpower was wearing thin. It was one thing to hold Imogene when she was sad and allow her to cry on her shoulder, but quite another to hold her close in an almost seductive dance. This was intimacy, an intimacy Catherine had been missing. The temptation was too strong and Catherine was too weak to keep her hands from dipping a little closer to Imogene's rounded backside. Her head was spinning, and she prayed the music would never stop playing.

How had she denied her need for this feeling? Catherine had given up even the hope of having this again, and why? For fear of being heartbroken again? Linda Nguyen was controlling. She called all the shots and destroyed Catherine as a result, but Catherine was different now, and Imogene wasn't Linda.

Catherine felt Imogene's breath hitch when she pushed herself against Catherine's firm body and wound her fingers through the fine curls at the nape of her heated neck. Then she slid her flattened palms down the front of the black jacket, coming to rest on her rapidly rising and falling chest. Catherine missed the cooling sensation of Imogene's touch but couldn't focus on that disappointment for too long. She shivered. Now Imogene was so close to Catherine's breasts, it was torturous. When Imogene looked up and met Catherine's gaze, she was so overwhelmed by her need that her knees began to shake. Once the song ended, Catherine pulled back.

"I'm going to use the ladies' room," she said, departing quickly for the safety only distance could provide.

Catherine leaned on the counter for support and took several heaving breaths. Not one woman or man in her past had reduced her to a shaky mess in front of a room full of people. She had never reacted this way to another person, not even Linda. She'd been too engulfed by fear and shadows to fully enjoy what she felt in Linda's company or to let herself lose control with her.

Catherine had never doubted her own self-control, but one

look into Imogene's wanting eyes and she was ready to take her right on the dance floor. As she looked at her own reflection, the flushed face and the reddened patches that crept up her chest, Catherine wondered what it was about Imogene that caused this volatile attraction. The other woman was gorgeous, sure. She was witty and funny, attributes Catherine always found alluring. She was also entering the bathroom. *So much for that distance.*

"I'm just about done." Catherine spoke in an unsteady voice as they looked at each other in the mirror. She pretended to check her makeup.

"Everyone paired off and I felt a bit lonely, so I decided to check on you. Are you okay? You left a bit abruptly." Catherine nodded as Imogene stepped forward and leaned against the counter beside her. It dawned on Catherine that they were alone, truly alone. Catherine looked at Imogene's ruby red lips, her crystal blue eyes, and the small sprinkle of freckles on her small nose. She cast a quick glance toward the door before she could change her mind.

She gripped Imogene's full hips and turned her so her backside was pressed against the counter. Before Imogene could move, Catherine kissed her. It only took a moment for the initial shock to wear off, then Imogene responded with equal passion. The kiss started out hard, but became slow and tender, a tiny ember among early flames. They savored each other's softness, relished the feel of their moist lips gliding together for never-ending seconds. Catherine traced the swell of Imogene's plump lower lip with the tip of her tongue. When the kiss went from tentative to deep, all the air seemed to leave the room.

Catherine broke the kiss, lowering her assault and running her lips along Imogene's feverish throat, then lower still. She kissed her bare shoulder and made her way back up Imogene's long, creamy neck, her thick wavy hair swept to the side. Catherine bit softly at a pulse point, loving Imogene's small gasp of surprise. When Catherine pressed her open palm on the counter behind Imogene to brace herself, the motion set off the faucet sensor.

The sudden noise of running water startled Catherine, then she and Imogene broke out into a fit of laughter. Catherine smoothed down the front of her jacket and motioned for Imogene to leave first. She knew they'd be looking less pristine than when they went in, but she didn't care.

Catherine steered them back to their table in time for the first course. She sat casually and ignored the stares from their friends. Catherine said the food looked delicious, and once the rest of the table was distracted by their dinners, Imogene leaned in and whispered into Catherine's pink ear.

"That reminds me, you taste better than I imagined."

She said it so nonchalantly that Catherine wondered if she had heard correctly. When she looked at Imogene, her expression was downright seductive. Catherine swallowed hard and checked the time. It wasn't late enough.

The rest of the meal passed without incident, though Catherine saw Sophia look at Imogene curiously. By dessert, Catherine thought Imogene seemed less sure of herself, lacking the confidence she had back in the restroom. Catherine placed her hand on Imogene's thigh, sighing when Imogene took her hand.

Once dessert was finished, the two married couples went off to bid on various items at the silent auction, leaving Imogene and Catherine alone for the first time in nearly two hours. For long moments they sat in comfortable silence that still crackled with underlying passion. Catherine drew lazy circles on Imogene's thighs. How it was possible, Catherine wasn't sure, but her lips still tingled in reminiscence of fiery kisses.

"What's next?" Imogene asked.

Catherine shook her head. She wasn't sure if she was ready to think beyond the present. Her desire faded to fear greater than she had known recently. Her heart started to beat with such force it made her feel sick, and her breathing became shallow. Could she trust Imogene not to hurt her? It would be a big step for Catherine, one she hadn't taken in nearly a decade.

"I don't know."

"What do you want?" Imogene asked.

"I don't know what's going to happen after tonight, and I can't promise you anything, but..." Catherine paused to breathe, feeling like a fifty pound weight was resting on her chest. "I know I want you and I don't want this night to end." Catherine looked at Imogene with desperation. She knew what she wanted and could even voice it, but she needed Imogene to take the lead and give her everything else she couldn't ask for. She needed Imogene to make the final decision.

"Let's go back to my place."

Catherine didn't even bother to search for their friends as she made her way to the coat check. She didn't wait for change for her fifty-dollar bill when she tipped the dapper young man who handed her two coats. Nor did she care that they were leaving before claiming the complimentary gift bag promised when she purchased the tickets.

❖

"What about this? A trip to Aruba—all-inclusive and child friendly." Dennis read aloud from the display card.

"I've told you before, I'm not bidding on a vacation," Alice said distractedly as she watched the other attendees closely, observing what everyone else was bidding on. "We can plan our own vacation, and if we go to Aruba, it will *not* be with the kids."

"What *do* you feel like bidding on?"

"Do they have that spa day package like last year? I was so upset when we lost that." Alice moved up the table of auction prizes.

"I'll look." Dennis walked off.

"I'm embarrassed by how late I am!" bellowed an enchanting voice from behind Alice. "I may have missed the food, but I will not miss the auction." Alice's ears perked up at a hint of familiarity. It wasn't unusual to run into people she knew at the annual fundraiser, but this voice was someone she hadn't heard in a while. Several guests swallowed the speaker from view, but that didn't deter Alice from craning her neck to sneak a peek.

"I have an important meeting in the morning that I needed to prepare for. I must've lost track of time."

"You know what they say about all work and no play," teased a gentleman.

"I know, but it's important to my company that the time spent with a new financial firm is productive. Time is of the essence with our business."

"Are you using a local financial firm? We have been thinking about switching recently, ours has been a bit too casual with responses to our concerns."

"I'm meeting with Marcati and Stevens in the morning. I'll email you a detailed review when all is said and done." Alice smiled proudly when the woman mentioned Catherine's firm. She was ready to interject with her own opinions of the company when the conversation started to end.

"Well, I appreciate that, and for the record, we're happy to have you in attendance, no matter what time you arrived." The large tuxedoed man who had been blocking Alice's view started to move. "Enjoy your evening, Ms. Nguyen."

"*Oh no.*" Alice froze.

"You as well, Mr. Engen." The sea of partygoers parted, and Alice got a good look at Linda Nguyen flitting casually about the auction tables. Alice scrambled for what to do. She rushed back to their table, only to be greeted by empty seats. In the distance she spotted Sophia and Chris dancing, but Catherine and Imogene were nowhere on the dance floor. Alice rushed back to her husband's side.

"Where's Cat? Have you seen her and Imogene anywhere? Where are they?" Alice asked with rapid-fire desperation.

"Whoa there." Dennis gripped Alice's shoulders. "I think they already left. Is everything okay?"

"Fine," Alice answered curtly. "I'll try to call her." She

removed her phone from the small purse she was carrying and dialed.

"She and Imogene are good together. I haven't seen Cat that happy in a long while," Dennis said as he filled out a bidding card.

"Yeah," Alice agreed with the phone pressed to her ear. "I'm trying to keep it that way."

CHAPTER SIXTEEN

The limousine was filled with a thick, suffocating tension that kept both women quiet for the short ride back from the banquet hall. Imogene's mind spun with the possibilities of what could happen once they arrived at her apartment, her imagination alit with all the things she wanted to do to the woman seated beside her. They sat closely. An inch of space kept them separated, but the heat they'd felt in the bathroom still vibrated along the void. Imogene watched Catherine check her phone from the corner of her eye.

"Anyone important?" Imogene asked casually.

"Just Alice." Catherine slid the phone back into her pocket. "She's probably dying to know where we ran off to." Imogene hummed in response, not really knowing what to say.

The rational side of Imogene's brain told her to call it a night. She'd learned from previous dating mistakes not to toy with a straight woman or allow a straight woman to toy with her. It would be so easy to fall for Catherine. Imogene was in dangerous territory, but what pushed her harder than rational thought was the way her heart hammered still and how wet she was for Catherine. *For just this once*, Imogene thought, *I'm going to do what* feels *right*.

"We're here." Imogene's voice, raspy and low, shattered the silence.

Catherine looked around. She slid across the fine leather seat and opened the car door before extending her hand toward Imogene for the second time that evening. Imogene stared at Catherine's offered hand and gripped it tightly. Never had she been with such a chivalrous date, and she wondered if Catherine would be as attentive in the bedroom.

They both stumbled awkwardly from the limo in an attempt to avoid patches of ice and piles of dirty snow that still lined the city sidewalks. Before Catherine could shut the door, Imogene stopped her.

"Are you sure this is what you want?" *Are you sure that I'm what you want?* Insecurity, fear, and small glimmer of hope filled Imogene as she waited for Catherine to answer her question.

"I'm not saying good night just yet." Catherine's voice held no expectation, just honesty.

Imogene stepped forward and reached behind Catherine, allowing herself to lean in closely enough to be blinded by the steam of Catherine's breath, and shut the car door. She watched as the limo drove away, knowing there was no turning back. She found her keys and gave Catherine a shy smile. Catherine was looking at the two-digit number that hung proudly to the left of the doorjamb. Imogene unlocked the door and swung it open.

"You coming?" she asked with a slight tilt of her head.

Imogene led the way up the stairs, turning a dim light on when they stepped inside. "Wine?" she offered nervously as she removed her coat and threw it over the back of the couch on her way to the kitchen.

"No, thank you. The martinis were enough." Catherine discarded her coat and tuxedo jacket and sank into the comfortable couch, crossing her long legs. Imogene joined her in a minute or two, sitting close enough to feel the warmth of Catherine's body without actually touching her.

"I'm not sure what we're doing here." Imogene spoke into her glass.

"Me either," Catherine said, "but I was telling the truth when I said I wasn't ready to say good night. Whether it's just for conversation or not, I want to enjoy your company for at least a little while longer."

"How do you do that?" Imogene asked in wonderment.

"Do what?"

"I'm a bundle of nerves right now, and you continue to be so damn charming." Imogene laughed at her own assessment. "For a straight woman, you seem incredibly relaxed, like you didn't just make out with another woman in a public bathroom."

"I'm pretty open-minded, Imogene." Catherine leaned forward and continued in a whisper, "The thought of kissing in a bathroom never fazed me. I've always wanted to try it."

"See!" Imogene slapped Catherine's arm. Although she was laughing, her tone remained serious. "You're even joking about it! You have to be feeling something, and as a non-predatory lesbian, I need to know you're okay before whatever may or may not happen next actually happens." Imogene started to fidget nervously and put her wineglass down on the table.

"It's been a long time since I've been with anyone." Imogene opened her mouth to speak, but Catherine quickly cut her off. "And it's been even longer since I've been with a woman. So the reason why I seem so relaxed is because this isn't completely new to me, and I feel very comfortable with you."

Imogene's heart pounded and then melted with Catherine's last few words. She, too, felt incredibly comfortable with her.

"When?"

"College. I never told anyone else about it because she was my professor. We were together for a few years, and then we weren't."

"What was her name?" Imogene asked.

"Linda Nguyen."

"What happened?"

"Well, as I said, she was my professor, so we had to keep

our relationship a secret. At first, that was kind of fun. You know, the taboo and the sneaking around? But even excitement like that can get old." Catherine shook her head and laughed. "I remember coming so close to telling my family about her but stopped myself because my dad was homophobic."

"What?" Imogene's shocked reaction was as shrill as it was comical.

"He flipped out once about my brother's teacher. She was a lesbian and that's how I took it at the time. I later realized he actually had a couple of gay friends, and I just used that as an easy excuse to keep myself from telling them about Linda."

"So you never told them?"

"No."

"Have you ever told anyone?" Imogene's curiosity was bordering on inappropriate, but she didn't care. "What happened between you and Linda?"

Catherine visibly flinched at the last question. "You're the first I've told, and it ended very, *very* badly." Imogene was about to fire off another question but Catherine beat her to it with the answer. "Badly enough to consider settling down with a man."

"Wow." Imogene sat back and let the new information sink in.

"Can I ask *you* a question now?"

Imogene nodded slightly and waited.

Catherine cleared her throat. "The dress, the color," she said. "Did you wear it on purpose?"

"Did you wear *that* on purpose?" She pointed to the small pocket square that now lay tossed aside behind Catherine.

"No."

"Me neither." The silence stretched on for a few minutes. "I only own two formal dresses, and the other was from my senior prom," she said with a self-deprecating smile. "Sounds funny coming from a woman that owns a boutique, I know."

"I just don't know what to believe anymore." Catherine

lowered her head, closed her eyes and started to rub her forehead with her fingertips. "From what Sophia said and what I know you know…"

"Putting everything Sophia told you aside," Imogene said, reaching over and taking Catherine's free hand, tracing the lines along her palm. "If I had worn a black dress tonight, would you still be sitting here right now?" Not receiving an answer immediately, Imogene pressed on. "Would you still have feelings for me?"

"Yes."

"And no matter what color anyone wore, I would have asked you back here." Imogene slowly moved closer to keep from scaring Catherine away. "I've been attracted to you since the night we first met, and if I allow myself to be completely honest, I've been falling for you since then, too."

"Even though I was an asshole?" Catherine asked with a raised eyebrow and a sideways smile.

"Even better, in spite of knowing *not* to fall for a straight girl." Imogene giggled, and then turned serious once again. She brought her right hand up and let her palm rest along Catherine's chiseled cheek. She leaned in, finally allowing herself to be sucked into Catherine's undeniable gravity. In a whisper, a voice so small it could have been lost in the breeze that whipped against the windows, Imogene begged, "Please tell me you feel it, too."

Instead of a verbal response, Catherine kissed her, lightly at first. Imogene relished the gentleness, knowing they didn't have to rush the way they did back in the banquet hall bathroom. The whole night belonged to them and their needs. After a few moments, the small kisses were no longer enough. Imogene felt herself being shifted as Catherine pressed against her. Imogene opened her plump lips and allowed Catherine to taste her thoroughly. Imogene's satiny tongue danced with Catherine's and a moan echoed through the apartment. Imogene was unsure of who was responsible for the feminine, sexy noise, but she was ready to hear it again. In one swift motion, Imogene bunched the skirt of her dress around her waist and swung one long leg over Catherine's thighs to straddle her lap. Imogene smiled when Catherine gripped her backside with both hands. She whimpered as the rough liner of her dress scraped against the cheeks of her ass left bare by her floral-printed thong.

"Oh God." She whispered the words against Catherine's mouth before she went in for another taste. The flavor was unique, bold, with a hint of vodka from the earlier martinis. Catherine was so addicting that Imogene actually whimpered when she pulled away. Her disappointment didn't last long, though. Catherine's lips reappeared at the base of her throat and continued south. They brushed along the swell of her breasts, and Imogene tangled both her hands in Catherine's thick brunette curls, pulling her impossibly closer. She gasped as she felt Catherine sink her teeth into her heated flesh. She lacked control, her movements erratic as she ground her hips and circled them on Catherine's lap. The friction was delightful, but not enough.

Catherine gripped the soft flesh filling her hands, digging in her fingertips, and flipped Imogene onto her back. Catherine settled between her spread thighs, her weight even over Imogene. When she paused for a moment, Imogene looked up into glittery dark eyes.

"You're stunning," Catherine said to her, brushing away the auburn strands that obstructed her view. "You're the most beautiful, mesmerizing woman I have ever met," she proclaimed in a whisper before kissing Imogene sweetly on the lips once more.

Imogene fought the tears threatening to rise at Catherine's words. "I think I love you." She didn't even know she actually spoke the words out loud until Catherine stopped dead. Her rapid breathing was hot against Imogene's neck, and neither woman said anything. Imogene braced herself for good-bye, fully convinced she had ruined the moment with her foolish confession.

Instead, Catherine reached up Imogene's dress and tugged at the flimsy excuse for underwear she was wearing, leaving them tangled around one ankle. Imogene ripped Catherine's shirt up, desperately seeking bare skin.

Imogene spread her legs so Catherine could settle between them. Catherine shifted a few times, bracing herself on her left elbow and knees. Imogene gasped as Catherine skimmed the fingertips of her right hand along the sensitive skin of Imogene's inner thighs. Imogene dug her nails into Catherine's skin, dragging them along and leaving angry red trails in their wake. She hoped Catherine would feel the sting for days to come and remember how badly Imogene needed to be touched, to be filled completely by her. Imogene groaned as Catherine trailed her long fingers along Imogene's moist outer lips before separating her flesh and delving deeper into her wetness, lightly circling her fluttering opening.

"Please," Imogene whimpered, "I need you inside me." Catherine drove into Imogene with two fingers until her palm was pressed firmly against her throbbing clit.

Imogene let out a howl. It was a scream born of the pure pleasure and ecstasy she felt at being so full and being taken so thoroughly. She moved her hips slowly, coaxing Catherine's long fingers, buried deep inside her, in and out. Imogene relished the perfect fit, in and out. She started to pick up the pace, and Catherine matched her easily. Imogene sighed each time she moved, and within minutes, she was calling out Catherine's name.

"Don't stop. Cat!" She bit her lower lip as she prepared for the fast-approaching orgasm and its inevitable intensity. "Harder," she demanded, digging her nails into Catherine's back, using her hips to increase the force of her thrusts. Her toes curled to the point of cramping. "Oh…I'm go—I'm com—" What started as a growl turned into every bit of air rushing from her lungs as her body locked in place. A second later, she shook as wave after wave of pleasure coursed through her body with an intensity she'd never experienced.

When she finally stilled, her body went numb as her muscles vibrated. A tear rolled down the side of her peaceful face as she continued to grind slowly, milking Catherine's fingers of every ounce of pleasure. When the final tremors subsided, Imogene relaxed enough for Catherine to remove her fingers. Imogene was tugged to her feet. She tried to protest but her meek offerings were silenced by reverent kisses being placed along her lips. She walked toward the bedroom with Catherine's hands in her own. With each step along the way Imogene was regaining her strength and started to plot all the ways she wanted Catherine's body. She sat atop her plush bedding and looked over Catherine as she stood before her.

"Take your clothes off," Imogene demanded, but before Catherine could undo two buttons, Imogene batted her hands away and did it herself. "I want this too much to let you have all the fun."

Once she had removed Catherine's shirt, Imogene began mapping out every inch of her toned upper body. She explored every dip, every valley, every ripple of muscle with such tenderness, tremors overtook Catherine's body.

"I knew you'd be soft," Imogene said, kissing one of Catherine's pulse points. Imogene went smoothly and slowly to Catherine's rounded shoulder and swiftly down to the lace trim of her bra. "So soft, so sexy..." she cooed as she undid the clasp and released two small, perky breasts with dark nipples. Without wasting a second, Imogene took one pebbled bud into her mouth for a tender kiss, wrapping her lips around it and tracing small circles along the raised flesh with her tongue.

"Kiss me," Catherine said.

Knowing that Catherine wanted her so badly turned Imogene's sated body on all over again. An excited and slightly pained whimper left Imogene's bruised lips as their mouths met fiercely. Imogene felt Catherine tugging at the small zipper of her dress frantically. The material pooling at Imogene's feet, Catherine wrapped her in her long arms as they kissed. Their tongues danced and moved against each other at a lazy pace while Imogene let Catherine remove the last bits of her mismatched clothing.

Imogene stood naked and vulnerable, watching Catherine take all of her in. Imogene was sure she could feel the path Catherine's eyes traveled like it was a physical caress across her bare flesh. Her pink nipples hardened instantly, and she could feel herself getting wetter. Without as much as a featherlight touch, she was on the brink again just from Catherine looking at her. The way Catherine stood naked from the waist up, still wearing her pointed heels and tight tuxedo pants, was the sexiest thing Imogene had ever seen, but she wanted to see all of her.

As if reading Imogene's mind, Catherine quickly removed the rest of her clothing and led her to the bed. They lay beside one another, Imogene on her back and Catherine on her side. Imogene started to squirm as Catherine explored every inch of her body. All Imogene had to do was moan at the attention being paid to a specific spot, and Catherine would linger, like the small mole behind her left knee or the patch of extra freckles just above a small triangle of red curls at the apex of her thighs. Still, she had kept it together and not gone out of her skin. She was about to congratulate herself on her patience and self-restraint, until Catherine palmed both of her breasts. She pressed her thighs together at the onslaught of pleasure overwhelming her. She lay prone and became a whimpering, thrashing mess as Catherine pinched her rosy nipples and rolled them between her expert fingers. She screamed out Catherine's name.

"I want you to do that again."

"Do what?" Imogene asked.

"Scream my name."

Imogene panted as Catherine descended from her chest to her thighs slowly, deliberately placing wet, open-mouthed kisses at random points along the way.

"Please, make me," Imogene begged. She spread her legs wide as soon as she felt Catherine settle on her stomach between them. The things Catherine was doing to her, the way she was setting her skin on fire with touches in all her most sensitive places, left her desperate and weak.

Imogene was relieved when Catherine didn't hesitate and immediately wrapped her lips around her rigid clit, only applying pressure for a second before sucking it between her lips fully. Imogene thrust her hips up, and she started to grind against Catherine's mouth, ready to reach a new high. Catherine explored every fold with the tip of her tongue, and Imogene mewed in response. She gripped the back of Catherine's head and pulled her closer. Imogene clenched her thighs around Catherine's head as Catherine penetrated her as deeply as her tongue could go. Imogene could feel the familiar fluttering come to life, and she became desperate to feel everything Catherine had to offer her.

"Catherine?"

"Hmm?" Catherine hummed against Imogene's wet opening.

"Fingers." Imogene slammed her head into the pillow when Catherine gave her exactly what she wanted. Catherine sucked gently and unrelentingly at her swollen clit as she pumped two long fingers in and out, curling just enough to find the sweetest spot that made her scream.

Imogene arched her back and called out Catherine's name with such force that it bounced from wall to wall. The feelings that started between her legs and came to life in her chest were violent, bold, and filled with an intensity that drove all other senses from her body. When she finally came down like a boneless mass, Imogene was partially aware of Catherine kissing her eyelids and cheeks, finally settling on her dry mouth.

"I can't—That was—You're…Wow." It was the most coherent sentence Imogene could put together. Her eyes had yet to open, and no matter how hard she tried to change that, they remained closed. There had to be poetic terms she could use to describe the array of colors that flashed behind her clenched lids or the way each and every nerve ending caught fire and cooled to ice, but she couldn't form words. She barely had enough energy to form anything beyond a simple "Mmm."

"Shh…" Imogene was pulled into Catherine's strong embrace. "Rest now, beautiful." Imogene's breathing evened out, and she slept as the clock on the wall ticked away the evening.

Chapter Seventeen

An unexpected heat woke Catherine from the most restful slumber she'd had in years. As she tried to clear her foggy mind she felt soft, naked flesh pressed against her side and a long, smooth leg thrown across her own. As the clouds started to dissipate in her mind, Catherine opened her eyes and saw a wild set of fiery blue eyes and tousled red waves. *Imogene.* Catherine moaned, realizing the heat that woke her was spreading from her center due to Imogene's slim fingers tracing the intimate flesh there.

"What time is it?" Catherine asked as she spread her legs slightly, giving Imogene better access.

"A little after two." Imogene placed a small kiss against Catherine's throat before continuing. "I had a dream that I was fucked senseless by a gorgeous woman, and then I woke up and realized it wasn't a dream." Imogene's use of such coarse language caused Catherine's breath to catch and wet pussy to clench. "I needed to return the favor." She captured Catherine's lips in a heated kiss as she spread Catherine's soaked folds, allowing the tip of her middle finger to tease her opening.

Wide awake now, Catherine threw her head back and burrowed it into the pile of pillows Imogene had on her bed. A needy moan escaped her lips as Imogene explored every sensitive inch of her womanhood.

"You're so wet," Imogene whispered into her hot ear. Catherine wasn't normally one for dirty talk or any sort of verbalizing during sex, but something about the way Imogene did it weakened Catherine and made her hope for more.

"You…" Catherine's voice crackled to life from deep within her tight throat. "You do this to me."

Imogene grinned. "Good." Catherine barely had the chance to register Imogene's response before she slid into her slowly, sinking into moist, welcoming heat millimeter by millimeter. Catherine wanted to keep her eyes open, but they kept fluttering shut as her hips came to life, rolling with abandon.

If Catherine thought she was turned on before, those feelings paled in comparison to what engulfed her body now. Having Imogene's complete attention focused on her hypersensitive body was almost too much to handle or allow. She found herself approaching the precipice a lot faster than she wanted to, but she was powerless against it. The way Imogene curled one finger deep inside her and circled her clit with the other, Catherine couldn't stop herself from giving in to a pleasure she wasn't even sure she deserved. The final straw was when Imogene bit down on her hardened nipple, sending Catherine over the edge with a guttural moan.

Her chest rose and fell as her abdomen contracted with the last few tremors of satisfaction. She smiled a blissful smile when Imogene's head came to rest over her rapidly beating heart. The last thing Catherine remembered before falling asleep was Imogene kissing her.

❖

The early morning sunlight made its way through Imogene's gauzy curtains, brightening the room with a hazy glow. Catherine awoke first and stretched her pleasantly sore muscles. At first she was disoriented by the unfamiliar smells and surroundings, then it all came flooding back. The bed was Imogene's, and the smell was sex. She smiled with satisfaction as she buried her face in the thick hair at the top of Imogene's head, tucked into her neck. Catherine felt the warmth of Imogene's arm across her abdomen and her bare, soft breasts pressed against her ribs, and she knew the true definition of contentment. She barely heard her phone buzzing, a sure sign of missed calls and messages.

Texts, calls, questions, answers—they all went hand in hand as reality hit Catherine with an alarming force. She didn't want to deal with all those things outside the walls of Imogene's apartment. Could she finally indulge in a happiness that once seemed so impossible and trust another woman to keep her heart whole? Another phone alert sounded through the room, and Imogene started to stir. Not wanting to wake her sleeping lover, Catherine made a move to get her phone.

Catherine gently extricated herself from Imogene's deceptively strong hold. She gathered her discarded clothing as quickly as possible and got dressed haphazardly. She sat at the kitchen table, scrolling through several text messages, mostly from Alice. Catherine deleted them without reading them, she knew what her best friend wanted to know. Catherine checked the voice mail list, finding Richard Thorton, Alice, and her mother.

"That's an odd combination to wake up to," Catherine grumbled before deciding to ignore Alice's messages. She tapped on Richard's name first and wiped the sleep from her eyes. She grimaced when she noticed her fingertips were stained black from her makeup.

"Hey, Catherine, it's Richard Thorton." His message was a little loud for Catherine's liking. She pulled the phone away from her ear a bit. *"I was calling to see when you'd like to get together again. Call me back."* She deleted the message the moment she heard it.

She tapped on her mother's name next and smiled when Martha Carter's warm voice filled her ear. *"Catherine, it's your mother. I'm not sure if you remember me since it's been so long since the last time I've heard from you. I know, I know, work has been busy.* " Catherine snorted and rolled her eyes. *"I'm just calling to remind you about your brother's birthday party next weekend."* Catherine stood and walked over to the bookcase, peeking around the corner at the snoozing Imogene as her mother's voice went on. *"Make sure you tell Alice to come, and if there happens to be anyone special in your life, feel free to bring them, too. Call me back, sweetheart."* Catherine concentrated so hard on those few words that she almost missed the end of the message. *Someone special,* she thought. *I have someone special now.*

The sun highlighted Imogene's pale, freckled skin as she slept. Catherine's heart swelled at the innocence of the moment. When she looked at Imogene's peaceful face, she knew she could trust this woman with her life, not just her heart, no matter how scary the idea was.

Catherine's phone buzzed again, and she swiped the screen. Mr. Adamson was calling an emergency meeting at ten o'clock. That gave her little more than an hour to get home, shower, dress, and get to the city. She rushed around the apartment to retrieve her coat and find a small piece of paper so she could leave a note for Imogene. She scribbled a quick sentiment and made her way out the door.

The walk back to her condo was brisk, and Catherine couldn't determine whether her cheeks hurt from the cold wind or the beaming smile she wore thanks to Imogene Harris and spending a night learning to love again.

❖

Imogene started to stir and stretched across her bed. A lazy smile crept across her sleepy face as she searched for her bedmate. She needed to touch her, but the sheets were cold in the empty spot beside her. Imogene sat up quietly and listened for any sign of Catherine even as her gut told her Catherine was already gone. She didn't hear any running shower or smell any breakfast being prepared. She stood and wrapped the light pink sheet around her naked body before walking out to the kitchen.

A certain vulnerability always accompanies the first morning after with a new lover. Waking up alone causes even the most docile of imaginations to run wild. After the constant push and pull she and Catherine had been through, Imogene tried to remain positive, but the painful throb in her chest made that a difficult feat to accomplish.

Maybe Cat went to get coffee or takeout for breakfast. I know she loves the café down the street. The excuses came too easily and then died just as quickly when she spotted the small rectangle of paper on her kitchen table. Imogene approached slowly, her heart beating wildly. She wanted to look everywhere but at the words scrawled neatly across the paper. She held her breath as she read.

Good morning, beautiful.
Money doesn't sleep in on the weekends.
I got called into an emergency meeting.
I'm sure I'll have a hard time concentrating thanks to you.
I'll call you later.
—Cat

Imogene started giggling. It wasn't until her stomach growled that she calmed down and finally started her day.

❖

"Good morning, gentlemen!" Catherine said as she nearly bounced into the bustling boardroom. Everyone had apparently received the same message, which usually meant a very large, very wealthy client was seeking their help.

"Good morning, Catherine," Mr. Adamson said from the

head of the table. He nodded subtly toward the seat to his right, but Richard blocked her way.

"Catherine." He spoke her name through a sideways smile. "You look nice this morning." Catherine rolled her eyes. Superficial compliments never meant much to her, and her choice of worn jeans and white wool sweater were hardly worthy of praise.

"Thank you." She tried to sidestep around Richard, but he spoke again.

"Did you get my message?"

"I did." Catherine pushed a handful of her curls to one side before scratching the back of her neck. She didn't want to have this conversation in the workplace, but it seemed like this was exactly where Richard preferred to talk about personal matters. "Look, Richard, I—"

"Okay everybody, let's get this show on the road. My brother-in-law is in town, and Saturday is for poker, so let's get this over with." Phillip Stevens sat opposite Mr. Adamson. Anthony Marcati was tapping his pencil against the tabletop to his right.

"We'll talk later." Catherine dismissed Richard and sat beside Mr. Adamson.

"Everything all right with the new hire?" he asked. If Catherine had been surprised by anything she had learned about Mr. Adamson over the years, it was how he loved being included in office gossip.

"Everything's fine," Catherine replied with a reassuring smile. "What's the emergency?" She opened her briefcase to pull out a worn leather portfolio. It was the same ritual she followed at every meeting. She opened it up to a fresh sheet of yellow lined paper and placed her favorite pen at the center of the page.

"A friend of mine called me out of the blue last night. He owns a large publishing company here in Manhattan, and he's in trouble. He's recently discovered…" The sound of the boardroom door opening didn't distract Catherine from her boss, but Mr. Adamson turned his attention to the latest arrival. "You know what? I think the company's senior editor and production manager would tell the story better than I." Walter Adamson stood slightly. He motioned to the person standing just within the room.

"Why didn't he come by him—" Catherine looked at the new arrival, and she froze when her eyes locked with too-familiar dark ones. "—self."

"Everyone, this is—"

"Linda." Catherine said her name before Walter, and he looked down at her curiously before finishing the announcement.

"Linda Nguyen."

An anxious buzz filled Catherine's ears as each staff member shook Linda's hand. When it came to her turn, Catherine remained seated and stared up at the only woman who could turn her back into the powerless young adult she once was.

"Nice to see you again, Cat."

CHAPTER EIGHTEEN

Catherine had never really been a religious person, but right now she was praying to every recognized higher power that Linda would never stop talking. If she continued talking, Catherine wouldn't have to face the feelings she had buried many years ago. She stopped taking notes long enough to look up at Linda, and her chest clenched. Feelings she *thought* she'd buried many years ago.

Linda was prim and proper and so intimidating that she often came across as cold. But as she stood before the small group in a tight black dress, Catherine remembered just how warm Linda could truly be. When she couldn't listen to Linda's smooth voice without forgetting what she sounded like in the bedroom, Catherine looked out the window at the gray sky and then tried to read her coworker's faces one at a time. The scene was so familiar: Catherine fidgeting in her seat as Linda addressed a room full of her peers. A secret undercurrent passed between them. Catherine's stomach twisted with the same tension she always felt in Linda's presence. Catherine sat back and took a deep breath, trying to calm herself.

"Are you okay, Catherine?" Mr. Adamson leaned in and whispered. His aftershave seemed overwhelming to her that morning.

"I'm fine, just a late night. Excuse me." Catherine stood

abruptly and rushed into the bathroom. The sound of the door shutting echoed behind her. Catherine took heaving breaths and paced the cool, white room.

"Get it together!" She berated herself aloud. "You're a professional, for Christ's sake!" She rushed over to the sink and filled her palms with cold water, splashing it over her pale face. She stood back and looked at her reflection. Water droplets fell from her chin and nose on to the countertop. Catherine's eyes were red but clear. She blinked the water from her lashes and reached for a paper towel. After drying her face, Catherine took one last breath and carried herself back to the boardroom on wobbly legs. She squared her shoulders with feigned confidence before she swung the large door open. Everyone's eyes turned to her.

"Sorry." Catherine made her way back to her seat. She could feel Linda's gaze follow her. She wondered how Linda remained so cool, so calm, and so collected. Then she remembered how nothing ever seemed to bother her. Even when they were a year into a hushed romance that could have cost Linda her job, she always remained so laid back. It was a quality Catherine envied, especially in that moment.

"So, in retrospect, we should have seen this loss a long time ago, but we really thought our accountant was trustworthy. We now see the fault in that and are hoping it's not too late, which is why I'm here." Linda summarized her presentation and took a seat. "Any questions?"

For the second time within minutes, all eyes were on Catherine. The team had come to expect Catherine to take point at every meeting, because she always had. She was the youngest and the most eager member. Catherine shook her head and remained silent.

"Really, Cat, no questions?" Linda scoffed playfully.

"It's Catherine," she nearly barked back. Linda was no longer privy to that nickname, nor was she allowed to speak to Catherine like she still knew her. The four men around the table looked from one to the other curiously, and Catherine's cheeks colored. Catherine wasn't comfortable that the room's attention was starting to shift from business to her personal life. "I have all the information I need right here." She tapped her index finger on the surface of a full note page.

Mr. Adamson spoke up. "I think we'll be able to help. I owe it to Roger to try at least. He published my niece last year, you know?"

"I heard." Linda bowed slightly and licked her lips. "Melanie Crowell, right? I loved her book, I hope she writes a follow-up soon."

"She's working on it right now, as a matter of fact."

"I can't wait." Linda batted her long lashes, and Catherine's face softened against her will.

"Okay, I think we have all the information we need." Catherine closed her portfolio and put an end to the charming, gut-wrenching exchange she was being forced to witness.

"We'll get started Monday morning, but I won't be angry if any of you start brainstorming today." Anthony, Philip, and Richard were quick to leave and start their Saturday afternoon while Walter Adamson stood and started to make his way over to Linda. Catherine stopped him.

"Mr. Adamson, this seems like a pretty straightforward case. Since my hands are a little full at the moment, I think it would be best for Antho—"

"I'm going to stop you right there, Catherine. Roger is a very good friend of mine, and like any friend, I'd want my best person helping him. You're my best person."

"Thank you, sir, but—"

"You're heading this operation. If that means you give one of your existing clients to Anthony or Philip for now, so be it. What about that private client? The Howdy Doody one?"

"Cowboy Fran's?" Catherine swallowed thickly as she thought of Imogene.

"Yeah, that one. It seems like you're pretty close to finishing up what you had to do there. Make Anthony the lead on that one, and that'll free up some of your time. You don't have a choice here, Catherine. This case is your top priority now." He patted her on the shoulder before he stepped around her to get to Linda.

Catherine sat back and watched their exchange with a look of pained wonderment on her face. This was her reality. It wasn't some twisted nightmare from which she'd wake. Linda Nguyen was back in her life, and she was just as beautiful as Catherine remembered.

"Catherine, may I have a word? Catherine?"

"What?"

Linda looked at her expectantly. "Can we talk?" Linda stepped over to where Catherine was seated and leaned her hip against the table. She tossed her long black hair over her shoulder. It seemed darker than Catherine recalled. Maybe she was trying to hide some grays. By Catherine's calculations, Linda would be turning forty-three that November.

"I can't. I have to be somewhere." She tossed her leather portfolio and pen into her briefcase and stood. Catherine had forgotten about their height difference until she was forced to look up at Linda. "I'll see you Monday."

"Please." Linda wrapped her hand around Catherine's wrist. When Catherine looked into Linda's pleading eyes, her determination waned and her tense stance sagged.

"Fine." Catherine shrugged away from the touch and tensed her jaw. "Talk." It had been eight years, but the anger still burned anew.

"Not here. Let me take you to lunch?"

"I'd rather not."

"How about brunch? I know how much you used to love brunch."

"Did you know I worked here?" Catherine inquired suddenly. She'd wondered that when she saw her in the meeting. Before she spent any time with her ex, whether for work or not, she needed to know the truth.

"What?" Linda stepped back. Catherine thought she seemed offended. *Good.*

"Did you know I worked here? Is that why you chose this firm?" Catherine's tone was accusatory and her voice higher than necessary, but she couldn't control herself.

"Roger Walton turned to his friend, Walter Adamson, for help. I had nothing to do with the choice of what firm we went with. I thought I covered all of this earlier, or were you not paying attention?"

"I heard every word."

"Then why are you questioning me now?"

"Because I don't know what to believe anymore!" Catherine shouted the sentiment for the second time within twenty-four hours. She heard a gentle knock at the door and knew they were being listened to. She turned back to Linda and spoke quietly between clenched teeth. "There's a place down the street. I can at least get a drink."

"It's barely noon."

Catherine chose to ignore her observation as she gathered her belongings.

As they exited the boardroom door, Catherine noticed Philip standing suspiciously against the wall beside the door. If anyone hung around to eavesdrop on her and Linda's conversation, she thought for sure it'd be Anthony.

"Poker starting late today, Philip?"

"Yeah, I uh…" He started to tug at the collar of his long sleeved polo. "I was just brainstorming a few ideas for Ms. Nguyen like Walter asked."

"Down here?" Catherine asked. "Your office is upstairs."

"Kind of an odd place for brainstorming, don't you think?" Linda giggled, and Philip's face reddened.

"You can't predict when ideas will come to you!"

"I really look forward to hearing those ideas on Monday, don't you, Ms. Nguyen?" The name felt odd on Catherine's tongue after all this time, but she still smiled, poking fun at her irritating coworker.

"I certainly do," Linda agreed enthusiastically. "See you Monday, Mr. Stevens." Linda turned toward the elevators, and Catherine was quick to follow after speaking a short good-bye. "Is he always like that?"

"Yes. He's always looking for something to hold against me," Catherine admitted as the elevator doors opened. They stepped on together and Catherine pressed the button for the ground level.

"He's just intimidated by your success."

Catherine narrowed her eyes. "What do you know about my success?" The question made Linda blush, and Catherine nearly stumbled when the elevator came to a halt.

"You work for Marcati and Stevens, of course you're successful." Catherine recognized the sound of Linda cracking the middle knuckle of her ring finger. It was one of her ex-lover's more obvious tells. "I have to grab my coat from my car if we're walking, or I can drive if you prefer," Linda said.

"What else do you know about me?" They stepped out of the building, and Catherine tightened her grip around the handle of her briefcase as a frigid wind whipped around the corner. A few strands of her curly hair covered her face. They rushed toward a row of cars parked in front of the building.

"This is me." Linda unlocked a cherry red sports car. After they both climbed in and slammed their doors, Catherine took a moment to breathe while Linda started the ignition and turned up the heat. An eerie silence fell over the car. Catherine jumped when Linda spoke again. "I've looked you up a few times over the years." Her voice was so fragile, Catherine could barely hear her words.

"Why?" Catherine asked in amazement.

"Professional curiosity? I like to know how my students fare in the real world." Linda shrugged while her eyes remained to the front. "At least that's what I told myself the first couple of times." She turned and looked at Catherine then, her dark, gorgeous almond eyes deeper than ever and her smile more radiant. "I just needed to know how you were doing."

"You could've called."

"No, I couldn't. We both know you didn't want to hear from me." The silence was back, but this time it was heavy with latent sadness. Something dawned on Catherine.

"But you said you didn't know I worked here."

"No. I said I didn't pick the firm, which is true. But I may have been an eager volunteer to come and do the face-to-face work." When Linda smiled, every tooth seemed to be on display. "It was an opportunity to see you again with no expectations."

"And under false pretenses," Catherine pointed out. She rubbed at her temples, trying to soothe the dull ache that had started there.

"It wasn't the most honest of moves, but I wanted to see you."

"You got exactly what you wanted, and you probably got a good laugh at my reaction when I saw you walk in, too." Though she tried to keep her tone light, the bitterness started to surface.

"I was actually quite speechless when I saw you." That was not the response Catherine expected. "Time has been very good to you, Catherine. You look wonderful. I was hoping we could talk. I'd like to apologize for the way things ended between us and clear the air, so to speak. I never had the chance to explain myself. There's so much that was left unsaid."

"You chose your job over me, what's to explain?"

"Let me take you to lunch, and I'll tell you."

"I—" She pulled out her buzzing phone, slid her thumb along the glass, and read Imogene's message: *I miss you already.*

Catherine frowned at the overwhelming guilt she felt at reading those four little words. She had barely thought of Imogene since slipping from her bed earlier that morning. She knew she should reply. It was the right thing to do, but she had no idea what to say. She sighed deeply.

"Do you have to take that?"

"No." Catherine pressed a button, and her screen went black. "Let's go." She sat back and fastened her seat belt. Catherine didn't look at the road ahead or at the driver, and she made sure to keep from looking at her own troubled reflection.

CHAPTER NINETEEN

Imogene absentmindedly tapped the tip of her fingernail against her teacup. The sound annoyed Vixen, who left the kitchen with a huff and found quiet shelter beneath the couch. Imogene was trying in vain to plan her day. It was barely after noon, and she was still in her robe, fiddling with the remnants of her late breakfast. She had started to change twice but decided against it because Catherine might come back soon. Imogene looked at her phone. She had sent that text a full half hour ago and had agonized over sending it for close to an hour before. The words were light and playful, but also true.

Imogene missed Catherine only a couple hours after her departure. At first she was unsure how to act after such a sudden shift in their relationship, then Imogene realized the shift wasn't so sudden. Nor was it one-sided. They'd been flirting since Alice's birthday party. They had been out several times, each outing feeling more like a date than the last. Finally, they fell into bed together. If anything, it was an average progression. Imogene shivered as she thought of the previous night. She checked her phone one more time. No messages. Not even from Sophia, but that wasn't strange. She knew how much Imogene enjoyed sleeping in after a night out. Imogene stood and stretched before clearing the table of the few dishes she used.

During the monotonous task of cleaning, she kept thinking

about Catherine's body, her hands, and her voice. Imogene remembered how Catherine had touched her and worked her body in a way she had never experienced before. By the time she'd finished cleaning her small kitchen, Imogene's face was flushed. "Bath," she said aloud and walked to her small bathroom.

Imogene stared at her reflection as the tub filled with steaming water. Bubbles collected densely beneath the steady stream. She could have sworn she had what the magazines called a "post-coital glow." *That's positively ridiculous*, she thought, *it's called sweat and exertion!* But she understood it now. She used a wipe to remove what was left of her eye makeup and took off her robe.

She dipped one toe, followed by her foot, and finally her whole calf into the water. Imogene's whole body pebbled with goose bumps as she lowered herself into the bath. The heat was bearable but still caused her breath to hitch. Her abdominal muscles contracted from the combination of pleasure and pain. As she moved her hands up her smooth thighs, the currents left by her fingertips' wake ghosted along the sensitive skin of her sex. Imogene sucked in a breath and replayed every one of Catherine's calculated ministrations.

She traced the outer lips of her vagina with her middle finger, and she recalled the way Catherine smiled cockily at her reaction. Imogene bit her lip and whimpered. She was still so sensitive. She ran the tip of her finger through the thick wetness that collected at her entrance. Even in the bath, Imogene could feel how ready she was to be taken again. She entered herself with one finger and grunted in disappointment. She had only spent one night with Catherine and she was already ruined for any other touch.

Imogene started to piston in and out slowly, matching the rhythm Catherine had set the night before to the best of her recollection. She cupped her left breast with her other hand and tugged roughly at her hardened nipple. Imogene pictured

Catherine's gorgeous face as she started to circle her own clit. It usually took her a while to get this worked up when she was alone, but she was already writhing beneath the bubbles. All it took was thinking about tasting Catherine from navel to waiting pussy, and she was screaming out into her porcelain surrounds. She fell back into the bath, sated, breathless, and smiling broadly.

Imogene showered quickly to wash her hair and emerged from the bathroom thirty minutes later, checking her phone. Still nothing from Catherine. Her face dropped and the worry she had fought all afternoon finally broke through. Imogene found it hard to believe a Saturday meeting would still be going on almost four hours later, but she supposed it was possible. With an office in New York City, anything was possible.

Imogene's stomach sank. Anything could have happened to Catherine. Trains got derailed, pedestrians were hit in crosswalks, and elevators failed all the time. *No.* Imogene scolded herself. *Stop thinking like that. Catherine is a workaholic. You knew this from the start.* She furrowed her eyebrows. Did that mean Catherine would always put her career first? Imogene dressed in her most comfortable weekend clothes, then she picked up her phone and typed out a message. One more message, that was all she'd allow herself. They had slept together once. Imogene didn't want to appear clingy, but she was concerned for Catherine's well-being. No harm in that. She typed rapidly, asking simply if everything was okay, and hit send. Before she could let go of the phone, it beeped with Catherine's reply.

Fine. Busy.

Imogene fell to the sofa and her heart fell along with her. Yes, they had only spent one night together, but Catherine's words were so dismissive they hurt. Didn't Catherine know she was falling for her? Maybe that was the problem. Maybe she had scared Catherine before she ever really had the chance to be with her. She couldn't let that happen, Catherine wasn't getting away that easily. Imogene felt her resolve building. This relationship was worth it. She trusted Catherine. She'd give Catherine her space for a little while, but they'd need to talk. Soon.

❖

Catherine tucked her phone into her pocket and graciously accepted a large glass of water from a dapper young waitress. She wasn't hungry, and as much as she'd love a strong drink in the moment, she'd settle for water. After three large gulps, she put the glass down and sat back. Catherine pushed her heavy curls back from her face and off her shoulders.

"How did you end up at a publishing company?" she asked Linda. "Your job was everything to you."

"It was."

"What changed?" Catherine inquired curtly.

"I got fired." Linda made the admission so easily, Catherine couldn't figure out whether Linda was proud or ashamed of it. "For having an affair with a student."

Catherine couldn't help but laugh. She rubbed roughly at her forehead and shifted in her freshly uncomfortable chair before tugging at the hem of her sweater. "What about your tenure?"

"Tenure doesn't make you invincible, Catherine," Linda said. *She still corrects people like a teacher*, Catherine thought. *She can make you feel like the head of the class or the bottom of the barrel.*

Linda sat so poised, so languid, and seemingly relaxed that Catherine found it infuriating. "But you were always so careful," Catherine said.

"I was, but she wasn't." Linda sat back as the waitress brought a bowl of creamy soup to the table.

Catherine fought against the jealousy she felt building because of this stranger, this other woman who had the same chance to experience Linda the way Catherine had. She watched intently as her ex-lover stirred the thick liquid with her spoon.

Steam bellowed up and disappeared as it collided with her thin lips and sharp nose.

Linda swallowed her mouthful of the hearty meal and said, "She wasn't you, though." The corner of Catherine's mouth pulled up, but she kept her eyes on the table. "After I was fired, I was forced to take stock of my life, look back at my achievements and regrets. I only had one regret."

"Getting caught?" Catherine winced as soon as the words left her mouth, and yet Linda seemed unaffected as she ate.

"No," she replied coolly. Linda pushed her bowl aside and leaned forward with her elbows on the tabletop. "I regret how things ended between us. I regret not being clear about how I truly felt for you. I regret not chasing after you that day when you left."

Linda reached for Catherine's left hand on the table. Catherine swallowed hard when Linda skimmed the top of her hand with cool fingertips. She didn't pull away.

"That's actually three regrets."

"Allow me to rephrase. I have a list of small regrets that boil down to one that shook me with its enormity: losing you."

After eight years of waiting, Catherine was hearing the words she had spent a year waiting for and another seven forcing herself to never imagine again.

"Spoken like a true English teacher." Catherine sighed and wiped a stray tear away with her right hand. She turned her hand over, subconsciously opening herself up to Linda once again. Catherine felt Linda tracing the lines of her palm down the length of her bare ring finger. She closed her eyes at her touch.

"I've missed you. I just didn't realize how much until I saw you again today, and I'd like to see more of you. Are you seeing anyone?" Linda asked with hushed confidence. Catherine's misty eyes shot open at the unexpected question.

Her breathing increased, and she pursed her lips. Looking into Linda's eyes, she easily conjured a vision of Imogene's smiling face. But the adult Catherine was no match for the wounded twenty-one-year-old deep within. After all these years, she finally had what she always wanted, and she couldn't turn her back on that. "No."

CHAPTER TWENTY

Somehow it was Tuesday. Somehow Imogene had managed to start her week just like any other, keeping busy with Cowboy Fran's spring collections and knickknacks. She had spent the remainder of her weekend fighting the urge to wallow. Monday, she spent reorganizing the boutique and dodging Sophia's calls. She didn't need a heart-to-heart right now. How was she going to answer any questions regarding her ambiguous relationship with Catherine when she was still so unsure of it herself?

Imogene sighed deeply and dropped the glass bead necklace she was holding on the countertop. She stared down into the swirling purples and blues of the beads and got lost in her thoughts. Maybe she *should* talk to Sophia. Who better to give her guidance than her best friend and spiritual advisor? Imogene chortled. *Haven't you had enough bad luck with advisors recently?* She grimaced. Maybe keeping Sophia out of it for now was best. Imogene picked up the necklace and started to return her attention to the display she was working on when the chime above the door rang out.

"Hello!" Imogene said in her artificially chipper store voice. "I'll be right with you in one minute." She hung the necklace from an ornate bronze hook display and turned her attention to the new arrival.

"Alice," she said, shocked into a momentary silence. "What a nice surprise." She struggled to keep her tone even. She had never seen Alice in her shop before. Was this bad news from Catherine? Why didn't she come herself? Imogene couldn't tell much from Alice's expression, but she didn't know her too well.

Alice walked carefully between the loaded racks until she was within a few feet of Imogene. "I was just in the neighborhood and wanted to stop by," she said as Imogene relaxed. "Catherine had told me so much and yet so little about your store that I had to see it for myself. I don't know how I missed it. I may have found a new favorite!"

"Do you shop on Washington Street often?" Imogene started to twirl a small section of her auburn hair nervously. Making small talk with the best friend of the woman she was desperately pining after wasn't the best way of keeping her mind off Catherine.

"Not as much as I'd like to."

Imogene wondered why Alice had come to the shop. Surely someone on her end of town had one of the Moroccan scarves she was running between her fingertips. Imogene could tell she wanted to say more.

"Is there something in particular you're looking for?" Imogene asked. "A gift or something for your—"

"Have you heard from Catherine?"

Imogene froze at the question. "Not since the night of the benefit." Alice appeared to be surprised by the answer. "Have you?"

"Nope. I was hoping to find out where the two of you rushed off to in such a hurry."

"Home," Imogene answered quickly without realizing the implications. Alice's smile turned into a triumphant leer. "*My* home, no! Separate—I mean…" Imogene stumbled over her words, and Alice's smile grew wider. She took a deep breath and cleared her throat. "I do not feel comfortable discussing what may or may not have transpired between me and Catherine

Friday night without her being present." She turned her back on Alice and went behind the counter. *Where are all the customers when I need them?*

"How diplomatic of you." Alice chuckled. "Imogene, I'm not here to get details, although I would *love* some. I'm just checking on Catherine. I called the office only to be told she's in meetings. I even went to her condo, and she wasn't there. She's not answering my calls or messages. I'm worried."

"Well, she's definitely not here." Imogene grumbled and started to play with a receipt that had been discarded on the counter.

"It's not like Catherine to disappear without at least a phone call or text—"

"She sent me a text Saturday." Imogene sighed in resignation. "She had an emergency meeting Saturday morning and when I tried to get in touch with her later, she told me she was busy with work. I haven't heard from her since." She watched as Alice processed the information, her green eyes narrowing a bit.

Alice approached the counter and grabbed Imogene's hand. "I don't know what Catherine is going through right now, and I will figure that out, but in the meantime, don't give up on her, Imogene. Please."

Imogene nodded in agreement but remained silent. She wasn't ready to give up on Catherine just yet.

Alice and Imogene said their good-byes, and Imogene switched off the neon Open sign as she ushered Alice out. The store needed straightening and so did her apartment, but Imogene couldn't manage either mindless task. She needed to talk. She needed guidance, and she needed to unload her burdens to the one person who'd created this whole mess in the first place. The idea of keeping any of this from Sophia seemed so foolish now.

❖

Imogene knocked violently on the front door of Sophia's single-family home. She knew she should have called first, but after a few days of wallowing and Alice's surprise visit, she didn't care what was polite. Imogene's face fell when Chris answered the door with a look of surprise.

"Imogene? What's up?"

"Hey, Chris." Imogene shifted from one foot to another, uncomfortably aware of the inconvenience of her sudden appearance. "Is Sophia home?"

"Not yet. She went for drinks with Gladys after work. Do you want to come inside and wait? She should be home soon."

When Imogene looked up into Chris's soft brown eyes she could feel her own tears coming to life. Every uncontrollable second of the past few days was coming to a head, and Imogene was heading into an emotional tailspin. He had always been so kind to her, never hesitating to step aside when she needed his wife. Chris treated Imogene like family, but she had never really spent time with him one-on-one before, so she surprised herself when she accepted the invitation and stepped into the warm home.

It was during times like this that Imogene felt her apartment lacked something that made this a real home. Every time she stepped into Chris and Sophia's home, she was transported back to the time she had helped them paint, deciding on the living room color herself after opening the wrong can of paint and getting started on the largest wall in the room. Truth be told, the bathroom looked better in mossy green than the living room ever would, and the pale yellow lit up the heart of her best friend's home. Memories of moving furniture and many drunken game nights warmed Imogene's heart, but that wasn't the indescribable *thing* that made this space any more special than her own. It was something else entirely.

"Can I get you something to drink?" Chris asked.

"Please," she said. *I'd love a distraction.* "Whatever you're having is fine." She removed her coat and tossed it on the arm of the sofa before falling onto the plush furniture. When Chris returned, he handed Imogene a frosty glass bottle. "What're we having?" She eyed the purple label suspiciously.

"A lager that had raspberries introduced during the final stage of the brewing process." Ever the beer enthusiast, Chris smiled broadly as Imogene tasted it.

"This is delicious!" The sweet bubbles lingered on her tongue as she savored the taste.

"I know!" He took a large gulp himself. "I keep trying to get Sophia to try it, but you know how she feels about beer."

"The greatest disagreement in your marriage." Imogene smirked.

Silence fell over the pair as they sipped at their beverages. Chris ran his palm along his dark, cropped head. "So, did you have fun Friday night?" It was a casual enough question, but it hit the sturdy walls Imogene had constructed like a sledgehammer. Tears started to fill her eyes. "Oh, no." Chris grabbed a square box from the coffee table and handed it to Imogene just in time to muffle the first sob that erupted. "I'm sorry?" The odd question hung between them.

"No, no, no." Imogene wiped at her wet cheeks. "Don't apologize. It's just been a bad few days, that's all." She blew her nose with surprising gusto.

Chris placed his bottle on a nearby coaster before clearing his throat and pushing his wire-rimmed glasses farther up his nose. "Tell me about it." The openness and empathy on his face eased Imogene immediately and she just started talking.

Imogene replayed the night of the benefit and the morning after, leaving out the details that would make her blush. She told him of her friendship with Catherine that had managed to flourish into something she could only label as love. She'd fallen in love with Catherine Carter. Every bit of her, every side and every detail she tried so desperately to hide. In just over a month,

Catherine had managed to do what several suitors over the past year could not: capture Imogene Harris's heart.

And for that, Imogene felt foolish.

"You love her?" Chris asked and sat back.

"I know it sounds crazy because I've only known her a month, but yes. God, yes." Imogene covered her face with her hands.

"Then you have to fight."

"What are we fighting for?" Sophia asked as she stepped into her home and caught the last few words of the conversation. She placed her purse on an end table and removed her coat.

"I was telling Imogene that if she loves Catherine, she needs to fight for her," Chris stated so matter-of-factly that Imogene actually envied him.

"Oh dear, what happened?" Sophia wedged herself between her best friend and her husband on the couch.

Imogene and Chris took turns telling the story this time. "My husband is right," Sophia finally said. "You need to fight or at least get some sort of answer out of her."

Chris stood and kissed the top of his wife's head. "I'll remember you said I was right. Another beer, Imogene?"

"No, thank you." Imogene watched the exchange, and the answer became so clear: love made a home into a sanctuary. "You're lucky to have him." Imogene's eyes remained on the man as he left the room.

"I am." Sophia's reply was quick. "Now tell me what you couldn't tell me in front of him—how was it?"

"I can't even begin to describe it." Imogene combed her fingers through her long tresses.

"That good?"

"Better." Imogene's cheeks reddened. "I won't go into too much detail, but I will say if I had worried before that we wouldn't connect on a physical level, those worries are long gone. She was so sweet and so soft with me, but not too gentle, you know? It was like she knew exactly how to touch me and where I needed her to be without any direction." Imogene's temperature increased as she reminisced. "It seemed like there was something so meaningful there…" She shook her head. "I guess I was wrong."

"You need to fight for her, Imogene. If you feel this strongly about her after such a short period of time, then she must be something special."

"I don't care what you saw."

"I'm not talking about my visions right now. I'm talking about what you, what my best friend is feeling. It's been so long since I've seen you react this way to another person. I was beginning to worry that you and Vixen were going to grow old together." Imogene laughed softly. Sophia grasped her hands. "She hurt you, and I'd love to see her suffer for that, but I think Catherine has been suffering for a long time now. Did she tell you about her past?"

"Yes."

"The whole story?" Imogene shook her head.

"Not in detail, no."

"You need to talk to her, tell her how you feel. At the very least, you deserve an explanation. You're worth more than a short text message."

"You're right, I know." Imogene pulled her clammy hands back to her lap. "I think I'm going to get going. I'm exhausted, and that beer is making me drowsy. Thank you and thank Chris for me. I'll talk to you tomorrow." She stood, pulled on her jacket, and walked to the door with Sophia close to her back. Sophia wrapped Imogene in a tight, protective embrace.

"I just want you to be happy again, Imogene," she said.

The whole way home, driving in a daze as snowflakes danced around her car, she thought of all the things she'd say to Catherine if given the chance. She needed to let her know how much she meant to her, and how she was willing to fight for a chance at something more than just one night together. As the snow passed the windows like shooting stars, Imogene's plan started to come together. When she arrived home and fell into bed, she knew what she had to do. She hoped it would all work out for the best.

CHAPTER TWENTY-ONE

*T*he month of May held green plush promise for the earth as well as Catherine's new life blossoming. She stretched her long limbs and whimpered quietly as her muscles protested. It was the final day of her junior year, and the final day of Ms. Nguyen's career as an English teacher at Rutgers University. This day had been two and a half years in the making, as was the satisfied smile pulling at the corner of Catherine's mouth. She reached out for Linda.

"Linda?" Catherine called out as she sat upright, the cool sheets pooling around her naked breasts. Linda emerged from the steam-filled bathroom, a damp towel wrapped around her waist and another around her head. Catherine's breath caught at the sight of her half-naked lover. She was sure she'd never grow tired of it.

"Good morning, Cat." Linda stalked toward the bed with an accentuated sway to her hips. "Rise and shine. Don't want to be late for your last day."

"Neither do you." Catherine wrapped her right arm around Linda's waist and pulled her onto the bed. Laughter resounded through the bedroom. Careful to keep one hand in contact with Linda's bare skin, Catherine pushed and pulled at the towel and sheets. "How much time do we have?" Catherine pressed her lips to the hollow of Linda's neck. She inhaled deeply and relished the spicy scent of her body wash.

"Not enough." Linda's voice was always steady and confident, a quality Catherine both wanted for herself and wanted to destroy. With little to no effort Catherine flipped Linda onto her back and spread her body along Linda's, pinning her into place.

"Let's make time." Catherine ground her pelvis down between Linda's legs. If it weren't for the slight widening of her almond eyes, Catherine wouldn't have been sure if Linda had felt the motion at all.

"We can't." Linda nipped at Catherine's lower lip. *"I have a meeting with the dean and my department head this morning."*

Catherine pulled back and looked down into her dark eyes. *"About you leaving?"*

"I suppose so. They hadn't said much to me since I sent in my resignation. This meeting was bound to happen." Linda kissed Catherine quickly and moved out from underneath her lithe body. *"You're coming by later, right?"*

Catherine leaned back on her elbows as she watched Linda riffle through her dresser for the perfect pair of panties. *"You won't be able to stop me."*

Catherine and Linda readied themselves quickly and left separately, as they normally did. Catherine rejoiced in knowing she'd never have to leave out the back or with a hood draped over her face again. She'd be able to throw away the awful oversized sunglasses Linda insisted she wear when she walked from her neighborhood in the morning. This would also be the last morning where she'd have to park around the corner. As Catherine walked to her car, she smiled at the way the sun was just lighting up the sky fully and how the birds were louder than ever. It was as if Mother Nature knew Catherine was about to start a new, better life with the woman she loved.

The day had passed much more quickly than Catherine had anticipated. Before the end of the semester had had the chance to sink into Catherine's brain, she found herself walking through Linda's front door without looking over her shoulder.

"I'm home!" Catherine called out with a newfound cheeriness that would normally annoy even herself, but today was the exception. Today she'd wrap her arms around her lover and not have to let her go. She'd entwine their fingers and walk along with her as they went for an early dinner. Catherine would be able to kiss Linda as they shared retellings of their day over a cup of coffee at a local café or while arguing about which books to buy at the bookstore. When she arrived at Linda's late that afternoon, Catherine felt so much possibility for them as a couple that she couldn't contain her glee. "Linda, where are you? Come out, come out, wherever you are!" Her voice hit a singsong pitch.

"Out back!" Catherine followed the voice that called out to her. She threw her duffel bag down by the back door and stepped out onto a small deck. Linda was in a lawn chair with a glass of wine. Catherine could tell her eyes were closed even behind the dark aviator sunglasses.

"Hey you." She lifted one of Linda's legs and placed it over her lap as she took a seat on the chair. Catherine leaned in and kissed Linda's wine-soaked lips. "Have you been home long?"

"About an hour." Linda took another swig of wine.

"Well." Catherine placed her hand on Linda's knee and ran it up and over her thigh. She applied more pressure as she came close to her apex. She leaned in and spoke, her breath ghosting across Linda's lips. "I made dinner reservations at Romero's, and I was thinking that maybe after we could finish what we started this morning."

Catherine snaked her hand around to the front of Linda's jeans and applied pressure to the seam just above her clit. Linda inhaled sharply.

"Wait—" Linda halted Catherine's ministrations with a gentle push to her shoulder.

"I'm sorry." Catherine sat back, unsure of herself and of why she just apologized.

"You don't need to apologize, but we do need to talk." Linda sat up straight and removed her sunglasses. Catherine's stomach twisted at the combination of clichéd prelude and the emptiness she saw in Linda's brown eyes.

"Talk about what?"

"My meeting."

"Let's talk about it over dinner." Catherine reached for Linda's hand, but Linda pulled it away.

"I can't go to dinner with you."

"I can make the reservation for another night." Catherine tried in vain to avoid what her subconscious was warning her was about to happen.

"They offered me tenure, Catherine." Linda stood up, and Catherine watched as the distance between them grew.

"What?" Catherine swallowed thickly against the nausea that rolled through her.

"They offered me tenure."

"Did you take it?"

"Of course I took it!" Linda looked down at Catherine incredulously. "Why wouldn't I?" Catherine flinched as Linda delivered the words like a punch to the gut. Despite the warm sun shining down on the deck, a chill ran up Catherine's spine.

"Us?" Catherine choked on the word. She was still seated, a look of shock emptying her face of any other expression. "Our plans?"

"The whole point of being a professor is to get tenure. No one just turns it down!" Linda scoffed indignantly.

"You promised me—"

"That promise was made before I knew I was being considered for tenure." The word "considered" wasn't lost on Catherine.

"When did they tell you?"

"Today—"

"Stop lying to me!" Catherine shouted. Her breathing was coming rapidly as she felt an uncharacteristic rage burn in her tight chest.

"I received an email the week after I sent in my letter of resignation," Linda said after taking a deep breath.

"That was a month ago!" Catherine's knuckles were white, and the muscles in her palms were strained as she clenched her fists.

"I knew how you'd react, so I figured it wasn't worth mentioning until they made their decision." Her reasoning was so sound, so logical, and so calculated, it made Catherine sick.

"Did I ever come first?" Catherine held back the sob. She didn't need Linda to know how broken her heart was. She was too afraid she'd see Linda's joy at the devastation she'd caused.

"You've always known how important my job is to me."

"Did I ever come first?" Catherine stood up as she repeated her question. With what little strength she had left, she stood in front of Linda and squared her shoulders. She wanted to look the woman in the eye as she accepted her response.

"No," Linda said.

One small word, wrapped in a soft voice and pushed through Catherine's heart like a dagger. But Catherine knew it was the most honest Linda had ever been to her, and that hurt more than anything.

Catherine stepped around Linda and grabbed her bag before heading to the front door. Linda shouted at her not to tell anyone, to keep it between them. A two-and-a-half-year love affair reduced to a secret. She should tell everyone she knew, but she wouldn't. She wouldn't even rush back to her apartment to cry on Alice's shoulder.

She climbed into her small car and sped away from the curb. She waited until she was a block away before pulling over and cutting the engine. A sob like no other erupted from her throat with such force that her insides felt raw. She realized that letting people in was more dangerous than shutting them out.

Catherine started as Philip stood up from the table. "All right, ladies," he said. "I think it's time to call it a night." She noticed his wrinkled slacks. The brown suit he wore had looked better that morning, but hours of being hunched over binders full of bank records had taken their toll on its crispness.

"Already?" Catherine swallowed a mouthful of room-temperature coffee that did little to soothe her dry throat. "We didn't even touch the stuff from 2011 yet!" She motioned to an overflowing box with her right hand.

"It's after ten o'clock, Catherine! This isn't exactly how I had planned on spending my Wednesday night."

Catherine looked at her watch and rubbed her eyes. She had been seated in the same chair, in nearly the same position for close to five hours and barely noticed it. She just wanted to review one last thing before heading home. One. Last. Thing.

"Philip's right, Catherine. We should call it a night." Linda's voice was soft and quiet, the perfect volume to accompany twilight. But Philip spoiled it slamming his briefcase closed.

"Good night, ladies. I'll see you both tomorrow." He left the room in a rush.

Catherine rubbed the back of her sore neck. "I'm sorry, I didn't realize how late it was getting."

"You don't have to apologize." Linda's gentle smile both soothed and alerted Catherine.

She had managed four days beside the woman who had turned her life upside down twice in her almost thirty years. They had started flirting much quicker than Catherine had intended, she loathed to admit she liked it. She liked it a lot. It reminded her of being a carefree college student again, discovering life outside the closet. But why was she allowing herself to do it again?

"I'm starved," Linda muttered as she stretched her arms above her head. Catherine's stomach growled in agreement. "Come on," Linda laughed and gently patted Catherine's thigh, "I'm going to feed you." Catherine followed Linda wordlessly as always. She never questioned Linda's decisions. Never. Just followed.

They walked together to the parking lot. With no direction necessary, Catherine climbed into her Mercedes and followed Linda's car as it bobbed and weaved through the city's evening traffic. The lights of New York's nightlife reflected off Catherine's windshield, and she squinted at the brightness of advertisements and store signs alike. She was so distracted by dodging wayward pedestrians and keeping an eye on Linda's sports car that she didn't think about what it was that she was doing.

She had spent the previous night lying restlessly in bed with her hands clasped tightly around her phone. Catherine had composed and deleted more than a dozen messages to Imogene, but none seemed appropriate. Maybe it was because she deserved more than inane excuses. Or maybe it was because Catherine didn't believe any of those excuses herself. She turned her car right and followed Linda into a quieter section of the city. In less than a minute, she pulled over to the curb in the heart of the Village and put her car in park. With a deep breath, Catherine recalled the one recurring line that made its way into each and every message she intended to send Imogene: *you deserve better than I could ever offer and someone better than I could ever be.*

Catherine turned off the car and waited. In the darkness, she could see Linda get out of her car and ascend the steps of a brownstone. Linda turned, stared at Catherine, and crooked her index finger. Catherine got out of the car and went to her like a hypnotized sailor ready to dash himself to death on the rocks answering the call of a Siren. When Catherine was within a foot of Linda, she finally spoke.

"Nice location." The winter winds whisked her breath away. As the small cloud dissipated and drifted, Catherine eyed the tall building.

"I like to be where the action is," Linda said with a tilt of her head as she went up the stairs and opened the front door of her home. If it hadn't been so cold outside, Catherine might have thought twice about coming inside. But the air was biting her face, and she knew just how warm space shared with Linda could be.

Once inside, Linda removed her coat and hung it on a nearby hook. She kicked off her heels and sank her feet into worn slippers waiting by the front door. "Make yourself at home." Linda rubbed her hands together briskly and left the foyer.

Catherine unbuttoned her long coat and hung it alongside Linda's before she looked around. This home was nothing like the one she had hoped to share with Linda in New Jersey. Straight ahead was a staircase that presumably led to any and all bedrooms and beyond that was a quaint living room set up as a home office. This didn't feel like a hideout, this felt like a home. Catherine was drawn toward a large bookcase, and she skimmed many titles, all fiction and classic. Each one just like the last.

"I seem to have led you here under false pretenses," Linda said from behind Catherine. She jumped. "You seem a bit on edge tonight, is everything okay?" Linda placed her hand on Catherine's forearm, but she brushed off the concern.

"False pretenses?" Catherine stiffened.

"I don't have a thing to eat other than some oatmeal." Linda smiled slyly. "It *is* a variety pack, however."

Catherine chuckled, and her tense muscles relaxed. "I'll take anything with cinnamon in it." Catherine watched as Linda led the way to the kitchen. Her hips swayed and brought to mind the memories that had taunted her earlier.

Linda filled a kettle and put it over an open flame. She set out two bowls and leaned back against the counter with her hands at her sides, looking beautiful and expectant.

"I'm actually surprised at the progress we've made," Catherine said. "It's only been a few days, but I think we've managed to sort through the majority of the mess—"

"Catherine?" Linda interrupted. She walked toward Catherine in the doorway. "I don't want to talk about work." Catherine looked down and started to fidget with her right cufflink. "Do I make you nervous?" Linda asked.

"Yes," Catherine replied instantly and she knew the follow-up question before Linda could even ask it. "I don't know what it is that you expect or want from me."

"I don't expect anything. I just wanted to spend time with you out from under Philip and Anthony's microscope." Linda went back into the kitchen, and Catherine took a deep breath. She returned a few minutes later with two bowls of oatmeal. "Here," she said, placing them on the small table. "It's not gourmet, but it'll fill you up."

"Thanks." Catherine first pulled out Linda's chair and then her own. She stirred her small meal, but she really wasn't hungry anymore. "So," Catherine said, desperate for anything but deafening silence and awkwardness, "this is much nicer than your other place."

"I like it," Linda replied around a spoonful of oatmeal. She chewed a few times and swallowed. "I guess with age comes better decorative insight." Both women laughed lightly.

"I guess."

"I've been thinking about us a lot," Linda said. "Working at your side for these past few days, I couldn't help but reminisce."

"Me either." Catherine grimaced.

"Judging by that face, I think it's safe to guess I was the only one focused on happier memories."

Catherine looked at Linda. "Good guess." She scratched beneath her starched collar and gave it a nervous tug for good measure. She pushed her bowl away.

"Like that weekend we spent in Philadelphia," Linda said. "We had so much planned, but we never left the hotel room." Linda touched Catherine's blushing cheek. "Or the New Year's you almost lost an eye to a runaway cork." Linda traced Catherine's meek smile with the pad of her index finger. "We had some really good times together, Catherine." Her palm came to rest on Catherine's cheek. Catherine fought to keep her eyes open at the sensation.

"I should get going." Catherine stood up abruptly. "We have

an early start tomorrow, and it's getting late." The excuse came quickly as she pushed in her chair and walked to the front door. Before Catherine could grasp her coat, she felt Linda at her back.

"You can stay if you'd like." Catherine felt Linda's firm grip on her bicep, encouraging her to turn around. Once Catherine was facing her, she drew closer and whispered the words that would've meant something to Catherine in the past. "Please stay."

Catherine looked into her hungry eyes and licked her lips. Linda, naturally, made the advance, closed the distance between them and claimed Catherine's mouth. At first, Catherine was unmoving. Linda flicked the tip of her velvety tongue along Catherine's lower lip, and she instinctively opened up.

Catherine pinned Linda against a nearby wall. She dug her fingertips into Linda's flesh and drove her tongue farther into her inviting mouth. Feeling Linda moan against her spurred Catherine on. With an uncharacteristic force, she pushed Linda harder against the wall and started to assault her throat. She bit at Linda, marking her pale skin as she gripped her ass. Catherine tried furiously to feel something for the woman writhing against her.

"Oh God, Cat," Linda moaned as Catherine palmed her left breast roughly and kissed her deeply. She reached blindly for Catherine's belt and undid it swiftly, snaking her hand under the waistband of her trousers. When she dipped her fingers between Catherine's folds, Linda's eyes snapped open. "Not wet yet? We'll have to do something about that."

Linda circled Catherine's clit with her nimble fingers, and all Catherine could think about was how she was trying to react. She was *trying* to feel something that was no longer there. She couldn't feel anything for Linda beyond professional respect and latent anger because nothing else was left. Any love or adoration Catherine held belonged solely to Imogene, the woman she had pushed aside without a thought the moment Linda entered her life again.

"Stop." Catherine tried to pull back but was held in place by the hand in her pants. "I said stop!" Catherine gripped Linda's wrist and removed her hand. "This isn't what I want."

"Oh come on!" Linda rolled her eyes. "This is what you want, it's what you've always wanted."

When Catherine looked at Linda, she saw someone completely different. She saw nothing more than a ghost of her past. The disheveled woman seemed older and sadder, selfish and unrewarded. Linda Nguyen was a fantasy that Catherine had held on to for too long. She smiled slowly.

"No, it's not." Catherine grabbed her coat and exited the front door. A sense of peace accompanied each step, her walk lighter than it had been in nearly a decade.

Chapter Twenty-two

That Thursday morning was bitter, the coldest morning Imogene had encountered yet, and it was gloomy. But the new day brought her a fresh sense of determination. She had decided to confront Catherine in a big way. The kind of way they did in movies, like standing outside in the pouring rain or chasing someone through a busy airport. Imogene woke up nervous and never got better. Though she did manage to dress quickly in spite of her shaking hands.

As she stepped out onto the gray Hoboken streets, she watched as unknown faces passed her by. She wondered what the old woman was thinking, where the sharply dressed businessman was heading, and how many times the dog walker had circled the same block. Safe thoughts like these would keep her from thinking about her final destination, the journey there, and all the possible outcomes that could change everything. When she had no more faces to study, when each and every passenger of the train she boarded exactly on time was buried in a paper, a phone, or a book, Imogene turned to the window. She smiled at her own reflection and then checked her watch. She'd be arriving in Penn Station in less than twenty minutes, and she knew there was no turning back.

She hadn't decided to do this in haste. Once Imogene had arrived home from Sophia's, she had wallowed and plotted, schemed and cried, trying to think of a way to fight for a woman who always ran away. Sophia was right. She did deserve more than a scribbled note, and at the very least, she'd walk away from today with an explanation. As the lights cut out in the train car, complete silence except for the smooth grind of metal on metal, Imogene dared to be optimistic. Maybe she'd make Catherine smile the way she had only seen a few times, laugh a hearty laugh like she did when they were in each other's arms, and just maybe she'd be able to take her out on a lunch date and discuss a future together.

"Next stop: New York, Penn Station," the robotic voice called out through the hushed space. Every passenger was a commuter and knew better than to move. They still had a tunnel to travel through, complete darkness for several long seconds, before emerging into their final destination. Imogene inhaled the semi-clean air deeply. She released her breaths slowly. The evening before she had mapped out everything in her mind, burning photographic images into her memory in an attempt to shorten her time in the city as much as possible. Those streets were once her best friends, and now she had to prepare for a reunion. The train doors slid open, and the passengers filed out slowly, leaving one lonely redhead seated. *I can do this*, she thought as she gripped the handle atop the seat in front of her and rose to her feet. Her legs were shaking, and her knees were weak with trepidation. *One foot in front of the other.*

❖

"Walton Publishing has to make up for hundreds of thousands of dollars they lost over the past five years thanks to their shifty accountant, and I'm not sure it can be done. If you take a look at their financial reports, you can see each and every hole. I'm afraid this may be a lost cause, Mr. Adamson. I'm sorry." Catherine spoke into the phone as she looked down at the thick blue folder she'd found on her desk that morning with a note from Linda attached. She wanted nothing more than to turn her back on this job and instead focus on how she could fix the damage she had done with Imogene.

"Catherine, just give it a shot, please. I'm not ready to tell Roger Walton that his family business is kaput. If anyone can do it, it's you."

Catherine found herself agreeing before she could think it through fully. "Okay. I'll take another look at it, but if I really feel there's nothing we can do, you'll have to take my word for it."

"Thank you, Catherine. I'll let you get to work, then."

Catherine sat back in her chair and closed her eyes. She had been in her office for nearly four hours, and she was exhausted. She had barely been able to sleep once she returned home after the disastrous night with Linda. Normally, a troublesome case would energize her, but this time the lack of sleep gave her dark circles beneath her eyes. She heard a quiet knock at her door.

"Come in," she called out, and rubbing the back of her neck.

"Good afternoon." Richard Thorton stepped into Catherine's large office.

"Richard," Catherine acknowledged in surprise. "What can I do for you?"

"I know I shouldn't bring this up at work," he said, closing the door, "but you didn't return my calls or answer any of my messages."

"I've been busy." Catherine stood up and made her way around her cluttered desk. She didn't like the feeling of being smaller, and being seated made her feel all the more vulnerable. She smoothed her palms down the front of her vest.

"Of course." Richard smiled kindly, a small twinkle filling his eyes. "I was wondering when I'd be able to take you out again."

"You're right, this shouldn't be discussed here." Catherine squared her shoulders.

"I know. Not only are we at work, but you're my boss. I get

it." He cocked one dark eyebrow mischievously. "Which is really sexy, by the way."

Catherine fought the cringe she felt crawling up her spine. "And because of that I don't think we should see each other again." The lie came easily. As much as Catherine hated lying, she knew the truth was better left unsaid.

"We wouldn't be the first superior-subordinate relationship here, Catherine." He took a step forward into Catherine's personal space, the desk behind her keeping her from backing away. He looked down at her with a confidence that bordered on an unattractive cockiness. "I think it's worth a shot."

"It's not. Now please leave my office." Catherine's voice took on a stern edge, and she stared at Richard until he started to retreat.

"Fine." He raised his palms in defeat. "But if you change your mind, you know where to find me." He left with a wink and closed the office door behind himself.

Catherine went to her office chair once again and fell into it with a sigh. She rolled her neck until she felt a pop and closed her eyes once more. She heard another knock. *For the love of...* "For the last time, I'm not—"

"Catherine?" Linda stood timidly in the doorway. "Do you have a minute?"

"Yeah, sure. Uh…come in." She stuttered slightly. Catherine had managed to avoid Linda all morning, and the last thing she expected was for Linda to seek her out. Linda closed the door and walked into Catherine's office with her head slightly down, stopping in front of Catherine's desk.

"I just wanted to apologize for last night," she said. "It was very presumptuous of me to think you'd be willing to give me another chance so soon."

"Or at all," Catherine replied coldly. She was torn between pride and disgust when she saw the wounded look in Linda's eyes.

"Or at all," Linda repeated to herself. She walked slowly around Catherine's desk and stood beside her. "I loved you so deeply, I guess I still hold some of that in here." She pointed to her heart.

"Our relationship is purely professional." Catherine looked Linda in the eye. "No more blurred lines. I meant what I said last night."

"Miss Carter?" Vivian's voice crackled through the intercom, and Catherine could barely contain her sigh of relief. She leaned forward and pressed the intercom button.

"Yes, Vivian?"

"There's someone here to see you."

"I don't have any appointments scheduled." She was sure her schedule was clear.

"I know. She just showed up and demanded to see you." Vivian's voice had that edge Catherine knew she couldn't ignore. It wouldn't be the first time a stressed client showed up unannounced to tell Catherine what they really thought of her and her "process."

"Name?" Catherine looked back at Linda, who was growing impatient.

"She won't—" A muffled voice cut Vivian off. Catherine could barely make out the words, but it sounded like her visitor was tired of waiting. "Excuse me! You can't go in there!" Just then Catherine's door swung open.

"Imogene?" Catherine's eyebrows flew up in surprise and then knit together in confusion. No amount of shock could keep the small smile from her lips.

"Jesus Christ! Why is it so hard to surprise people these days?" Imogene grumbled to herself before she looked at Catherine, then Linda, then the minimal space between them. "Surprise?"

"I am so sorry, Miss Carter." Vivian said. "Would you like me to call security?"

"What?" Imogene looked at the short, middle-aged woman in alarm.

"What? No! No, that won't be necessary." Catherine shook her head.

"Am I interrupting something important?" Imogene asked, her eyes on the woman beside Catherine.

"No," Catherine said.

"Yes," Linda answered simultaneously.

"Oh." Imogene started to fidget nervously, pulling at each finger separately before wringing her hands together.

Catherine tried to think of a way out of the awkward situation without calling any attention to who Linda was, but the gods seemed to be against her.

Linda stepped forward and asked, "Are you a client of Catherine's?"

"Are *you?*"

Catherine's eyes widened.

"I'm Linda Nguyen." She extended her hand, which hung empty for a moment before she withdrew it.

Catherine's mouth fell open. This was a nightmare.

"I represent a client of Miss Carter's." Linda's eyes narrowed, and Catherine recognized that look. She tried to interrupt but was too slow. "But we go way back. Don't we, Cat?"

"Linda?" Imogene's voice was shaking and Catherine's heart clenched.

"And you are?"

Catherine managed to find her voice. "Imogene, what are you doing here?"

"I needed—*we* needed to talk, but I think I got my answers." She looked to Linda.

"It's not what it looks like, Imogene."

Linda snorted. "I thought you said you weren't seeing anyone."

Imogene turned for the door. "She's not."

"Imogene, wait!" Catherine called out after her. "Please!" Catherine rounded her desk and went to leave her office only to bump into Richard.

"Whoa, Catherine, slow down."

"Dammit!" Catherine hissed. She turned back to her office and politely excused a very confused Vivian before stalking toward Linda. "You!" She pointed. "Your account will be transferred to Anthony and Philip by five o'clock. I am done, *done*, with you."

"Catherine—"

"Get out of my office, and I would appreciate it if you kept your distance during the remainder of your business here." Catherine stood tall as she spoke. This was the last time Linda Nguyen would affect her life, because Linda was no longer the one Catherine was afraid to lose.

CHAPTER TWENTY-THREE

Imogene sat in Penn Station for over two hours, missing each train that would've taken her home. But what was waiting for her at home? Nothing more than silence and a moody cat. She replayed the scene from Catherine's office over and over in her head as she watched commuters race to their designated platforms. She ignored the way her phone had been buzzing constantly since she fled Catherine's office. There was nothing left to say. This was why she had avoided dating since her split with Aria. She always wound up being lied to or getting hurt. Catherine, though, she was a doozy.

"It's not what it looks like," Imogene mimicked aloud, earning a curious look from the woman beside her. She scoffed at Catherine's plea. *What a cliché. Maybe all those messages are her just thanking me for my business. Oh my God, maybe she's going to charge me now!* Imogene took a deep calming breath. *No, Alice would kill her if she ever did that.* Imogene focused on Catherine's best friend. Alice seemed like a good, smart woman who only wanted happiness for Catherine. Imogene considered her impromptu visit from earlier in the week. *Don't give up on her*, Alice had said.

A young couple caught Imogene's attention as they weaved their way through the crowds. A clean-cut young man held the woman's hand as he led her toward a boarding train. When he turned his back toward Imogene, the letters FDNY embroidered on the back of his jacket caught her eye. Would the reminders ever stop? She left Penn Station and hailed the first taxi she saw.

The cab ride to the memorial was short but still brought forth a multitude of memories for Imogene. Each building, no matter how updated or unchanged, was still burned into her mind—small corner stores where she'd pick up produce for her Dad so he'd have a healthy snack; large billboards for shows that were still on Broadway, shows she'd probably seen more times than most people saw their favorite movies. Even the numerous carts selling edible and possibly hazardous snacks brought a sight or a smell or a sound back to Imogene. Everything was familiar except for the destination they arrived at.

Now Imogene stood quietly, getting lost in the feel of warm tears traveling down her frigid cheeks. She had long since become numb to the wind whipping around her. It was no longer biting, gnawing at her thighs through her pants.

A gentle voice startled her.

"Are you all right?" asked a tall middle-aged gentleman.

Imogene blinked away the tears that blurred her vision before saying, "I'm fine."

"You don't look fine."

"I am, it's just—" Imogene pointed to the vast edifice before them. It was significant in both size and meaning. It had taken Imogene over an hour to find her father's name etched into the surface, and she had been standing there motionless ever since. "It's my first time."

"Oh," he said, his aged face softening. "Did you lose someone?"

"My father, he was a firefighter." From the corner of her eye, Imogene saw him nod.

"I'm sorry for your loss, but grateful for his bravery." He looked at Imogene for a moment before explaining. "My wife worked in the second tower, but a fireman saved her that day. He went in and pulled her out." He cleared his throat roughly. "He died later when a section of rubble caved in. I never got his name, I never got to thank him or his family, so I come by here once a month to say a little prayer of thanks for getting another chance with her." Imogene sniffled as renewed tears welled up.

"I'm sorry." Imogene felt foolish.

"Don't be. Here." The stranger opened his long overcoat to reach into his inner pocket, but Imogene's heart seized when she noticed his pocket square. It matched the one Catherine chose for the benefit. She took a few tissues from him.

"Thank you." Imogene expected him to say more, but he offered her nothing other than a small smile before walking away.

When she was alone once more, Imogene walked up to the wall lined with names. She ran her finger along the letters, tracing her father's name several times before kissing her fingertips and laying them down gently.

She could hear his stern, reassuring voice so clearly in her head: *I know you're hurting, Imogene*, he'd say so rationally. *But try to see her side, too. What if it was the other way around?*

"I can take a hint, Dad." She gave Francis Harris a watery grin before making her way back to the train station.

❖

Catherine was nursing her second glass of red wine since arriving home early that evening. After explaining as vaguely as possible to Mr. Adamson why it was in everyone's best interests for her to be off this account, she decided it would also be best for her to take some personal time. Just a couple of days through the weekend, which should be enough to pick up the pieces of her life, right?

She had left Imogene several voice mails and sent out countless texts, each more desperate than the last for a chance to explain her stupidity and terrible decisions. If she could just tell Imogene the whole story from the start, she could make her understand and maybe she'd even be forgiven. *Maybe.* Her heart leapt up at a knock at her door. She stood quickly and squared her shoulders. She lit her face up with the brightest smile she could manage, a smile that fell the moment she opened the door.

Linda stumbled inside. "Such mixed signals, Cat." Catherine watched her make herself at home by kicking off her heels and sitting back on the couch. "First you want me gone, and now you're happy to see me. I don't think you know what you want." She laughed.

"I thought you were someone else," Catherine explained. "How did you get my address?" she asked and closed the door.

"You make it sound like the company directory is top secret information." Linda took a sip of Catherine's wine. "Although I must say, you've trained Vivian very well. She wouldn't tell me a thing." Catherine noticed an uncharacteristic slur in Linda's speech.

"Have you been drinking?"

"Yes," Linda answered coolly.

"Great," Catherine said as she took the glass from Linda's hand and pulled her to her feet. "Come on, I'm calling you a cab."

"But I'm not ready to leave." Linda whined and wrapped her arms around Catherine's neck. Catherine had only seen her like this one other time, and it hadn't ended well.

"I think you are." Catherine stepped back, but Linda advanced nearer, pressing the length of her body against Catherine's.

"I'm not happy with how our reunion turned out, and I thought we could make one more good memory to carry with us."

"Have you always been this desperate?" Catherine bit off.

"I'm not desperate, sweetheart, I'm horny. And you playing hard to get turns me on." Linda thrust her hips forward as if to punctuate her point. Their faces were inches apart, the tart scent of wine mixed with stale liquor turning Catherine's stomach. "One more night together, and I'll be gone. I need to have a taste of this woman you've become." Linda pushed Catherine toward the sofa, causing her to sit abruptly. Linda settled herself on her lap.

"Linda, listen to me," Catherine said, looked into her glassy eyes. "I don't want you, I don't want any of this, and if I'm being completely honest, I don't think I ever did."

"Oh please."

"I'm serious."

"Is this because of that woman who came to your office today?"

"Yes," Catherine replied.

"And yet I knew nothing about her." Linda started to unbutton her blouse. "That's pretty telling, don't you think?"

"It is telling," Catherine said as she grabbed Linda's hands. "It's telling that I'm an idiot for seeing more than there was between us and for letting myself get carried away by something meaningless. It wasn't until you kissed me that I knew I had made a mistake." Catherine gripped Linda's hips and tried to shift her away. "There's only one woman I want and it's not—" Catherine's words died against Linda's lips. She was being kissed again and this time there was no accompanying confusion, only anger. She tore herself away and before she could berate Linda for her unwanted advances yet again, a soft knock sounded in the room.

Catherine stood abruptly, throwing Linda off her lap on the floor. "Stay here." She raced to the door and opened it enough to see Imogene standing on the other side. *Shit!*

"Imogene! What a surprise!" Catherine slid out into the hallway, closing the door behind her.

"I know, I'm sorry. I shouldn't show up unannounced twice in one day." Catherine watched Imogene bounce from one foot to another nervously.

"It's okay, really. I'm very happy to see you. I wanted to explain—"

"No," Imogene held up her hand. "Let me talk because I have

to. I have to say some things first because this is how it's meant to be." Catherine looked at Imogene curiously as she rambled on. "I stayed today, you know. I stayed in the city, and I went to the September Eleventh Memorial for the first time, and there was this guy and his pocket square..." Imogene looked directly into Catherine's eyes. "I'm meant to be here. For whatever reason, I needed to see you again." Catherine wanted to jump right into her explanation and apology but Imogene wouldn't let her.

"Can we go inside? I feel a little weird talking like this in the hallway." Imogene chuckled warmly, and Catherine's heart seized.

Catherine breathed deeply and bit her inner cheek. "How about getting a drink?"

"I'd much rather it be just you and I someplace quiet and comfortable."

"Inside isn't..." Catherine paused and stared into the hopeful blue eyes looking at her. "Inside isn't good right now."

"Why?" Imogene's question was so innocent. Catherine remained quiet, but she knew her fallen, guilt-ridden expression said it all. Imogene reached around her and opened the door. Just inside, Linda stood buttoning her blouse.

"Imogene, please let me explain." Catherine grabbed her hands.

"If you say 'it's not what it looks like' one more time..." Imogene pulled against Catherine's grip.

"It's not! She just—" Catherine tried in vain to explain.

"You must think I'm stupid!" Imogene stopped struggling and looked into Catherine's eyes. She looked so defeated, it twisted Catherine's gut. "You keep hurting me, and I just keep coming back for more. I *am* stupid." Imogene's voice dropped to a whisper. "I'm pathetic."

"No, you're not stupid or pathetic. Please, Imogene, let me explain," Catherine said frantically.

"There's nothing left to explain, you got what you've wanted all along and one day maybe I'll even be happy for you."

"Linda isn't—"

"Just let me go, Catherine." Imogene interrupted. "This was a mistake." Imogene started crying forcefully. "Please just let me go. Let me go!" She nearly begged Catherine with a panicked tone. Catherine released her hands, and Imogene ran from her.

Catherine's eyes flinched as they began to burn with gathering tears. She stood in the hallway and stared. The overwhelming reality that she had spent all her chances hit her in the chest. When she walked back into her apartment, she wondered how things had gotten so twisted and so out of control. Linda was perched on the edge of the sofa, a sober look on her face.

"I owe you an apology, Catherine."

"You owe me more than that." Catherine's voice hardened enough not to crack under the weight of her emotions.

"But you owe me one as well."

"Excuse me?" Catherine asked indignantly.

"I pursued you because I was under the impression that you were single. You had told me as much," Linda pointed out. Catherine looked at the floor in shame. "After what had happened earlier today, I should have walked away, but my ego was wounded and after a few drinks, I felt like I had something to prove." Linda stood before Catherine. "I needed to prove that I could still have you if I wanted you." Catherine's head shot up and she looked Linda in the eyes.

"I don't—" Linda silenced Catherine with an index finger over her lips.

"I can't have you because you love her, I get it," she said. "But what I don't understand is why you let her go." Catherine didn't have a reason to give. Linda stepped back and made her exit as Catherine stood silently in the wake of her words.

Once Catherine was alone, she knew that was the last she'd see of Linda. But the sickening grip she felt tightening around her stomach told her the same was true for Imogene.

Chapter Twenty-four

I told the guy to dress up for court, and you know what he showed up in? A plaid shirt, jeans, cowboy boots, and a bolo tie!" Catherine's rotund uncle Mark laughed. "That may be formal attire down South, but this is New Jersey!" His round belly strained against his sweater. "There was no chance I was going to win that case, but you know what? I did."

Catherine sipped at her white wine and watched as several of her nieces and nephews slid across the polished hardwood floors. She willed one of them to fall so she could escape the conversation she found herself stuck in. Luck was on her side as she watched her six-year-old niece, Tina, tumble to the floor.

"Excuse me, Uncle Mark." She rushed to the aid of the small child, who wasn't hurt nor did she need any care. Tina looked slightly confused when her aunt thanked her, but she stood, brushed off her knees, and ran to join her siblings. *So much for an escape.*

Catherine continued to the back of the Carter estate. It was never easy for her to return to her childhood home. Every time she stepped foot in the house, she felt as if she had to defend every decision she had made in her life and act as though she had everything she ever wanted. But that Saturday afternoon felt like the biggest lie of all, because she put on the "perfect rich daughter" show seamlessly as she thought about Imogene.

When she smiled her fake smile, she kept dreaming of the bright smile Imogene put there effortlessly. When her aunt from her mother's side asked if she had a boyfriend, she just laughed the question off and told the old woman she didn't have time to date. She didn't mention anything about Imogene. Nobody needed to know those details. Or wanted to. Catherine just flashed her perfect smile and kept her family on safe territory, like her plan to purchase a vacation home. When she grew bored, she'd simply excuse herself for an important phone call and disappear into an empty room for a half hour. When she slid into the first-floor guest bedroom, she came face-to-face with her least favorite sister-in-law, Rachel.

"Need some quiet time, Cat?" The artificial blonde was fixing her overapplied makeup in the mirror. Catherine hated when Rachel used that nickname for her, but she learned to hide her disdain well. When her oldest brother announced his engagement to Rachel, Catherine's whole family was in shock. For such a brilliant young man, Patrick Carter was blind when it came to how harsh the real world could be. Rachel was obviously after his money but Patrick didn't want to hear one negative word about his wife. So the rest of the Carter family sat back and watched as Rachel bought what she wanted, had the surgeries she felt were necessary, and changed luxury cars more often than she changed her designer underwear.

Catherine shook her head as she watched Rachel apply pink lipstick to her overly enhanced lips.

"What's new, sis?" Rachel asked. "It's been a long time."

"Nothing much." *I'm not your* sis.

"Still single?" Rachel turned and smiled a sweet smile that turned Catherine's stomach and made her right eye twitch. "It'd probably be a bit easier for you if you glammed it up a bit."

"I've been dating, but I'm not ready to subject an innocent person to the family yet." Lying to Rachel was easy, and she usually believed them.

"Any plans for the big three-oh? It's right around the corner."

"Just a little over two months." She watched as Rachel eyed her up and down, judging the way she chose to dress. Her black slacks and the shirt Imogene had given her didn't seem to pass the test. "I probably won't celebrate."

"That'd be a shame." Rachel stepped around Catherine's side and opened the bedroom door, motioning to the crowd outside. "You should have a party like this, at least. Celebrate with your family."

This is the last way I'd like to celebrate my birthday, Catherine thought and chuckled.

"You know, Cat, I have to admit I really expected you to find someone by now." Rachel walked toward Patrick. "I guess some of us are just late bloomers." *How does she always manage to hit all my sore spots?*

For the first time in a while, Catherine really observed her family from the doorway, studied their faces and thought about where life had led them. Patrick seemed happy but that probably had something to do with the trophy wife he only saw on weekends. His bank account was large, and he had everything that everyone wanted, but no one had seen him laugh openly and freely since childhood.

Her other brother, Russell, stood tall but without a smile. His two young children ran circles around his legs, and he didn't even bother to stop them. He seemed closed off to the world as he drank down the rest of his aged bourbon in one gulp. His wife, Cynthia, decided to stay home, claiming she was feeling under the weather. Catherine couldn't remember the last time they had attended a family gathering together, and she had a feeling they did so in order to avoid anyone noticing how unstable their marriage was.

Catherine realized her brothers followed the example set for them, met their self-imposed deadlines, and strived to be the exact person she was striving to be. She couldn't help but wonder if she'd be another frown amongst the crowd next year if she continued to make the poor choices she had. Her relationship with Imogene was the only decision she made with her heart, and that hadn't gone well. She decided to find her parents and say good-bye. It had been a long few days since Imogene had run from her office Thursday morning and she was exhausted. She spent each night berating herself or dreaming of a reconciliation she knew was futile. She had called Imogene several times only to get her machine.

She looked through the crowded main rooms and finally found her father in his study. The eldest Carter was cradling Russell and Cynthia's newborn, wearing a large smile. Catherine didn't want to disturb him, so she turned back toward the kitchen where she found her mother sitting quietly at the table.

"Sit," Martha Carter demanded as if she had been waiting for Catherine's arrival. Looking at Martha, one would never believe she'd had three children, the youngest about to turn thirty. Her pastel pink polo tee showed off her trim torso, and her face was nearly wrinkle free for a woman in her early sixties. Catherine obeyed, accepting the fine china tea cup her mother pushed in her direction. "We need to talk."

Both women sipped their tea for close to five minutes without speaking a word. Catherine started to fiddle with the delicate handle. *This has to be serious*, Catherine thought. *You usually can't shut her up.*

"You should call more," Martha finally said. It was a gentle scolding, and it accompanied every conversation they had. Catherine apologized and Martha accepted. They spoke of work, how the grandkids had been, and how they both missed Alice's bubbly personality at the party. In record time, the benign conversation turned personal.

"I couldn't help but notice you arrived alone. I said you could bring someone special." Martha looked expectantly at Catherine.

A vivid vision of Imogene's saddened eyes and Linda's triumphant snarl entered Catherine's mind. "There isn't anyone."

"You should at least be enjoying the single life. Go out and meet people!"

"I'm not getting any younger," Catherine grumbled.

"You're not even thirty yet! What is it with my children feeling the need to do exactly as their father did? Just because your father and I were married with kids by thirty doesn't mean that's how it always should be. We were lucky to find love so early in life and have it be strong enough to withstand so many years." Martha pinned Catherine with a stare. Catherine remembered that intimidating stare from when she was a girl. That look alone would stop her from doing whatever devilish deed she had planned. "Marriage shouldn't be a goal you set out to accomplish. The only goal you should focus on is being happy. The rest will follow." Martha clicked her tongue at her youngest.

Something became open between mother and daughter in that moment, giving Catherine the confidence necessary to ask the question she needed answered. "What if I find someone that makes me happy, but I do something stupid enough to lose them?"

"If it's meant to be, all the stupid things in the world won't keep the two of you apart." Martha grabbed Catherine's hand.

Catherine asked quickly, "How does anyone even know if it's meant to be?"

"Oh Catherine." Martha's lips spread into a slow, soothing smile. "You just know. You'll know because that person will be your equal in the least obvious ways. You'll want to protect this person, and you'll want to help them when they feel utterly helpless. They'll make you feel more comfortable in your own skin and damn near invincible." Martha chuckled, and her dark eyes took on a dreamy quality. "You'll feel born again."

"Wow. I had no idea you were such a romantic."

"Shush." She slapped Catherine's hand lightly. "Tell me, dear, have you given anyone a real chance since college?"

"No. There hasn't been—" Catherine stopped when her mother's exact words registered. She had never spoken of any romantic relationships in college. Before she could question her mother, Tina ran into the kitchen demanding a cookie. Catherine watched quietly as her mother stood and cleared their empty cups before forcing her granddaughter to ask politely and getting rid of her.

"Whatever happened with Linda anyway?" Martha asked.

"What do you mean?" Catherine was ready to deny everything.

"Don't you dare play coy with me, Catherine Elizabeth. Your mother is not deaf, blind, nor stupid."

"I'm sorry." Catherine heard her own words. *What I am apologizing for? How does she do that!*

"Every time we spoke, you'd go on and on about that woman. If I can be completely honest with you, every phone call I was waiting for you to announce your engagement or tell me that you eloped!" It was clearly a one-sided joke since only Martha was laughing. The older woman grew somber before continuing. "But then you came home the summer after your junior year, and you never mentioned her again. Something changed in you then. You haven't seemed happy since. It broke my heart because you were always such a happy child."

"Martha!" Her father called out from the study. "Stephanie won't stop crying!"

"I'm coming, Terr." Martha hurried toward her husband, but Catherine heard her clearly on the way out. "I was hoping you'd be the one to bring home a normal girl."

Catherine was left at the kitchen table with her mouth agape. All the new information was dizzying, yet she felt more clearheaded than she had in years. She stood immediately and made her way to the door without as much as a good-bye to her family and fellow guests. She needed to talk things through before she made any drastic plans and she knew just the person who would be perfect on the other end of her rant and revelation. Once she got to the safety of her car, she turned the ignition and set the heat to high before dialing her phone.

"You're alive! "Alice answered on the second ring.

"Are you home?"

"No, I'm at the touch museum. I probably won't be home for another hour. Are you okay?"

"I need to talk to you."

"Dennis can do the next round without me. I need to talk to you, too. I know Linda is back and working with your company."

Catherine let that information sink in. *This is why I shouldn't ignore phone calls,* she thought as she took her time responding.

"Have you always known?" Catherine asked.

"No, I just saw her at the benefit. I tried to call you—"

"I don't care about that, I'm talking about college," Catherine clarified.

"Yes," Alice answered with a sigh.

"Why didn't you say something?"

"Because you never told me." Catherine could tell by Alice's curt and quick response that she was hurt.

"I'm so sorry." Her bottom lip started to quiver as she finished the first of many apologies she owed to Alice. "I'm sorry for not telling you."

"It's okay, sweetie. I know you didn't do it to hurt me."

"My mom knew about Linda." A lengthy silence followed the significant words. "She asked me why there hasn't been anyone since." Catherine looked back at her childhood home as she spoke. She hugged herself, and only partially because of the cold.

"Did you tell her about Imogene?"

"No, there's nothing to tell." Catherine whispered the bitter response.

"Will you tell me about Imogene? Please, tell me what happened."

"It doesn't matter." Catherine looked down at her pale hands. "We can't be together."

"Why not?" Alice asked with vehemence.

"I really fucked it up, Alice. She won't even take my calls."

"What in God's name did you do?" Catherine heard a muffled

commotion on the other end of the phone. "This is a museum for children, not a library!"

"Alice?"

"Sorry, some old man had the nerve to shush me. Anyway, I went to see Imogene last week and she seemed eager to hear from you again."

"You saw her? When?" Catherine sat up straighter.

"The Tuesday after the benefit. I knew Linda was back in the picture. I hadn't heard from you, and I was starting to worry that she had something to do with it. I went to Cowboy Fran's hoping to find you shacked up with your new lover. She told me about your text. A *text message*?"

"I was busy."

"How mad?" Alice asked, confusing Catherine with the sudden question.

"What do you mean?"

"How mad am I going to be with you once you tell me everything that has happened since we last spoke?"

Catherine considered Alice's question carefully and decided to just get it over with.

"Imogene and I spent the night together after the benefit. I got a nine-one-one from work the next morning, so I left Imogene a little note saying we'd talk soon. I got to work, sat down, and prepared for the usual meeting. Then Linda Nguyen walked in. She's representing our newest client, who happens to be a good friend of my boss, Walter," Catherine told her in a rush.

"And when you sent Imogene that text, where were you?" Catherine scratched at the back of her neck, purposely tugging at a few sensitive hairs as a distraction. "Cat?"

"I was going to lunch with Linda."

"Catherine." She cringed. Hearing Alice say her full name was worse than having her own mother do it. "That's disgusting."

"I know."

"The very next day?"

"I said I know!" Catherine defended weakly.

"Do you still love Linda?"

"No! That's just it! I don't feel anything for her anymore, but I got sucked right back into the idea of her." Catherine waved her free hand emphatically. "I got lost because I was blinded by that small part of me that's still back in college wanting a second chance with the love of my life."

"The love of your life? Seriously? I saw what became of you after things ended. Why did things end, by the way? I've always wondered."

"She promised to quit Rutgers for me, hid the fact that she was being considered for tenure, and then chose her career over our relationship." Broken down to such a simplistic sentence, the relationship tasted bitter on Catherine's tongue.

"You wanted another chance with that?"

"The deplorable college student in me did, yes, but when Linda kissed me, I knew it was a mistake."

"She *kissed* you? Oh my God, Catherine please tell me that's it." Catherine remained silent. "For the sake of my respect for you, I don't want to know any more details, just cut to the chase and tell me why Imogene won't speak with you."

"Imogene came to my office and found out about Linda before I had the chance to tell her." Catherine hesitated. "She found out when Linda introduced herself."

"That had to be ugly." Alice's comment made Catherine snort derisively.

"That's not the worst of it." Catherine swallowed harshly as vivid scenes from that night replayed in her mind. "After I kicked Linda out of my office, I called Imogene dozens of times, leaving message after message begging her to hear me out. So when I heard a knock on my door that night I was thrilled until I opened it to see Linda standing on my doorstep," Catherine told Alice bitterly.

"Did you not tell her to take a hike?"

"I did, very clearly, but she had been drinking and was determined to spend one more night with me."

"Cat, I'm going to have to stop you there," Alice interjected. "I bet I can guess what happens next, but I desperately hope I'm wrong."

"You wouldn't be wrong." Catherine sighed. "Imogene showed up while Linda was there. I swear, Alice, I was going to tell Imogene everything. I was going to tell her that I love her." Catherine dropped her voice and picked at a loose string on her jacket.

"You love Imogene?"

"I do, and I have no idea when it happened."

"You need to not only apologize for your pitiful behavior, but you also need to get her back! Grovel like you've never groveled and beg until you lose your voice."

"I can't—"

"Yes." Alice stopped her. "You can and you will because she is the best thing that has ever happened to you. If you don't, then you're an idiot. And I know for a fact that you are a brilliant woman, so hang up with me and call her."

"I told you, she's not taking my calls."

"If only you had a mutual contact that would be willing to help."

"You don't think Sophia would help, do you?"

"Good-bye, Cat." The line went dead, and after a moment Catherine finally pulled away from the snow-covered curb.

❖

The empty wine bottle mocked Imogene from the coffee table. Earlier in the evening, it had seemed like such a good idea to spend her Saturday night with merchandise catalogs and her favorite cabernet, but her head was spinning an hour after she made that decision. Ever since seeing Catherine on Thursday, Imogene felt as though her world had been knocked off its axis. She hadn't known her long enough for her to have such an impact on her life, but she did.

She wasn't supposed to have fallen in love with her. But once she had gotten to know the woman hidden beneath the stony exterior, just friendship was never an option. From the moment Catherine introduced herself the second time, Imogene knew she was dangerous. She should've turned away, but instead she got closer to the flames and now she sat scorched. Her heart and body betrayed her and now she was left with nothing but memories and heartache.

Angry at herself for shedding more tears on Catherine's behalf, Imogene grabbed her phone and called Sophia, much like she had every night since meeting Linda. "Fucking Linda," Imogene muttered under her breath. She kept a lot of details to herself, but just hearing her best friend's reassuring voice helped her through her lonely nights.

"Another rough night?" Sophia asked.

"Yeah. Why am I letting her get to me like this?" Imogene threw herself back onto her couch and curled up into a fetal position. Her matching green sweatpants and sweatshirt sported a few stains from red wine.

"Because you liked her, and it was bad timing. Your grandfather had just passed away."

"Yeah," Imogene sighed.

"I know you really don't want to talk about it, but are you ever going to tell me exactly what happened?"

"You know the most important bits," Imogene lied, her words slightly slurred due to the wine. She was reluctant to tell Sophia that she went into the city to see Catherine. Admitting such a thing would prove just how significant Catherine was to her, and that made Imogene feel foolish. "I spoke to my mother today."

"Oh? And what did Dottie have to say?"

Imogene decided to indulge Sophia, she knew how much her friend enjoyed tales of Dorothy Harris. She thought back to the earlier phone call.

"Of course the first time my baby falls in love in years she has to fall for a stupid bitch!"

"Ma!"

"What? It's true! First she strings you along as a client and then a friend, then she schmoozes you out of your panties and leaves you the morning after for an ex? She's an idiot and clearly doesn't deserve you. I will not have my daughter shack up with a playgirl!"

"Same shit." The alcohol was lubricating Imogene's lips. She rarely swore, but now she was wondering if it'd be a worthy habit to pick up.

"I beg your pardon?" Sophia laughed.

Imogene cleared her throat and put on her best Dorothy voice, her minimal Southern drawl became more pronounced. "Imogene dear, you're too good for her. It obviously wasn't meant to be. You're too smart and beautiful to cry over a woman you just met."

"She's right."

"This is all your fault, and Chris's, too. If you guys hadn't introduced us, this would've never happened." Imogene spewed blame, night after night, every time they talked that week. "And then you filled my head with that fate bullshit and look where it got me! What was my role supposed to be exactly? Make sure she was ready for when her first great love returned? Fan-*fucking*-tastic!" The exclamation echoed in her apartment. Vixen got up and left her spot on the back of the couch. "Why did I think I had a chance?" Imogene broke down into quiet sobs and Sophia's phone beeped.

"Sweetie? I have another call, can you hang on for a minute? I'll be right back." She clicked over to the other line, slightly worried that the ID showed up as private. "Hello?"

"Sophia?" The voice on the other end was deep and hoarse, but familiar.

"Yes?"

"It's, um," the caller hesitated, "it's Catherine Carter."

"Catherine." The name slipped out as a harsh group of syllables. Sophia's first instinct was to be rude, cut this woman down to size, but a small voice told her to listen before acting. "What do you want?" But that voice didn't tell her she had to be nice about it.

"I'm sure I'm the last person you want to talk to—"

"Understatement."

"But," Catherine continued, "I need to know. Was it Imogene all along? The car and her apartment number. The dress, her eyes—her beautiful eyes." Catherine's voice broke before she took an unsteady breath. "She was inevitable."

"Imogene is really hurting. I shouldn't even be talking to you."

"I know, and I'm sorry. I know I can't apologize enough."

"You shouldn't be apologizing to me."

"She won't talk to me. Not after what had happened at my office and then my apartment."

"She went to your office?" *She never told me that.*

"Yes, and it was a disaster."

Sophia finally answered Catherine's initial question with a query of her own. "Imogene went into the city for the first time in almost fifteen years to win you over. *You.* The woman who had already hurt her by disappearing. Forget about colors, don't you think *that's* enough of a sign?" A long stretch of silence filled the phone before Catherine spoke again.

"Do you think Imogene would agree to see me? Tomorrow?"

Sophia smiled wickedly before telling Catherine exactly where and at what time Imogene would indeed meet her tomorrow. They hung up shortly after, and Sophia was shocked to hear that Imogene was still holding on the other line.

"I'm so sorry about that, Imogene. It was my mother, and you know how that old bird loves to chirp."

"It's fine. All I did was cry anyway." Imogene's voice was now stronger but still sounded weak with pain.

"How about we meet up for a few drinks tomorrow? My treat." As Sophia relayed the details to her friend and ended the phone call with a menacing laugh, she felt the need to give herself a pat on the back. Maybe Imogene would get her happy, if not well resolved, ending after all. Thanks to her trusted and sneaky best friend.

Chapter Twenty-Five

The late afternoon sun was setting on the last Sunday in February. Imogene double-checked the address she had scribbled down the previous night and thought Sophia's choice of meeting place was odd. They had a tendency to frequent the same bars and restaurants and didn't usually try something new. Imogene didn't question her friend, though. She thought maybe it was an attempt to distract her from the pain that continued to reside in her chest. As she approached the large wooden door to the bar, she wondered whether the psychic knew the building was no more than a few blocks from Catherine's condominium. The door swung open, nearly knocking Imogene backward.

"I'm sorry!" A middle-aged gentleman reached out to help her steady herself. "They should really have a door with windows." He smiled brightly in Imogene's direction as he held the door open to her.

"That'd ruin the mystery." Tempting smells and the sound of loud chatter floated through the air, and Imogene eyed the building curiously. She had never noticed it before. "It's my first time and it piqued my interest." She started to make her way through the wide doorway just as the deep voice spoke once more.

"I recommend the house drink. You won't regret it."

Imogene appreciated the suggestion but could've done without the wink that accompanied it. "Thanks." She turned away quickly and walked toward the bar. The large space was well lit and crowded. Wood surfaces and a large fire roaring in the far corner gave the space a warm homey feel. Almost every seat was taken around the bar. Imogene scanned the rest of the space in hopes of spotting Sophia before the awkward feeling of standing alone in a crowded room set in. She noticed one corner of the room glowed amber and orange, with a small square table occupied by one lonely woman.

"Catherine." She couldn't raise her voice above a whisper. In a panic, she looked around again for Sophia, but didn't spot her anywhere. Imogene weighed her options. She could leave, call Sophia and tell her that she just wasn't up for going out, or she could be a better woman than that. She'd probably run into Catherine eventually, and she couldn't hide from her every time. She could get the hard part out of the way now while the pain was still fresh and then maybe they'd be able to have some version of a friendship down the line. With false confidence, Imogene made her way across the bar toward the small table.

As Imogene approached the table, she slowed down to evaluate Catherine's appearance. She looked tired, disheveled, and troubled. Her hair was far from styled as it normally was. Her curls were frizzy, and her face was makeup-free, highlighting the dark circles that haunted her clouded brown eyes. She wore a wrinkled black blouse untucked from her loose-fitting jeans. Imogene scolded herself for thinking Catherine was breathtaking regardless, but she was satisfied to know that the other woman was suffering as well. She nearly gasped when Catherine looked up and their eyes met.

"Imogene." Catherine smiled brightly, and Imogene forced herself to remember why she was there in the first place.

"I'm here to meet Sophia, but I saw you sitting here and in an attempt to avoid a potentially awkward situation, I decided to say hello. So, hello." She shifted uncomfortably and clasped her purse tighter against her side. She turned to retreat as quickly as she appeared.

"Sophia's not coming," Catherine blurted out like a murderer confessing his guilt on death row.

"What?" Imogene's voice rose in response. She looked Catherine in the eye for a brief second before something bright blue caught her eye. On the starched white tabletop was a bouquet of familiar flowers. *Bluebonnets.*

"I asked her to set this up. I needed to see you, and I knew it'd be a while before you'd agree if I asked."

"So you used my best friend? You got her to lie to me and force me into doing something you knew I wouldn't want to do?" She turned to walk away, but Catherine had a strong yet shaky grip on her arm.

"Please." Catherine's voice was weak. "Give me five minutes and then if you don't want to see me ever again..." She cleared her throat. "I'll do whatever you ask of me."

Imogene looked back into Catherine's eyes and felt powerless. Even if she wanted to punish the woman, she couldn't. Not when her eyes were so soft, inviting, and earnest. "Fine." She removed her coat and took a seat across from Catherine. Her black, long-sleeve Henley shirt hugged every curve perfectly. She fingered a small, velvety blue petal. The sentiment didn't escape her, but it would take more than flowers to earn her forgiveness. She pushed the bundle aside.

"Looks like you took a page out of the Catherine Carter wardrobe handbook." Imogene looked at her with icy eyes.

"Five minutes." Imogene crossed her arms across her chest and leaned back in her chair. Their waiter arrived a moment later. Catherine ordered a red wine and Imogene blurted out the first thing that came to mind. "I'll have the house drink." *She owes me more than a drink.* Imogene encouraged Catherine to speak with a wave of her hand.

"I wanted to apologize," Catherine said. "I made a lot of mistakes over the past two weeks, each one worse than the last. And please, don't be mad at Sophia. I begged her to do this for me."

"Too late."

"Okay then." Catherine looked down, seemingly regrouping her thoughts. "I had no idea Linda was going to be a client. When I got to work that Saturday, I was caught completely off guard. I didn't ask her to come into my office that morning and I sure as hell didn't invite her over on Friday night. At first I was confused about how I felt toward Linda being a part of my life again, so I disappeared."

"You were too confused to manage a text or phone call?"

"I cannot apologize enough for my behavior."

"You got that right." Imogene checked her watch. "Three minutes." Time couldn't pass quickly enough. Imogene was angry about being lied to and agitated because she wanted to forgive Catherine. Catherine was hitting all the right notes and Imogene wanted nothing more than to get lost in that melody, but she couldn't ignore the small voice in the back of her mind.

"What happened between you and Linda?" Imogene's stomach twisted when she recalled the scenes from Catherine's office and apartment. She thought she had the answer, but she needed to know the truth.

"Imogene, I didn't just ask you here to apologize." Warning bells went off in Imogene's head because Catherine was avoiding her question and her eyes.

"You didn't ask me here, you *tricked* me into showing up." An eyebrow quirked in challenge. "Answer the question."

"We spent some time together. We talked about our past, and she wanted to have a future. I told her no, again and again. She stopped by my place that night and drunkenly forced herself on me, I swear."

"What about in your office, you seemed pretty cozy then, too." Imogene checked her watch again.

"She was there to apologize for the night before—"

"What happened the night before?" Imogene wasn't sure why she asked because she wasn't entirely sure that she even wanted to know.

"Imogene, I don't want to hurt you."

"What happened?" Imogene repeated her question through a clenched jaw. Catherine didn't answer immediately, so she asked exactly what she needed to know, small facts that would tell her whether to stay or whether Catherine was just like every other woman from her past. "Did you kiss her?" She didn't wait for a response before asking, "Did she *touch* you?" The silence that engulfed their table told Imogene everything she needed to know. "Go fuck yourself." Imogene stood and tugged her jacket from the back of her chair so forcefully that its legs clattered against the floor.

"Imogene, please, wait!" Catherine called out. She looked around nervously before chasing Imogene to the door and putting a hand on her shoulder. "I stopped her because it didn't mean anything! I couldn't stop thinking about you!"

"I'm so sorry you couldn't get your rocks off with your professor because of me." Imogene pulled away and opened the large wooden door. "You're unbelievable, you know that? You treat someone like this and expect an I'm sorry and a bouquet of flowers to fix it? At first I thought you were sad and a little lonely, but now I see you for what you really are, Catherine: a user and a liar. Stay away from me." The door thudded closed in Catherine's face.

Catherine took her seat at the table and sat still while staring aimlessly at the small bouquet of flowers, impossible to get during the winter in New Jersey. She wanted to cry, she wanted to scream and throw things. But she couldn't muster up the necessary energy. Her shoulders slumped forward, and her head hung low. All the good things she had grown accustomed to in the past month had just drained from her life.

"Red wine for you, and our house special." The young waiter put the drinks in the center of the table. Her mouth puckered and her stomach turned at the thought of consuming anything, but she did a double take at the sight of Imogene's cocktail. The martini glass was filled dangerously high with an electric blue liquid and garnished with a red cherry. She threw forty dollars on the table and rushed past the young man in an effort to catch up to the best thing that had ever happened to her.

Out on the busy streets, Catherine strained to see over the heads of the pedestrians before her. She was moving quickly, weaving between bodies and even pushing a few out of her way while muttering short apologies. She looked from car to car, face to face, and when she reached a busy corner, she spotted Imogene hurrying across the street.

"I'm in love with you!" Catherine felt possessed as the confession tore from her throat. Imogene froze. Catherine took the opportunity to catch up and run across the busy intersection, saying a silent thank you to the yellow light that slowed the cars. When she finally came face-to-face with Imogene, she grabbed her freezing hand.

"I've known you for just over a month, and you're all I can think about. I wonder what you're doing, if you're happy, if the shop is busy, or if you're thinking about me. I haven't been able to concentrate at work because every time I try to focus, I catch myself daydreaming about your smile, and then I remember how good it feels to make you laugh, and the way your nose scrunches when you do." Her breathing was rapid from running and the cold air burned her chest and cheeks, but that wasn't going to stop Catherine from pouring her heart out on the city street in a crowd of strangers. "I *was* sad and lonely, and, yes, I did make several really bad choices lately, but I never used you, and I didn't lie. I can promise you everything I've told you until now has been the truth. I can have Alice vouch for me, hell I'll even let Sophia read me!

"I have a little more than two months until my birthday. I thought I'd have everything I've ever wanted by then, but I realize now if I don't have you then I have absolutely nothing. You've changed me, Imogene Harris. You've brought back a piece of my life I thought was gone forever." Her deep brown eyes widened in realization. "I feel born again." Catherine was spurred on by the way Imogene tightened her grip. "Linda was nothing more than a mistake fueled by my own stupidity, and I'll regret that for the rest of my life. I'll apologize every day if you just tell me I have a chance. Please," Catherine's voice started to shake and her vision was distorted by tears. "Please tell me I have a chance."

A simple yes would've been a wonderful answer, but the kiss Imogene planted on Catherine's chilly lips was the best response she could have ever hoped for. Imogene wrapped her arms around Catherine's neck and pressed the length of her soft body against her. Their kiss accepted every apology and washed away any hurt suffered. Catherine's past had finally faded to black.

"You have a chance," Imogene whispered against Catherine's moist mouth. "Only one more."

"That's all I'll need."

They held on to one another long after their lips had parted, just breathing one another in and reaffirming the solidity of each other's presence.

"And I hope you're still falling in love with me, too," Catherine whispered into Imogene's ear.

"I couldn't have stopped myself even if I tried." Imogene stepped back. "One small request, though."

"Anything." Catherine looked down into Imogene's shining eyes.

"Can we please go someplace warm? I'm freezing!" Imogene giggled through a violent shiver.

"My place is right up the street." Catherine had already started to lead the way.

"That's why you picked that bar?"

"I had my reasons." A sinister smile spread across Catherine's face. "I was prepared for any and all outcomes. I'd be able to drink copious amounts of alcohol if you denied me, and if not, it's just a short distance home."

"Very sly, Catherine, and well planned."

Catherine spun Imogene around and held her tightly. "Please don't call me Catherine, ever again."

"Okay, Cat, I won't." Imogene's bright smile could've lit up the night sky. "Unless you're in trouble, then I'll use your middle name, too."

"You don't know my middle name."

"I'll get it from your mother." Imogene looped her arm through Catherine's bent elbow as they continued to walk.

"She'll never tell you."

"Sweetie, I'm so charming she'll be ready to show me nude baby shots after our first conversation."

Catherine looked at her and knew she spoke the truth.

They walked together arm in arm, laughing freely and dreaming of what the next day would bring. Imogene teased and Catherine laughed as she wondered what it was she had done so right in her life to be able to have everything that mattered just in the nick of time.

EPILOGUE

"Happy birthday." Alice leaned in and gave Catherine a kiss on the cheek before turning back to the large front door. "I love you and don't forget dinner on Friday. Mackenzie has been asking for Imogene, you know."

"The woman is stealing the kids from me already? I'll have to have a talk with her." Catherine chuckled.

"Good-bye, Cat." They shared another quick hug before Alice departed, speaking on her way out the door. "Bye, Mr. Carter."

"Always a pleasure, Alice." The door shut with a heavy thud, leaving father and daughter in an odd silence.

"You've done very well for yourself," Terrence Carter said. "I'm very proud of you, Catherine." He towered over his youngest child and gave her a firm pat on her back.

The candles had been blown out hours prior, and Catherine had been counting the minutes until she and Imogene could leave.

"Thanks, Dad. That means a lot coming from you." She wrapped her arms around her father and hugged him. At times like this, she felt like a small child again. Their relationship had come a long way and she was grateful.

"You should bring Imogene around more, she's a delight."

"We'll try to make it out here more often. I'm sure Mom would be happy about that as well." She laughed as she thought of how her mother had scolded her multiple times that day for not meeting Imogene sooner. "Where are those two anyway?"

"They're still in the kitchen." Catherine tried to ignore the panic she felt at the thought of her mother having Imogene all to herself for more than two uninterrupted minutes. She stood with her hands in her pockets, bouncing on her heels, impatiently waiting for Imogene to join her by the front door.

"Hey, Dad?"

"Yes?"

"I need to ask you something." She turned and looked up to her father. "Ms. Henderson."

"Who?"

"Patrick's junior year English teacher."

"Right." His tan face relaxed. "What about her?"

"You were so disgusted when you found out she married her girlfriend." She didn't need to continue, the unasked question was in the air between them. The odd memory from her childhood had bothered her for some time, and that moment seemed as good as any to bring it up.

"My feelings toward Ms. Henderson had nothing to do with her sexual orientation, but they had everything to do with the fact that the woman was a drunk." He snorted.

"What?"

"A few of my friends from the club had seen her stumbling from bars at all hours, several days a week, even if it was a school night. Your mother and I approached the board of education about it, but her father was some sort of a bigwig within the district. No amount of legal know-how on my part could help."

"Oh."

"You didn't think I had a problem with her being a lesbian, did you?"

"No, Dad. You were Max's best man when he married John. That's why I was so confused, actually." Catherine's smile was reassuring as she bumped her shoulder into Terrance's arm. "It certainly does explain a lot, though."

"What do you mean?"

"Patrick still thinks 'irregardless' is a word." Their shared laughter resounded loudly in the open entryway.

❖

Meanwhile, in the kitchen, Imogene squirmed in an embrace that had been going on for far too long. She heard laughter coming from the other room and wanted nothing more than to make an escape.

"It was really nice to meet you, Mrs. Carter." Imogene gave the older woman a pat on the back in hopes of being released from an oddly firm grip.

"I told you to call me Martha." Her arms tightened around Imogene. "I'm just so happy! I never thought this day would come." She finally released her, but Imogene's relief was short-lived when Martha gripped her face between her hands. "You're the best thing that has ever happened to Catherine." Imogene was startled by the similarities between mother and daughter. She knew exactly what an older Catherine would look like, and she felt all the more lucky for it.

"Don't you dare hurt my little girl."

"I would never."

"Good! Now get going! I know how impatient that one can get."

The women emerged from the kitchen and laughed at the sight that greeted them. Catherine was pacing back and forth in front of the door, worrying at her thumb's rough cuticle. Her eyes lit up when Imogene entered the room.

"Ready to go, *Catherine Elizabeth*?" Imogene smiled warmly at Catherine's endearing impatience.

Catherine looked at her mother. "What did she do to get that information from you?"

Imogene laced her fingers between Catherine's and gripped her hand.

"All she did was ask." Martha winked at Imogene.

"Okay, we're leaving before she can ask about anything else!"

Together, Catherine and Imogene said their good-byes and made promises of another get-together soon. They walked into the springtime breeze holding hands and smiling.

They spent the drive home in comfortable silence. Imogene kept the conversation she had with Martha to herself, and Catherine hummed softly to the song on the radio. She gripped the steering wheel with one hand while she laid the other on Imogene's thigh. They didn't speak until they arrived at Catherine's condo, a space that had become a home to Imogene over the two months in which they were inseparable.

"That went well," Imogene said, both women stumbling through the door laughing quietly.

"I told you that there was no reason to worry." Catherine spun Imogene around and pinned against her front door. Winter had died and May had come quickly, bringing along with it unusually warm days. The trees outside Catherine's condominium building bloomed fully and stood proudly in the spotlight of the late evening sunset. The wide array of pinks and purples made the view from her large windows look more like a million-dollar pastel than real life.

"I wasn't worried, just nervous. The Carters seemed like an intimidating group." As Imogene spoke, she fingered the collar of Catherine's sky blue polo shirt. She stared back into Catherine's sparkling chocolate eyes and tried to focus on the playful emotion within them instead of the playful fingers that were sliding beneath the hem of her skirt.

"And what do you think of them now?" Catherine moved in closer, pressing her body along Imogene's full length. Their noses were an inch apart, and Imogene was finding it hard to focus on the question. She was sure she'd never tire of the effect Catherine had on her.

"They're a little stiff, but incredibly kind people. Just like you were when I first met you, before you made fun of my best friend." They both laughed and as Catherine tried to step back, Imogene pulled on her brown leather belt to keep her in place. "Your father was quite the gentleman. Your brothers, however—"

"Were incredibly jealous." Catherine finished Imogene's sentence in a husky voice. "Their eyes almost fell out when they saw you, and Rachel didn't speak to me once the entire time." Imogene sighed as Catherine nipped at her lower lip. "Best birthday ever."

"After you blew out your candles," Imogene paused to untuck Catherine's shirt from her pants, "Patrick turned to me and said, 'I can't believe my baby sister has the hottest chick in the room!'" Imogene did her best impression of Patrick's deep voice. "You're clearly the well-spoken one of the group."

"Well, he was only speaking the truth." Catherine slid her palms along the surface of the door until they were stretched above Imogene's head, bringing their bodies impossibly closer. Catherine leaned in and continued, "You were the most jaw-dropping, gorgeous woman in the room, and I'm grateful that you're mine." Catherine dropped her hands and caressed Imogene's shoulders. "It feels good to have something they don't." Imogene grew worried when Catherine's expression turned serious.

"What's that?" Imogene's brain wasn't working quickly enough to solve the riddle, not when Catherine was so close and touching her with such promise.

"They don't know what it's like to truly be in love." Imogene smiled and Catherine turned her attention to the tiny, torturous buttons on Imogene's blouse. She unbuttoned them one by one.

"I still have to give you my gift." Imogene's voice cracked as Catherine's hot, moist lips made their way to her throat and all the sensitive spots that caused her knees to grow weak.

"I'm unwrapping my gift now." Catherine took off Imogene's delicate blouse and gripped her breasts in her reverent palms. She teased Imogene's hard nipples through a barrier of indigo lace.

Imogene grasped at the small of Catherine's back, fingernails digging in just as her sensitive peaks were being circled for the second time. She squeezed her thighs together to alleviate some of the pressure that had turned into a persistent throb.

"It's tickets to an art show in Boston and a weekend at a fancy hotel." Their lips met in a fierce, long, wet kiss before separating with a loud pop. "Now take me to bed." Catherine threw Imogene over her left shoulder.

An hour later, as they lay naked in one another's arms, Catherine drew lazy shapes along the bare plane of Imogene's freckled back. The violet comforter and lavender sheets were tangled at their feet and discarded long ago. Imogene lay languidly across Catherine's prone body, her head atop her lover's chest, and she let her thoughts dance along to the rhythmic beat of a steady heart. "Was it everything you hoped it would be? Your birthday, I mean," Imogene said, her voice husky from lovemaking.

In a tone heavy with exhaustion, Catherine said, "I hoped I'd be married with at least one kid by now."

Imogene could hear the smirk that accompanied Catherine's words. "Slow down, tiger, one step at a time." She patted Catherine's abdomen.

"Fine. But you better watch out, because I am coming for you." She pinched Imogene's backside before whispering, "I still have those real estate options we talked about when we first started working together."

Imogene's heart started to beat faster. "The houses you thought would be a good idea for me to look at? Ones I could start a family in?" She felt Catherine nod.

"I'd have to get an updated list, but yeah."

"You want to look at houses with me?" Imogene looked to Catherine with wide eyes that shone a hopeful cerulean.

"You said one step at a time." Catherine ran her fingertips along Imogene's jawline. "I love you, Imogene, and I'm ready to take the next step if you are."

"Yes." Imogene's chin started to quiver. "If my financial

advisor thinks it's a sound investment decision, then yes. Of course, yes." Her smile was brilliant and she laughed as she leaned into a promising kiss that sealed the deal.

It was just like every night since Imogene had given Catherine another chance. The two women fell into a peaceful slumber pressed firmly against each other, entwined in a delicate partnership. They held hands and shared not just a pillow, but also pleasant dreams well into the night. Catherine fell asleep while giving silent thanks to whatever greater power it was that brought Imogene into her life, while Imogene thought of all the ways she could show Catherine how much she truly loved her. When the sun rose on a new day, they knew the future held an unpaved path they'd walk together toward a life filled with happiness, love, and good fortune.

About the Author

M. Ullrich has always called New Jersey home and currently resides by the beach with her wife and three boisterous felines. By day, M. Ullrich works full-time in the optical field and spends most of her free time working on her writing. When she's not trying to capture her imagination on paper (a rare occasion), she enjoys being a complete entertainer. Whether she's telling elaborate stories, performing karaoke, or making bad puns, M. Ullrich will do just about anything to make others smile. She also happens to be fluent in three languages: English, sarcasm, and TV/movie quotes.

Books Available From Bold Strokes Books

24/7 by Yolanda Wallace. When the trip of a lifetime becomes a pitched battle between life and death, will anyone survive? (978-1-62639-619-7)

A Return to Arms by Sheree Greer. When a police shooting makes national headlines, activists Folami and Toya struggle to balance their relationship and political allegiances, a struggle intensified after a fiery young artist enters their lives. (978-1-62639-681-4)

After the Fire by Emily Smith. Paramedic Connor Haus is convinced her time for love has come and gone, but when firefighter Logan Curtis comes into town, she learns it may not be too late after all. (978-1-62639-652-4)

Fortunate Sum by M. Ullrich. Financial advisor Catherine Carter lives a calculated life, but after a collision with spunky Imogene Harris (her latest client) and unsolicited predictions, Catherine finds herself facing an unexpected variable: Love. (978-1-62639-530-5)

Dian's Ghost by Justine Saracen. The road to genocide is paved with good intentions. (978-1-62639-594-7)

Soul to Keep by Rebekah Weatherspoon. What won't a vampire do for love… (978-1-62639-616-6)

When I Knew You by KE Payne. Eight letters, three friends, two lovers, one secret. Can the past ever be forgiven? (978-1-62639-562-6)

Wild Shores by Radclyffe. Can two women on opposite sides of an oil spill find a way to save both a wildlife sanctuary and their hearts? (978-1-62639-645-6)

Love on Tap by Karis Walsh. Beer and romance are brewing for Tace Lomond when archaeologist Berit Katsaros comes into her life. (978-1-62639-564-0)

Whirlwind Romance by Kris Bryant. Will chasing the girl break Tristan's heart or give her something she's never had before? (978-1-62639-581-7)

Love on the Red Rocks by Lisa Moreau. An unexpected romance at a lesbian resort forces Malley to face her greatest fears when she must choose between playing it safe or taking a chance at true happiness. (978-1-62639-660-9)

Tracker and the Spy by D. Jackson Leigh. There are lessons for all when Captain Tanisha is assigned untried pyro Kyle and a lovesick dragon horse for a mission to track the leader of a dangerous cult. (978-1-62639-448-3)

Whiskey Sunrise by Missouri Vaun. Culture and religion collide when Lovey Porter, daughter of a local Baptist minister, falls for the handsome thrill-seeking moonshine runner, Royal Duval. (978-1-62639-519-0)

Dyre: By Moon's Light by Rachel E. Bailey. A young werewolf, Des, guards the aging leader of all the Packs: the Dyre. Stable employment—nice work, if you can get it…at least until silver bullets start to fly. (978-1-62639-662-3)

Fragile Wings by Rebecca S. Buck. In Roaring Twenties London, can Evelyn Hopkins find love with Jos Singleton or will the scars of the Great War crush her dreams? (978-1-62639-546-6)

Live and Love Again by Jan Gayle. Jessica Whitney could be Sarah Jarret's second chance at love, but their differences and Sarah's grief continue to come between their budding relationship. (978-1-62639-517-6)

The Fifth Gospel by Michelle Grubb. Hiding a Vatican secret is dangerous—sharing the secret suicidal—can Felicity survive a perilous book tour, and will her PR specialist, Anna, be there when it's all over? (978-1-62639-447-6)

Stealing Sunshine by Tina Michele. Under the Central Florida sun, two women struggle between fear and love as a dangerous plot of deception and revenge threatens to steal priceless art and lives. (978-1-62639-445-2)

Starstruck by Lesley Davis. Actress Cassidy Hayes and writer Aiden Darrow find out the hard way not all life-threatening drama is confined to the TV screen or the pages of a manuscript. (978-1-62639-523-7)

Cold to the Touch by Cari Hunter. A drug addict's murder is the start of a dangerous investigation for Detective Sanne Jensen and Dr. Meg Fielding, as they try to stop a killer with no conscience. (978-1-62639-526-8)

Forsaken by Laydin Michaels. The hunt for a killer teaches one woman that she must overcome her fear in order to love, and another that success is meaningless without happiness. (978-1-62639-481-0)

Infiltration by Jackie D. When a CIA breach is imminent, a Marine instructor must stop the attack while protecting her heart from being disarmed by a recruit. (978-1-62639-521-3)

Midnight at the Orpheus by Alyssa Linn Palmer. Two women desperate to make their way in the world, a man hell-bent on revenge, and a cop risking his career: all in a day's work in Capone's Chicago. (978-1-62639-607-4)

Spirit of the Dance by Mardi Alexander. Major Sorla Reardon's return to her family farm to heal threatens Riley Johnson's safe life when small-town secrets are revealed, and love may not conquer all. (978-1-62639-583-1)

Pathfinder by Gun Brooke. Heading for their new homeworld, Exodus's chief engineer Adina Vantressa and nurse Briar Lindemay carry game-changing secrets that may well cause them to lose everything when disaster strikes. (978-1-62639-444-5)

Prescription for Love by Radclyffe. Dr. Flannery Rivers finds herself attracted to the new ER chief, city girl Abigail Remy, and the incendiary mix of city and country, fire and ice, tradition and change is combustible. (978-1-62639-570-1)

Ready or Not by Melissa Brayden. Uptight Mallory Spencer finds relinquishing control to bartender Hope Sanders too tall an order in fast-paced New York City. (978-1-62639-443-8)

Summer Passion by MJ Williamz. Women loving women is forbidden in 1946 Hollywood, yet Jean and Maggie strive to keep their love alive and away from prying eyes. (978-1-62639-540-4)

The Princess and the Prix by Nell Stark. "Ugly duckling" Princess Alix of Monaco was resigned to loneliness until she met racecar driver Thalia d'Angelis. (978-1-62639-474-2)

Winter's Harbor by Aurora Rey. Lia Brooks isn't looking for love in Provincetown, but when she discovers chocolate croissants and pastry chef Alex McKinnon, her winter retreat quickly starts heating up. (978-1-62639-498-8)

The Time Before Now by Missouri Vaun. Vivian flees a disastrous affair, embarking on an epic, transformative journey to escape her past, until destiny introduces her to Ida, who helps her rediscover trust, love, and hope. (978-1-62639-446-9)

Twisted Whispers by Sheri Lewis Wohl. Betrayal, lies, and secrets— whispers of a friend lost to darkness. Can a reluctant psychic set things right or will an evil soul destroy those she loves? (978-1-62639-439-1)

The Courage to Try by C.A. Popovich. Finding love is worth getting past the fear of trying. (978-1-62639-528-2)

Break Point by Yolanda Wallace. In a world readying for war, can love find a way? (978-1-62639-568-8)

Countdown by Julie Cannon. Can two strong-willed, powerful women overcome their differences to save the lives of seven others and begin a life they never imagined together? (978-1-62639-471-1)

Keep Hold by Michelle Grubb. Claire knew some things should be left alone and some rules should never be broken, but the most forbidden, well, they are the most tempting. (978-1-62639-502-2)

Deadly Medicine by Jaime Maddox. Dr. Ward Thrasher's life is in turmoil. Her partner Jess left her, and her job puts her in the path of a murderous physician who has Jess in his sights. (978-1-62639-424-7)

New Beginnings by KC Richardson. Can the connection and attraction between Jordan Roberts and Kirsten Murphy be enough for Jordan to trust Kirsten with her heart? (978-1-62639-450-6)

Officer Down by Erin Dutton. Can two women who've made careers out of being there for others in crisis find the strength to need each other? (978-1-62639-423-0)

Reasonable Doubt by Carsen Taite. Just when Sarah and Ellery think they've left dangerous careers behind, a new case sets them—and their hearts—on a collision course. (978-1-62639-442-1)

Tarnished Gold by Ann Aptaker. Cantor Gold must outsmart the Law, outrun New York's dockside gangsters, outplay a shady art dealer, his lover, and a beautiful curator, and stay out of a killer's gun sights. (978-1-62639-426-1)

White Horse in Winter by Franci McMahon. Love between two women collides with the inner poison of a closeted horse trainer in the green hills of Vermont. (978-1-62639-429-2)

Autumn Spring by Shelley Thrasher. Can Bree and Linda, two women in the autumn of their lives, put their hearts first and find the love they've never dared seize? (978-1-62639-365-3)

The Renegade by Amy Dunne. Post-apocalyptic survivors Alex and Evelyn secretly find love while held captive by a deranged cult, but when their relationship is discovered, they must fight for their freedom—or die trying. (978-1-62639-427-8)

Thrall by Barbara Ann Wright. Four women in a warrior society must work together to lift an insidious curse while caught between their own desires, the will of their peoples, and an ancient evil. (978-1-62639-437-7)

Side Effects by VK Powell. Detective Jordan Bishop and Dr. Neela Sahjani must decide if it's easier to trust someone with your heart or your life as they face threatening protestors, corrupt politicians, and their increasing attraction. (978-1-62639-364-6)